PRAISE FOR SHACKLES
AND BILL PRONZINI'S
"NAMELESS DETECTIVE" SERIES

"THE PACE NEVER SLACKENS! . . . The detective Nameless, so seemingly simple a character, continues to evolve into one of the most complex and rewarding series heroes in the genre." —*Booklist*

"NAMELESS . . . IS PROBABLY THE CLOSEST THING TO A REAL-LIFE DETECTIVE IN DETECTIVE FICTION. . . . It is fascinating to see [his] personality change subtly under the strain of his predicament, which, in the end, forces him to confront some truths about himself and his values. . . . Worth the attention of any PI maven."
—United Press International

"PRONZINI HAS QUIETLY ESTABLISHED A REPUTATION AS A MASTER OF THE MODERN MYSTERY. . . . An appearance of Pronzini's Nameless Detective is always a promising event; in his latest case . . . Nameless delivers on that promise with more punch and sensibility than ever. . . . *Shackles,* with its many satisfactions, should move right to the top." —*Publishers Weekly*

"THIS IS THE BEST OF THE SERIES. . . . The author writes of minds and emotions, rather than of guns and car chases. His stories are for thinkers, perhaps philosophers. They are also top-drawer entertainment, and getting better all the time." —*Drummer News,* Vandalia, Ohio

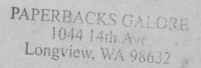

QUANTITY SALES

Most Dell books are available at special quantity discounts when purchased in bulk by corporations, organizations, and special-interest groups. Custom imprinting or excerpting can also be done to fit special needs. For details write: Dell Publishing, 666 Fifth Avenue, New York, NY 10103. Attn.: Special Sales Department.

INDIVIDUAL SALES

Are there any Dell books you want but cannot find in your local stores? If so, you can order them directly from us. You can get any Dell book in print. Simply include the book's title, author, and ISBN number if you have it, along with a check or money order (no cash can be accepted) for the full retail price plus $2.00 to cover shipping and handling. Mail to: Dell Readers Service, P.O. Box 5057, Des Plaines, IL 60017.

SHACKLES

Bill Pronzini

A DELL BOOK

Published by
Dell Publishing
a division of
Bantam Doubleday Dell Publishing Group, Inc.
666 Fifth Avenue
New York, New York 10103

ISBN: 0-440-20523-9

Reprinted by arrangement with St. Martin's Press

Printed in the United States of America

Published simultaneously in Canada

February 1990

10 9 8 7 6 5 4 3 2 1

OPM

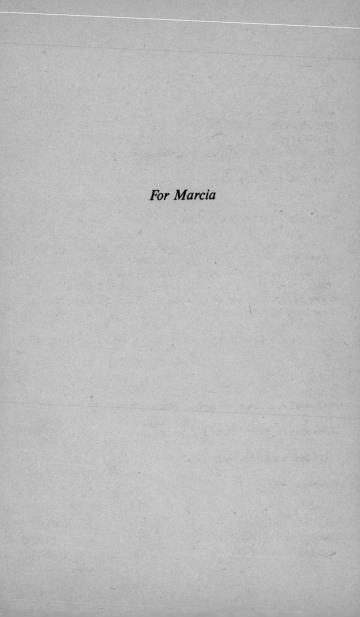

For Marcia

Prologue

THE LAST
NIGHT

Eberhardt's new girlfriend was named Barbara Jean Addison, though she preferred to be called Bobbie Jean. She was from Charleston, South Carolina, she had been divorced twice, and she worked as a secretary to a real estate broker in San Rafael, and one of her hobbies was skeet shooting. All of which, given Eberhardt's recent taste in female companions, built up an image of her in my mind as blowsy, bawdy, bottle-blond, bubble-headed, and the possessor of both a large chest and a drawl so thick you could use it to make a peach parfait. A sort of southern-fried version of Wanda Jaworski, the pride of Macy's downtown footwear department, whom Eberhardt had almost married not long ago while in the grip of temporary insanity.

Despite his protestations that she was "a sweetheart, nothing like Wanda," I persisted in carrying my image of Bobbie Jean Addison right up until the night I met her, a month or so after they'd started dating. The meeting took place in Eb's house in Noe Valley—the first leg of a planned evening of drinks and then dinner across the bay in Jack London Square. I had been dreading it for three days, ever since I finally weakened and let him talk me into it. So had Kerry, as she had told me often and voluably during those three days. Kerry also had a Wandalike mental image of Bobbie Jean, not to mention memories even more painful than mine of a dinner at San

Francisco's worst Italian restaurant; that was because the
dinner had culminated in Kerry, more than slightly
squiffed on white wine, decorating Wanda's empty head
and stuffed bosom with a bowlful of something resembling
spaghetti in marinara sauce. Still, as a favor to me—"Misery loves company," was the way she'd put it—she had
agreed to come along. Underneath, I think she was as
curious as I was to see just what sort of freak Eberhardt
had hooked up with this time.

Well, Bobbie Jean was no freak. That was the first surprise. The second was that, after spending twenty minutes
in her company, I found my previously low opinion of
Eberhardt's taste and mental health climbing several
notches to hover around normal. The third surprise was
that by the time we left in my car for the East Bay, Kerry
and Bobbie Jean were not only getting along but on their
way to becoming fast friends.

Bobbie Jean resembled Wanda Jaworski in no way
whatsoever. She was in her late forties, slender, attractive
in an unflashy way. She had shag-cut brown hair lightly
dusted with gray, and a normal-sized chest, one that
would not support a couple of midgets performing an
Irish jig. She was quiet, intelligent, frank. She owned a
nice wry sense of humor and spoke with only the faintest
of Carolina accents. And she did not paw Eberhardt in
public as Wanda had done, or refer to him as "Ebbie" or
"Sugar Buns."

If she had any flaw, it was the one she shared with him:
Up until now she had shown poor judgment in her deal-
ings with the opposite sex. Her first husband, whom she'd
married at age eighteen, had left her after fourteen months
and gone off to Texas, where he intended to fulfill a life-
long dream of making big money as a laborer on the Gal-

veston docks. ("He had a head *this* big," Bobbie Jean said at one point, holding her hands about six inches apart. "My God, even as young as I was, how could I have married a man with a head the size of a cantaloupe?") A few years later she'd met and married an electronics engineer, and eventually moved out to the Silicon Valley with him and her two young daughters. The marriage had been rocky all along, but she probably would have stuck it out for the sake of her daughters, she said, if she hadn't found out that hubby was having an affair with one of his coworkers—one of his *male* coworkers. By this time the older daughter had married and moved north to Marin County, so Bobbie Jean took the other girl and came north to live with the married one until she could find a job and a place of her own. She'd had the job and the place two years now, the second daughter was eighteen and out on her own, and by Bobbie Jean's own admission she was "reasonably content" with her new life as a middle-aged single woman. "Single till I die," she said. "I've learned my lesson. As far as I'm concerned, marriage is a dirty word."

That comment endeared her to Kerry, if not to Eberhardt. He scowled when she said it; he thought marriage was a sacred institution, one that everybody should be locked up in, and had been looking to be recommitted ever since his divorce from Dana a few years back. Kerry and Bobbie Jean yakked about the evils of marriage all the way to Jack London Square. Eberhardt didn't have much to say and neither did I. I didn't necessarily agree with his attitude toward marriage, but on the other hand I was hardly a militant opponent. I wouldn't have minded being institutionalized with Kerry; I had even proposed to her a couple of times. But she'd had a pretty bad marriage herself. In fact, her ex-husband was a certifiable lunatic. He'd recently discovered fundamentalist religion (after first discovering Eastern religion and living in a commune), was now a member of the Right Reverend Clyde T. Daybreak's Church of the Holy Mission in San Jose, and as of a few weeks ago had been hassling Kerry to renew their old vows and join him in his weekly fireside chats with God. He seemed to have given up on that last quest as a result of a little talk Kerry had had with the Right Reverend Clyde T., but with a wacko like Ray Dunston you couldn't take anything for granted.

So it was no wonder Kerry was sour on marriage. I couldn't blame her for not wanting to tie the knot again, especially with an overweight private detective who was more than a dozen years her senior and who wore his poor lovesick heart on his sleeve most of the time. But there were times—tonight, for instance, while I listened to her and Bobbie Jean verbally abusing the concept of matrimony—when I still wished I could talk her into legalizing our relationship.

We had dinner at a place called the Rusty Scupper, just off the Square. Margaritas for the ladies, Beck's Dark for Eberhardt and me. Seafood and sourdough French bread all around. The restaurant was built on pilings out over the Inner Harbor, and we had a window table. It was one of those cold, clear December evenings when the stars seemed to burn like icefire and all the night shapes stand out in bold relief against the hard black of the sky. The water sparkled with reflected lights from the ships anchored across the harbor at the Alameda Naval Supply Center, and from the pleasure boats down at the Pacific Marina and the Alameda Yacht Harbor. The ambience was one of the reasons we were all enjoying ourselves; the other was the company. The fare was good, but we could have been eating junk food and it wouldn't have mattered a bit.

We were having coffee when Kerry and Bobbie Jean got up and went off in tandem to the powder room, the way women do. When they were out of sight Eberhardt leaned across the table and said, "Well? What do you think?"

"I think she's too good for you."

"Yeah, I know," he said seriously. "I told you she was a sweetheart, didn't I? Isn't she a sweetheart?"

"She is, and I apologize for doubting you."

"Yeah." He drank some of his coffee. "Damn," he said then.

"What?"

"She makes me nervous, a little. Like a damn kid."

"How so?"

"I dunno. She just does. We haven't been to bed yet."

"Did I ask?"

"No, I mean I want to, I think she wants to, but I can't ask her. I try but I can't get the words out."

"Give it time. Sex isn't everything, pal."

"I think I'm in love with her," he said.

"Eb . . ."

"Don't say it. I know what you're gonna say."

"All right, I won't say it."

"I'm not rushing into anything, believe me. But I think about her all the time. I never felt this way about anybody else, not even Dana. I mean that."

"Eb, you heard how she feels about marriage—"

"Who said anything about marriage? I told you, I haven't even been to *bed* with her."

That struck me funny and I burst out laughing. He let me have a displeased glower. "Damn hyena," he said, and gave his attention to the lights rippling on the water until the women came back.

There was some discussion about prolonging the evening—a drive, drinks in the city somewhere—but Eberhardt seemed to want to get back to his place. Maybe he had firmed up his resolve, as it were, and intended to pop the bed question to Bobbie Jean; or maybe he just wanted to be alone with her for platonic reasons. At any rate she didn't seem averse to the idea and so we headed straight back across the Bay Bridge, bound for Noe Valley.

When we came through the bridge's Yerba Buena tunnel, the lights of the city struck me as having a kind of magical quality tonight—towering skyward in squares and angles in the Financial District, strung out over the hills and down along the Embarcadero and Fisherman's Wharf, outlining the familiar symmetrical shape of the Golden Gate Bridge to the north. Everything looked new and clean and bright, real and yet not real, as if this were a mock-up for a Disney realm called San Francisco Land. Fanciful notion, but that was the sort of mood I was in. I reached for Kerry's hand, held it as I drove. It was a good night to be with someone you cared about, a good night to be alive.

It was almost ten-thirty when we dropped off Eberhardt and Bobbie Jean. We said our good nights in the car. Eb allowed as how he'd see me at the office in the morning, forgetting that tomorrow was Saturday and he never went to the office on Saturdays except in an emergency. I didn't correct him; he had things on his mind, poor bastard.

As we pulled away Kerry said, "I like her," as if she were still a little surprised by the fact. "Don't you?"

"Quite a bit."

"I think she'll be good for him."

"Me too. If he doesn't screw it up."

"By going too fast, you mean?"

"Well, you know how he is sometimes."

"I wish I didn't."

"He says he thinks he's in love with her."

"Oh God."

"Thinking with his crotch again, maybe. His number one priority right now seems to be getting laid."

"I can relate to that," she said.

"You can, huh?"

"Take me home and I'll show you my etchings."

"Good old etchings. I know 'em well."

"Could be I've got some you've never seen."

"I doubt that. But I'll take a look, just to make sure."

I swung over onto Diamond Heights Boulevard and drove up into the Heights. Kerry's apartment house clung to one of the steeper hillsides, and like the others strung out on both sides, it had a minimum of parking facilities. Street parking could be a problem, especially on weekends —typical San Francisco neighborhood in that respect— but tonight I got lucky: There was a space less than a hundred yards downhill from her building.

Kerry's place was pretty nice, if a little too feminine in the decor she'd chosen. Large rooms, large fireplace, and a twelve-foot-wide balcony that commanded a skyview of the city, the bay, and the East Bay. The view was worth about $300 a month extra, or so we estimated considering what an apartment of comparable size and amenities would go for in a neighborhood that *didn't* offer a view. But she could afford it. My lady works as a senior copywriter for an advertising agency called Bates and Carpenter, and she pulls down more money in six months than I do in an average year of skip-tracing, insurance investigation, and general poking and probing into other people's lives.

Her annual salary was one of the reasons I kept nurturing the notion that I could retire, or at least semiretire, within the next few months: It would help underwrite my Golden Years.

She went into the kitchen to get us something to drink and I went out onto the balcony. The night panorama was even more impressive from this vantage point. San Francisco really is a beautiful city when you see it like this, from high up, with the distance and the light-spattered darkness hiding the ugliness and the people who create the ugliness, who keep spreading it like a plague in ever-increasing numbers. Those were the people I had to deal with on a day-to-day basis. And they had put an ugliness in me, too—scars on my body that I could see when I stood naked before a mirror, invisible cankers on the inside, in the form of bitter memories and recurring nightmares, that pained me more with each passing year.

In not too many months I would be fifty-six years old; I had been a cop of one kind or another for nearly two-thirds of my life. I'd seen too much suffering, suffered too much myself. The time had come for a change, a new outlook, a saner way of living out my days. The time to turn the agency over to Eberhardt, who had no intention of ever retiring. For a while maybe I could go in one or two days a week and take care of paperwork and miscellany, just to keep a hand in, but I would draw the line there. No more field work. No more stakeouts, or prying questions, or physical skirmishes, or sudden confrontations with death. No more ugliness.

I'd already broached the idea to Kerry, in a tentative way, and she seemed all for it. In the time we'd been

together, she had seen me shot up, beaten up, used up
psychologically, and she'd grown to hate the kind of work
I did. So why shouldn't I retire, make us both happy?
Money was no problem. The last few years had been good
and I had some cash in the bank; I could draw a token
salary out of the agency, and Kerry would willingly supply any more I might need. I had no male hangups about
that sort of thing, because it had nothing to do with char-
ity or an incapacity in me. She was much younger, tal-
ented, and more ambitious; the odds were good that she
would one day be made a junior partner at Bates and
Carpenter. And we were practically living together anyway, practically married even if she didn't care to make it
legal. She had her apartment and I had my flat in Pacific
Heights, but we spent lots of nights together in one place
or the other. None of that would have to change.

As for my time, I could find plenty of ways to fill it.
Spend more hours with Kerry, doing the things we enjoyed doing together. Read, go fishing, take little trips, get
out to sports events. Maybe teach a criminology course at
UC Extension or take on some consultancy work if I
found myself getting bored. In any case, relax, enjoy the
rest of my life. Fifty-six years old, I'd put in my time, I
was entitled, wasn't I? Damn right I was. Damn right.

The whole idea scared hell out of me.

I couldn't forget the period, not so long ago, when I'd
lost my license for two and a half months. It had seemed
as though I'd lost my reason and zest for living along with
it: I had done little more than vegetate during those
weeks. I kept telling myself this was different because it
was voluntary, because I was older, more financially se-
cure, and ready and willing to get shut of the full-time
investigating grind. And yet there was the nagging fear

that I would have the same reaction if and when I did get shut of it—the same sense of displacement, uselessness, emptiness. That I would be like the old firehorse put out to pasture and chafing constantly because he knew there were fires he could be helping to put out, and never mind that he might get burned in the process. Well, maybe I *couldn't* do it; maybe I had grown so used to the harness that I could no longer live without it. But I felt that I had to try. And so I had set an arbitrary target date of January 15, a little less than six weeks from now. Holidays would be over then, and I'd have some things I was working on wrapped up. I hadn't told either Kerry or Eberhardt yet, but I would before too much longer. Eb would need a few weeks' notice to get used to the idea. He wouldn't like it at first but he'd come around; eventually he would see it as a challenge, a way to prove what he'd always believed—that he was the better detective. And maybe he was, at that. Things didn't bother him, fester in him the way they did with me. He did his job with a minimum of emotional involvement. I envied him that, because in the long run it is the one quality more than any other that allows you to survive in our profession.

I watched the starlight and the city lights burn in the surrounding dark. And I thought: This is the right away to look at the city, from a place where you can't see the ugliness. Yeah, I've got to try.

It was too cold to sit on the balcony; when Kerry reappeared with the drinks we had them inside. Then, without hurry, we went to bed and made love, and it was particularly good because of the kind of night this was.

Kerry's digital clock said a quarter of one when I got out of bed and pulled on my clothes. She said sleepily, "You really want to go home?"

"No. What I really want to do is hump you all night long."

"So why don't you?"

"An old man like me? I'd be dead by morning."

"Nice way to go."

"I'll consider it when I'm eighty-seven and you're seventy-four." I tucked in my shirt and zipped up my pants. "You have to get up early, remember? And I'd like to sack in tomorrow. Won't hurt us to sleep alone one night this weekend."

"Damn Saturday meetings," she said. "I hate to work on Saturday."

"You're on your way up, kid. It'll be Bates, Carpenter and Wade before long."

She muttered something; she was half-asleep already. I leaned over and kissed her and said I'd call her around five, and she said, "Mmmm," and turned over. I put on my jacket and overcoat, left the bedroom, and managed not to make any noise letting myself out.

Outside the street and sidewalk were both deserted. The wind had picked up and the temperature had dropped a few more degrees, but the night still had that hard, brittle clarity: December in San Francisco. Kerry and our lovemaking were still on my mind; I started to whistle off-key as I walked down toward my car. I felt fine—free and fresh, not sleepy at all. Alert.

Even so, I had no inkling that I wasn't alone. He must have been waiting in the shadows in one of the cars parked along the curb, and he was quick and light on his feet. He didn't give me a second's warning as he came up behind me.

I was at the driver's door of my car, getting the keys out of my coat pocket, still whistling, wondering idly if Eberhardt had managed to talk Bobbie Jean into bed, when I felt the sudden sharp pressure against my lower spine, heard the voice sharp and whispery close to my right ear, "Don't move. This is a gun and I'll use it if you force me to."

I stood still, very still. It was so sudden, so unexpected, that my mind went blank for three or four seconds while it shifted gears. When it began functioning again I sucked at the inside of my mouth, to get saliva flowing, and said, "My wallet's in the inside jacket pocket, left side. If you want me to take it out—"

"I don't want your wallet," the whispery voice said. There was something odd about it, something stilted, as if he were making a conscious effort to disguise it. "This isn't a mugging."

"Then what *do* you want?"

"You'll find out. Turn away from the car. Walk back uphill until I tell you to stop."

I had an impulse to twist my head, try to get a look at his face, but I didn't give in to it. Turned and began to walk instead. The pressure remained tight against my lower spine; I could feel him crowded in close behind me. There was a faint medicinal odor about him, one that I couldn't quite place.

My mind was hyperactive now, and one thought it whirled up was: Jesus, one of those random street things. Psycho out looking for an easy target. But he didn't act or sound like a psycho: no edginess, no excitement. Calm, almost businesslike. Man with a purpose.

"Stop," he said, and I stopped. The street was still deserted, the night hushed except for the murmur of the cold wind blowing in off the ocean. "The car on your immediate left—walk to it, open the rear door, and get inside. Lie facedown across the seat."

"Listen, what—"

"Do as you're told. I won't hesitate to shoot you. Or don't you believe that?"

I believed it. I pivoted without saying anything, walked slowly to the car at the curb. Medium-sized, dark-colored, probably American made—that was all I could tell about it in the starshine. There was fear inside me now, a cold steady seepage like trickles of icewater, but it was as much a fear of the unknown as any other kind. Who was he? Why was he doing this? Those two questions were raw in my mind as I tugged open the rear door, hesitated with my hand still on the handle. The dome light hadn't come on; he must have unscrewed the bulb.

"Get inside," he said in that odd whispery voice. "Lie facedown across the seat with your hands clasped behind you."

"And then what?"

"Do as I say."

He prodded me with the gun . . . I had no doubt it *was* a gun. I ducked down, dry-mouthed now, and crawled onto the seat and flattened out with my cheek against cold leather, my arms splayed back and the hands joined on my buttocks. He took the gun out of my back while I did that, but not for long; he shoved in after me, leaving the door open, and jabbed my spine again. I tried to turn my head enough to get a look at him, but it was thick-dark in there and the angle was wrong. He was just a peripheral man-shape hulked above me, doing something with his free hand.

Metal clanked and rattled; I felt the cold bit of it around my left wrist, heard a sharp snicking sound. Christ

—handcuffs. He snapped the other circlet tight around my right wrist. But he wasn't finished yet. The gun muzzle stayed firm against my spine.

I smelled the medicinal odor, sharper this time—and realized what it was just before he leaned forward, pressed something rough-textured and damp over my nose and mouth. "Don't struggle," he said, but I struggled anyway, fighting helplessly against the suffocating dampness, knowing I would lose consciousness in a matter of seconds. And then losing it, feeling it swirl away on the sickening fumes from a cloth soaked in chloroform. . . .

Part One
ORDEAL

THE FIRST DAY

EARLY MORNING

I came out of it feeling dizzy, disoriented, sick to my stomach. It was seconds before I remembered what had happened, realized I was still lying prone on the backseat of the car, my hands still shackled behind me. We were moving now at a steady pace, not fast and not slow, traveling in a more or less straight line on an even surface. Highway of some kind, probably a freeway: I could hear the faint desultory passage of other cars. But when I opened my eyes I couldn't see anything except heavy blackness. There was something over me, covering my head—a blanket of some kind. I could smell its coarse, dusty fabric, and the odor stirred the roiling nausea in my stomach.

I tried to move, to throw the blanket off. Pain erupted in cramped muscles all along my body, sharpest in my drawn-back shoulders and arms. More pain, a quick blaze of it, seemed to sweep through my head from temple to temple, then modulated into a fierce throbbing. That goddamned chloroform. . . .

Bile pumped up into the back of my throat. I managed to twist my body enough to get my head off the seat, hang it down close to the floorboards, before the vomit came boiling up—spasm after spasm that left me weak and shaking. A thick hot sweat oiled my skin. My head felt as if it would burst from the thunderous banging pressure within.

"Christ, that stinks."

Him up there behind the wheel, the son of a bitch with the whispery voice. He sounded offended. I heard him crank down his window, heard more clearly the sounds of light traffic outside. Chill air came into the car, but it didn't reach under the blanket, didn't ease the sweaty feverishness.

I needed that air, needed to breathe it; I was beginning to feel claustrophobic with the coarse wool of the blanket still draped over my head. Painfully I clawed up at the fabric with my fingers, got a grip on it and dragged at it until it came away from my head and neck. The wind was like a rejuvenating drug. I struggled onto my side, turning and raising my head, and sucked the cold air openmouthed.

Reflected headlamps and highway signs made occasional flickering patterns of light and shadow across the headliner, the seatback. The light hurt my eyes; I narrowed them down to slits. And then lifted up onto one elbow, trying to see over the top of the seat.

He whispered out of the darkness, "Don't try to sit up. If I see you in the mirror I'll stop the car and shoot you through the head. Do you understand?"

"I understand." The words came out thick and moist, as if they had been soaking in the same oily sweat that filmed my body.

"Good. Lie back and enjoy the drive."

"Where are you taking me?"

"You'll find out."

"When? How far is it?"

"Quite a ways. Do you like snow?"

"Snow?"

"A white Christmas," he said, and laughed. There was nothing wild or crazy about the laugh; it was low-pitched, wry. He seemed to be enjoying himself, but in a grim, purposeful way.

I said, "Who are you? Tell me that much."

"Don't you have any idea?"

"No."

"My voice isn't familiar?"

"No."

"Keep listening, keep thinking about it."

"We've met before then?"

"Oh yes. We've met before."

"When?"

"A long time ago."

"Where?"

"Think about it. You'll have plenty of time. And don't vomit anymore, will you? I really don't like that stink."

I shifted around on the seat, trying to find a less cramped position. Lying supine was impossible because of the shackles and the folded-back arrangement of my arms; but I managed to get turned enough onto my right hip so that I was able to tilt the back of my head against one armrest. That way, I could look out through the opposite window on the driver's side. Not that there was anything to see, just starlit darkness and intermittent flashes of light as cars passed going in the other direction. Once a highway sign flicked past but I couldn't read the lettering on it. I had no idea where we were or how long we'd been on the road.

The cold air had helped my head, lessened the throbbing somewhat so that I could think more clearly. Why was it so important to him to keep his identity a secret?

No idea. No idea, either, where or when or under what circumstances he and I might have crossed paths . . . except that it must have been in connection with my work. Possibly while I was on the SFPD, but more likely at some point during my twenty-odd years as a private investigator. But twenty years is a long time, and I had made so damned many enemies. . . .

I gave it up when the mental effort began to resharpen the pain in my temples. Bile still simmered in my stomach; I locked my throat and jaws to keep it down. *And don't vomit anymore, will you? I really don't like that stink.* All right, you bastard. You're in charge for now. But I'll find a way to turn this around. Then we'll see how *you* like lying back here with handcuffs on.

"What time is it?" I asked him, to break the silence.

"Why do you want to know?"

"It must be late. There's not much traffic."

"It's not late. It's early."

"How early?"

"The beginning," he said, and again he let me hear his laugh. "Tell me, are you afraid?"

"No."

"You're lying. You must be afraid."

"Why must I?"

"Any man would be in this situation."

"Just what *is* the situation?"

"You'll find out. I don't want to spoil the surprise."

My mouth tasted raw and bitter from the vomit; I worked saliva through it, swallowed into a dry, scratchy throat. The fear was still inside me—he was right about that. But it was dull now, with nothing immediate to feed on; I had no trouble keeping it at bay. Not until a thought worked its way to the surface of my mind, a thought that ignited the fear like dry tinder under a match.

I tried to keep it out of my voice as I said, "How did you know where to find me tonight?"

"Kerry Wade, advertising copywriter, Twenty-four-nineteen Gold Mine Drive, Apartment Three. You sleep with her off and on, have for years. You see? I know a great deal about you and your lifestyle."

"How do you know so much?"

"Oh, I have my sources."

"Does Ms. Wade know you?"

"We haven't had the pleasure. Are you worried about her?"

"No," I lied.

"Of course you are. You're afraid I'll do something to Ms. Wade."

I didn't say anything. I did not want to provoke him.

"She's attractive, isn't she?" he said. "Yes, very attractive."

This time I had to bite my lower lip to keep words from coming out.

Deliberately he allowed the silence to build. After a minute or so he said, "I *could* torture you with the idea. Make you think I intend to harm your woman. It's tempting, I'll admit . . . but I don't think I'll do it. No need for it, really. There's such a thing as overkill, after all." Another laugh. "Overkill—that's very funny," he said then. "Don't you think so?"

I let myself say, "We were talking about Kerry Wade."

"Yes, we were. I told you I won't torture you that way and I meant it."

"Does that mean you'll stay away from her?"

"You needn't worry. I have no interest in her now that I have you."

He could be lying, playing head games with me. How could I believe anything he said? And yet, I *had* to believe it. If I didn't, if I tortured myself with thoughts that Kerry might be in jeopardy, I would not be able to concentrate on the jeopardy I was in.

I said, "So you've got me. Now what?"

"You'll find out."

"You keep saying that. Why keep it a secret? I know what you plan to do with me."

"Do you? I don't think so."

"Not the details, no. The end result."

"And that is?"

"My death." The words were as bitter in my mouth as the vomit taste.

"You think I intend to murder you?"

"It's obvious, isn't it."

"Not to me. You're wrong, you see. I'm not a murderer. When you die it will be of natural causes. Or by your own hand. You may want to commit suicide after a while—but if so it will be *your* decision, not mine."

That last sentence frightened and repulsed me more than anything else he'd said. *You may want to commit suicide after a while.* . . . My mind cast up all sorts of nightmare visions. Sweat broke out on my body again and my skin crawled and prickled with it. This was what it was like for the helpless victims of psychotic serial killers. This was what it was like when hell opened up and you saw what lay in the Pit.

For a few seconds a kind of wildness took hold of me, a mixture of hatred and fear and impotent rage. I thought of trying to work my hands under my buttocks, down around my shoes and up in front of me; of rising up, throwing them around his neck, throttling him with his own handcuffs—and take my chances on surviving the wrecking of the car. But it was a crazy idea, even if it were possible. And it wasn't. My arms and lower body were so cramped it would take long, agonizing minutes to make the switch, if I could do it at all. And there was no way I could manage it without making noise, without having to rise up on the seat. Once he heard or saw me he would realize what I intended to do and stop the car and either shoot me or administer another dose of chloroform.

The wildness went out of me all at once, leaving me limp and shaken. Neither panic nor rash action was going to get me out of this. It would have to be guile, cunning, my wits against his. Now, trapped here in transit, there was nothing to do but wait it out until we got to wherever we were going. And not let my imagination create any more horror-film scenarios. Reality was never quite as hideous as anything you could dredge up from the depths of your subconscious.

He seemed disinclined to talk anymore for the time being, and that was to my benefit. The less I heard of that calm, whispery, goading voice, the better off I would be. I lay still, emptying my mind, concentrating on what I could see of the night outside.

Clouds obscured some of the stars now, fast-moving and thick. Rain clouds? Thunderheads? I couldn't tell. Couldn't tell anything about our surroundings, either, except that the lower part of the sky and the underbellies of the clouds were stained with a faint shimmery glow. City lights created a sky glow like that. But so did densely populated smaller towns and suburbs.

Time passed in silence broken only by the sporadic

swish of passing cars. Hardly any traffic at all now; must
be very late, after three at least. Almost one when he
abducted me . . . that would put us two to three hours
away from San Francisco. But there was nothing much in
that. Several highways led out of the city, to all sorts of
connecting roads. We could be just about anywhere.

The silence began to get to me after a while. I did not
want to start him talking again, but I wished he would
turn on the radio. No chance. More miles, more silence.
And then a rhythmic snicking sound filled the car: He'd
flipped on one of the directional signals. We slowed,
swung off to the right. Secondary road this time, one that
ran straight for several miles. There was virtually no traffic here. The darkness outside was clotted, with more of
the gathering clouds cutting off the starshine altogether.

We came into some kind of town, lights at intervals on
the outskirts, a chain of lights as we got into the center of
it, then flashing signal lights where we made a left turn
onto still another road. This one was a little bumpy, not
quite as straight; the jouncing motion began to affect my
stomach, start it churning again. I shut my eyes, rolled
onto my side. It was an effort of will to keep from throwing up.

A long time later lights came into the car, and when I
glanced up I saw that we were passing through some kind
of village: streetlamps, the silhouetted tops of old-fashioned buildings pressing in close on both sides. Then we
were out of it, into darkness again. And more miles of
silence, and tortuous curves, and the constant struggle to
keep from emptying what was left in my stomach.

He slowed again, without putting on the directional signal this time, then pulled off onto the side of the road and
stopped. He put on the emergency brake but did not shut

off the engine or the lights. Outside, there was nothing to see except dark and a spot of reflected light somewhere in the distance. I thought: End of the line?

But it wasn't. He said, "Have you figured out yet who I am?"

"No."

"Good. Then roll onto your belly and turn your head toward the seatback. Don't look around. I'm going to get out and make sure you're covered with the blanket."

"Why?"

"There's a service station up ahead and we need gas. When we drive in there I want you to lie perfectly still and make no sound. If you do anything to alert the attendant I'll shoot both of you. Is that clear?"

"Clear enough."

"On your belly, then. Face toward the seatback."

I did as I was told. He must have leaned up to watch me because he didn't get out until I had finished moving. The rear door opened, letting in a gust of icy air scented with pine and fir and tinged with snow. Mountain country, I thought. Somewhere to the northeast, east, or south of San Francisco: You weren't likely to find mountainous pine and fir forests and the threat of snow in any other direction.

He leaned in, arranged the blanket over me, leaned back out. Pretty soon we were under way again, but only for about a minute. Then we turned off the road, came to a stop: the service station. He got out, shut the door, but I could hear him unscrewing the gas cap, getting the hose off the pump, inserting it into the tank opening. A voice came from somewhere, asking a question I couldn't make out. He said from close by the rear window, in that same disguised voice, "Cash. I'll bring it over when I'm done."

I could feel him looking in at me as he filled the tank. I lay motionless, sweating a little, waiting.

It seemed to take a long time before he finished. I heard the hose nozzle rattle as he extracted it, heard the gas cap rattle as he replaced that. He went away, came back, got into the car. Then we were moving again, out of the light into heavy darkness.

"Very good." he said. "You didn't even twitch."

"Yeah."

"You can come out from under the blanket now. But don't try to sit up. I wouldn't like that."

I squirmed around on the seat, pulled the blanket down, got my body turned so that I could look out through the window. We passed occasional lighted buildings, and in the glow from them I could see the tops of evergreens. And a thin sifting of snow, slanting down from the direction in which we were heading.

I said, "How much farther?"

"Oh, not far now. Another forty-five minutes or so. Unless I have to stop and put on chains, but I don't think that will be necessary. There hasn't been much snow here lately."

"We're up in the mountains."

"Yes, we are. You're such a good detective."

"Which mountains?"

"Not relevant," he said.

"I'd like to know."

"Be quiet now. You'll know all you need to soon enough."

We made a right turn, drove on an even surface for ten minutes, made a couple more turns. Then we were on a road with a rougher surface, and climbing before long through a series of endless turns that grew sharper, now and then became hairpins and switchbacks. Sickness simmered up into the back of my throat; I closed my eyes again, swiveled my head downward toward the floorboards. Gagged once but didn't let anything come up.

On and on, on and on. Turn, turn back, turn, turn back. The road surface got bumpier, seemed to be studded here and there with potholes; the jarring vibration as we bounced through the holes set up a fresh pounding in my head. Wind whistled outside, tugging at the car. He put the windshield wipers on: I could hear their steady clack-clacking. Must be snowing harder now, limiting visibility. He had also slackened speed, so that we were moving at less than twenty-five.

We had been climbing steadily, and the higher up we got, the worse the road surface became. For a time we seemed to be following an up-and-down roller coaster course; then the terrain flattened out and we were into more twists and turns. I opened my eyes, looked out through the window. Nothing to see but dark restless clouds emptying snow in thin, wind-swirled flurries; the upper branches of trees silhouetted against the clouds, most of them wearing thin jackets of snow. There was a layer of frozen powder on the ground here, too: the rear tires spun in it from time to time, briefly losing traction before he maneuvered free of the deeper patches. We were down to a crawl in low gear.

God, I thought, how much longer?

Ten minutes. Or maybe fifteen; my mind was fuzzy and I no longer had a clear conception of time.

The car cut away to the left, tires crunching on thinly packed snow; went up and over some kind of hill, down through a dip and up a long gradual slope on the other side, and finally came to a halt. "Here we are," he said.

The words brought a small measure of relief: I could
not have stood much more of that jarring and jouncing.
But I didn't say anything, didn't move. Just waited.

Pretty soon he said, "All right. On your belly again,
face to the seatback."

"Does it really matter if I see you?"

"Do what you're told."

"What happens now?"

"You go to sleep again for a little while."

"More chloroform? Listen, there's no need—"

"There's a need."

"It makes me sick to my stomach."

"That's too bad," he said with mock sympathy. "No
more talking, now. I'm tired and I want to get this done
with. On your belly."

Pain flared in my back and arms as I rolled over. My
left arm was so badly cramped the tips of the fingers on
that hand were numb. When I was in position I heard him
get out, open the trunk, shut it and then open the rear
door and lean in. Smelled the snow and the evergreens,
then the sharp odor of the chloroform.

I didn't struggle this time when he clamped the damp
cloth over my mouth and nose. No point in it. Let it
happen, let the chloroform do its job, wake up and find
out where we were and what he had in store for me, wake
up and find a way out of this. . . .

MORNING

This time, when I came out of it, there was disorientation
and an even more savage headache, but no nausea. I lay
still for a cluster of seconds, until the mind-swirls settled

and I could think clearly again. My first perception was
that I was on my back, lying on a surface thinner and
more resilient than a car seat. Then I realized that my
hands and arms were no longer shackled behind me; they
were resting at my sides, palms up, and there was a tingly
weakness from fingers to armpits. I tried to raise my right
arm but it wouldn't work right, wouldn't come up more
than a few inches.

I got my eyes open, blinked them into focus. Ceiling.
The rustic variety—knotty pine crisscrossed by beams of
some darker wood. I turned my head to the left. Wall, the
same knotty pine as the ceiling, with an uncovered window down past my feet. To the right, then, and I was
looking at part of a room, shadowed, empty of both people and furnishings of any kind. A fireplace bulked at the
edge of my vision: native stone hearth, no logs and no fire.
Cold in here. The awareness of that made me shiver. I
looked back to the left again, up at the window. From this
vantage point I could see a wedge of sky, smoky gray
veined with black, and little dusty flutters of snow.

My mouth and throat were dry, raw. I worked up a
thin wad of saliva, moved it around from cheek to cheek,
managed to swallow it. The tingly sensation was stronger
in my arms and hands: improving circulation. I thought
about trying to sit up, to get a better look at where I was.
Moved my arms a little, experimentally, and then my
legs—

There was something tight around the calf of my left
leg, something that made a metal-on-metal scraping noise.

I tried to lift my head enough to see what it was, but the
pain from neck and shoulder cramps was too intense. I
tried again and again, jaws locked against the pain. On the
fourth try I managed to raise up enough to see down the

length of my body—and what I saw made the hair pull all
along the back of my scalp.

The thing around my calf was a band of iron five or six
inches wide. Attached to it through a welded metal loop
was a length of thick-linked chain, the other end of which
was fastened to a ringbolt set into the wall below the window.

A swell of nausea pushed me down flat again. I lay
motionless until it subsided, until the ache in my head
dulled again into a tolerable throbbing. Then I flexed and
rubbed my hands and arms, worked them through the
pins-and-needles stage to where I could use them to push
up slowly into a sitting position. It took three tries to get
all the way up, to get my right foot off and onto the floor
as a brace.

What I was lying on was a folding canvas cot, the kind
campers use. I noted that with a portion of my mind; it
was the leg iron and the chain that held my attention.
There was a lot of chain, much more than I'd first
thought. Most of it lay in a loose coil between the cot and
the wall—at least a dozen feet of it. *Why?* But my mind
was not ready to deal with that yet; it shied away from the
question, threw up a barrier against it.

I leaned forward for a closer look at the leg iron. It was
a pair of hinged jaws that interconnected one over the
other for an adjustable fit and had then been padlocked in
place. The padlock was one of those industrial types with
a staple a quarter of an inch thick. The chain loop was on
the opposite surface and one end of the chain had been
welded through it; the other end was fastened to the ringbolt in a similar fashion. The bolt itself appeared to be as
thick as a spike. You would need a heavy-duty hacksaw to

cut through link, loop, staple or bolt, and at that it would probably take hours to accomplish the task.

I quit looking at this new set of shackles and eased my body around on the cot so that I could see the rest of my surroundings. At first they made no more sense than the chain and leg iron. Or maybe it was that my mind refused to let them make sense just yet.

At the head of the cot was a square folding card table, the top of which was littered with an odd assortment: portable radio, several pads of ruled yellow paper, pens and pencils, a large desk calendar open to this week, a stack of paper plates and another of plastic glasses, a tray of plastic knives, forks and spoons, one of those little hand can openers. Next to the table on one side were a pair of heavy wool blankets; on the other side were a long squat space heater and an old brass floor lamp with an unshaded bulb, both of which looked as though they had come out of a Goodwill thrift shop. Against the outer wall stood a white-painted bookshelf, also of thrift-shop origin, that was jammed with canned and packaged foodstuffs. An ancient two-burner hot plate rested on top of the shelf. And in the corner where the side wall—the one with the uncovered window in it—and the room's back wall joined were three cardboard cartons: rolls of toilet paper and paper towels in one, magazines and paperback books in the second, a miscellany of kitchen items in the third.

That was all. The rest of the room—the main room of somebody's mountain cabin—was barren. No furniture, no carpeting, no adornments on any of the walls, no cordwood or kindling for the fireplace. Nothing except what was in this cluttered corner where I had been chained.

Four doors gave access to the room. Three were shut; the fourth, in the near back wall some ten feet from the

cot, stood open. Through it I could see a cubicle that
contained a toilet and sink. The door in the front wall
opposite seemed to be the cabin's main entrance; it was
flanked by windows, both of them shuttered. The remaining two doors must have led to other rooms—bedrooms,
kitchen. There were just the three windows, and all of the
light in the room came through the unshuttered one near
the cot.

I dragged my arm up to look at my watch. After nine
now: I had been unconscious this time for three or four
hours. The whisperer—where was he? If he was in one of
the other rooms, he was being damned quiet about whatever he was doing. There was no sound in the cabin, nothing but the plaint of the wind outside.

I eased my chained leg off the cot, managed with some
effort to stand up and stay up. But the left leg buckled on
my second wobbly step, as I started around the lower end
of the cot, so that I had to lunge ahead into the wall and
clutch at the windowsill to keep from falling. I leaned
there, breathing hard, looking out through the rime-edged
glass.

A cleared area maybe fifty feet wide stretched the width
of the cabin, patched here and there with snow. More
snow drifted up against a shed of some kind toward the
rear. Otherwise trees were all that I could see—white-
garbed spruce and fir, densely grown, climbing beyond the
shed into a misty obscurity. Cold, silent world out there,
ruled by the elements. High-mountain country—but
where? I pressed my cheek against the glass, squinting
toward the front. White and gray and dull green, nothing
else. If the whisperer's car was still here, it was parked
somewhere around front or on the far side.

I did some goose-stepping in place, to loosen the mus-

cles in my legs. Then I squatted to examine the ringbolt
set into the wall beneath the window. It was in there solidly—driven in with a sledge, maybe, or wedged through
a tight-bored hole to the outside and then locked into
place with a bolt plate. I took up a handful of the chain,
stood again, backed off a few paces, and yanked backward
with all the strength I could muster. Nothing happened
except that I scraped some skin off one palm; there was no
give at all from either the chain or the ringbolt. Wasted
effort, as I'd known it would be. But you have to try.

I let go of the chain, rubbed sweat off my face with the
sleeve of my coat. I was still wobbly but I didn't want to
sit down again, not yet. Walk, I thought. And I walked,
taking short shuffling steps until I was sure of my balance.
Behind me the chain made a slithering rattle on the
rough-hewn floor. I went toward the front wall first, but
the chain stopped me well before I reached it. I couldn't
have touched that wall, let alone the front door, if I'd
gotten down on my belly and stretched out full length. I
came back toward the rear at the chain's full extension. It
let me get almost to the center of the room, then within a
few feet of the fireplace. But there was no way I could
reach the fireplace, either—no way to find out if any of its
mortared stones were as loose as some of them looked. As
for the other two closed doors, they might as well have
been in another county.

The bathroom cubicle was accessible, though, when I
lifted the chain over the cot and over the card table. I
could use both the toilet and the sink. He had also supplied three bars of soap, a frayed hand towel, a new tooth-
brush and a tube of toothpaste, and a mirror with a jagged
crack in one corner that hung from a nail above the sink.
A window no larger than a porthole, with a pebbled glass

pane, was cut into the outer wall. But it wouldn't budge
when I tried the sash. Nailed shut, probably. I tried the
one sink tap to see if there was running water. There was
—ice-cold and clear.

Out of there, over to the packed bookshelf. Cans of
soup, beef stew, Spam, tuna fish, sardines, spaghetti and
ravioli, macaroni and cheese, chili, vegetables, a variety of
fruits. Packages of crackers, cookies, tea bags. Two six-
teen-ounce jars of instant coffee. A smaller jar of nondairy
creamer. Sugar. Salt. Pepper. The more I looked at all of
this, the more my stomach clenched and knotted—and
not with hunger.

I bent for a closer look at the cartons on the floor. In
the one of kitchen miscellany there was a dented saucepan, an enameled coffee pot and matching cup, another
stack of plastic glasses, a packet of batteries that would
likely fit the portable radio. The magazines in the second
carton were rumpled back issues of several different titles;
the paperback books were a similarly mismatched secondhand assortment. It seemed these things, too, had been
carelessly swept off thrift-shop shelves.

That's what he did, I thought. Went into a thrift shop
somewhere, bought all this crap at once, transported it up
here with the provisions. Just for me. Built this little corner, this little cell, just for me.

Why?

You may want to commit suicide after a while. . . .

I shook my head, shook the words out of my mind.
Pawed through the stuff on the card table without finding
anything I hadn't noticed earlier. The light in there was
starting to fade, and when I glanced over at the window I
saw that the snowfall had thickened, was blowing now in
swirls and gusts out of a sky that seemed to hang blackly

above the trees. I leaned over to flip the switch on the floor lamp. It worked all right; light from a twenty-five-watt bulb chased away some of the shadows. Was the cabin hooked into a main power supply? Or did the electricity come from some kind of portable generator? It made a difference in how high up in the mountains, how isolated, this place was.

I left the lamp on—small comfort—and paced for a time, with the idea of strengthening the muscles in my legs. Ten paces toward the front, turn, ten paces toward the rear. But it wasn't long before the weight of the dragging chain began to do more harm than good to my leg muscles. I stopped moving finally, lowered myself onto the cot.

At first I just sat there, mind blank, listening to the wind work itself up into a frenzy and hurl snow against the window glass. Then the cold began to seep through my clothing, to bump and ripple the flesh along my back. I got up again, shook out one of the folded blankets, wrapped it around me like a sarong. I switched on the space heater, too, and moved it so that when it warmed up it would throw its heat against my legs.

I sat huddled inside the blanket, and pretty soon I thought again: *Why?* The question filled my mind. No shying away from it now. Time to deal with it, and with all its implications.

He was somebody with a killing grudge against me, that was certain. So much of a grudge that instead of murdering me outright, he wanted me alive and suffering a good long time—weeks, even months. That was what this little cell was all about. There couldn't be any other explanation for the foodstuffs, the magazines and books, the access to toilet facilities. And yet, why give me a selection of food, things to read, a radio, blankets, the heater, the bathroom? Why not a *real* poverty cell, a makeshift Inquisitor's dungeon where I would be forced to survive in squalor rather than in relative comfort?

If I knew who he was, what his grievance against me was . . . but I didn't know, I didn't have a glimmer of an idea. All I knew was that I must have had direct contact with him at some point. Otherwise he wouldn't be so coy about letting me see his face, wouldn't have kept asking me if I remembered him.

Playing head games with me. Psychological torture. This place, these shackles—they were part of it, too. He had to be unbalanced, no matter how rational he seemed on the surface, but this wasn't a random persecution any more than I was a random victim. He had a reason, a purpose for all of this. Revenge was at the bottom of it, but there was more to it than that—nuances of motive and intent that I couldn't even begin to guess at now.

Jesus, I thought, he must really hate me. And that made what he was doing all the more terrifying: someone hating you with enough virulence to plot a thing like this, someone whose life had touched yours in a way that was so meaningless to *you,* you might even have forgotten he existed. It was the stuff of nightmares, of gibbering paranoia. If you had ever made an enemy in your life—and what person hasn't—could you ever feel completely safe?

Where was he now? Still around here somewhere; I felt sure of that. Sleeping in one of the other rooms, maybe—he'd admitted to being tired when we got here, before he administered that last dose of chloroform. I felt sure of something else, too: He wasn't going anywhere without talking to me again. That was also part of the psychological torture. Now that he had me here, chained up in his little cell, he wouldn't pass up the opportunity to watch me squirm.

Wait him out, then. And no more speculating, because that was what he wanted me to do—that was playing right into his hands. Sooner or later he would show himself. And when he did, I would find out at least some of the answers.

I sat swaddled in the blanket, bent forward at the waist so that some of the warmth from the space heater reached my upper body. And I waited, mind empty—a big white vegetable, because vegetables have no emotion, vegetables are not afraid.

MIDAFTERNOON

It was almost three when he finally came.

I was lying on the cot, still wrapped cocoonlike in the blanket, eyes closed, not sleeping but not quite awake either. Drifting inside myself. When I heard the door open and then close, it seemed an unreal perception, part of a vaguely formed dream. But then I heard his steps, one, two, three, and in the next second I was sitting bolt upright, blinking to get my eyes clear.

He was there, on the other side of the room. In one hand he held a chair, a straight-backed chair, and he put it down and stood beside it. Average height, slender. Wearing a bulky knit Scandinavian-style ski sweater, dark trousers, some kind of boots.

Wearing a ski mask.

It covered his entire head, hiding everything but his eyes—and I couldn't see those in the half-light beyond the reach of the pale lampglow. The mask and the gloom gave

him a surreal look, as if he were some sort of phantom I
had conjured up out of the dark recesses of my subconscious. I stared at him for long seconds in the room's cold
silence. And the fear came back, not all at once but in a
slow, thin seepage like liquid flowing through cloth.

Finally he moved the chair a little, scraping its legs on
the floor, and said, "Taking a nap, were you?" He was still
speaking in the whispery voice, and the ski mask muffled
it and added another dimension of surreality to him.

"No."

"Well, I had a good long one myself—in one of the
bedrooms. Did you suspect I was here in the cabin all this
time?"

"The possibility didn't occur to me."

He laughed. "Tell me, how do you like your new
home?"

"I don't. Is this your cabin?"

"It doesn't matter whose cabin it is."

"I'd like to know."

"Of course you would. But I'm not going to tell you."

"Tell me where we are, at least."

"No," he said, "I don't think I will."

He sat down on the chair in a posture that was almost
formal: legs together, back straight, hands resting palms
down on his knees. I tried to look at the hands, to see if
there was anything distinctive about them, but they were
just pale blobs in the weak light.

For a time we sat motionless, watching each other.
Then he said. "I see you put the heater on. Work all right,
does it?"

"Yes."

"Better use it sparingly. It's old and the coils might
burn out on you."

"How long are you going to keep me here?"

"Well, that's up to you."

"I don't know what you mean."

"Don't you?" There was a sly edge to his voice now.

"No."

"It all depends," he said. "There is enough food on those shelves behind you to last thirteen weeks. But if you're careful, eat only one or two small meals a day, you might stretch it out to, oh, four months or so."

"And then?"

"Then you'll starve to death. Unless, of course, you decide to take your own life before that happens. I haven't provided you with a knife, but the lid from one of those cans would be sharp enough to open the veins in your wrists."

The words were calculated to draw a reaction; he leaned forward slightly as he said them, anticipating it, because he could see my face clearly in the lampglow. I made sure that he didn't get it. The one thing I would not do, not now, not at any time, was let him see my fear.

I said, "I'm not going to kill myself. And I'm not going to starve to death either."

"Really?" He laughed again and sat back, not quite as stiffly as before. "You can't possibly escape, you know."

"Are you a hundred percent sure of that?"

"Oh yes. You must have already examined the leg iron, the chain, the wall bolt. Escape-proof, wouldn't you say?"

"No, I wouldn't."

"The brave exterior—just what I expected of you. But underneath you must know the truth. The padlock on the leg iron is the strongest made; it can't be opened except with the proper key. And I've given you nothing you could use to saw through the chain or remove the bolt from the wall." He paused, and then said matter-of-factly, "You *could* try cutting off your leg with one of the can lids. The equivalent of an animal chewing off a limb caught in a trap. But I imagine you'd bleed to death long before you were free. Besides, a can lid won't cut through bone, will it?"

I didn't say anything. I thought: If I could get my hands on him right now, I'd kill him. No hesitation, no compunction. I would kill him where he sits.

He said, "Your only other hope is that someone will come and rescue you. But that won't happen."

"What makes you think it won't?"

"This cabin is isolated, more than a mile from its nearest neighbor. No one would have any reason to come here in winter. No one but me, and once I leave I won't be back until after you're dead." Another pause. "I have a burial spot all picked out for you. And you mustn't worry —I'll dig your grave deep so the animals won't disturb you."

I said in a flat, emotionless voice, "How long are you going to keep me company?"

"Not long. I'll be leaving this afternoon, as soon as we've finished our talk. Did you think I would wait around and watch you suffer? No, that wouldn't be right, that isn't the way it's done. You'll be here alone, all alone, until the end comes."

He waited for me to say something to that, and when I didn't he went on in his sly way, "I wonder how you'll stand up to it. The aloneness, I mean. Some men would go insane, chained up as you are, all alone here for three to four months. But you're not one of them . . . or are you?"

"No. But you'd like it if I were."

"That isn't so. I wouldn't like it. I'm not without compassion, you know."

I said nothing.

"Well, I'm not," he said. "That's why I've given you the radio, the books, and magazines. The paper and writing tools, too. Why, with all that paper you could write your memoirs. I'm sure they would make fascinating reading."

I had nothing to say to that, either.

"At any rate," he said, "if I hadn't provided all those things to occupy your mind, you surely *would* go insane. So you see? That isn't what I want at all."

"I know what you want," I said. "If I stay sane, then I suffer even more. Right?"

"Suffering is what punishment is all about."

"Punishment. All right, why? Why all of this?"

"You still don't know?"

"No."

"Think hard. Try to remember."

"How can I remember if you don't give me some idea of who you are, what you think I did to you?"

"What I *think* you did to me?" Suddenly, violently, he came up out of the chair, almost upsetting it, and pointed a shaking finger at me. "Damn you, you destroyed me!" he said in a voice shrill with rage—his normal voice, I thought, but still too muffled by the ski mask to be recognizable. "You destroyed my life!"

"How did I do that?"

"And you don't even remember. That's the kind of man you are. The kind of *detective* you are. You destroyed me and you don't even know who I am!"

"Tell me your name. Take off that mask and let me see your face."

"No! You'll remember on your own. Sooner or later

you'll remember and then you'll know and then you'll be dead and I'll have my peace. That's the only way I'll ever have my peace, when you're dead, dead, dead, dead!"

He spun on his heel, half ran across to one of the closed doors, yanked it open, disappeared into the room beyond. Reappeared seconds later, and he had his gun—a snub-nosed revolver—upraised in one hand. He stopped along-side the chair and pointed the gun at me. I saw his thumb draw the hammer back and heard the click it made, saw the way his arm was shaking, and I thought in that mo-ment he was going to shoot me. Thought he'd lost his tenuous grip on sanity, forgotten his purpose in bringing me here, and in a matter of seconds I would be dead. It took all the will I possessed to sit still, keep my eyes open, keep the fear dammed up so it wouldn't leak through to where he could see it when he pulled the trigger.

But he didn't pull the trigger, just stood there holding the revolver extended in his trembling hand. It was sev-eral pulsebeats before I understood that he wasn't going to use the gun, had never intended to use it, had himself back under control despite the shaking or maybe had never lost control in the first place. That behind the ski mask he was probably smiling. That this, too, this little charade, was part of the psychological torture.

He let it go on for another half minute, wanting me to break down and beg for my life, hungering for it with a kind of feral lust that I could almost smell. I sat very still, showing him nothing, hating him with some of the same visceral hatred he had for me, and waited him out.

When he finally lowered the revolver he did it in slow segments, inches at a time, until the muzzle pointed at the floor. Then he said, still carrying out the charade, "No.

No, I won't do it, I won't make it easy for you. I'm not your executioner. I'm only your jailer."

He wanted me to say something; I said nothing. There was a hot dry burnt taste in my mouth, like ashes fresh from a stove fire.

I watched him pick up the chair with his left hand. "It's time for me to leave," he said, and he turned, carrying the chair, and went across to the same door and then stopped again and turned back—all of it calculated, like the game with the gun. "One more look at you," he said, "one last look at the condemned man. Do you have anything else to say before I go?"

"Just this," but the words got caught in the dryness in my throat and I had to cough and swallow and start over. "Just this. If I survive, if I get out of here alive, I'll track you down no matter where you are and I'll kill you."

"Yes," he said, "I don't doubt that. But it's a moot point. Because you won't survive."

He put his back to me again, went through the door and shut it behind him.

I sat there, not moving, not thinking, listening. Faint sounds in the room behind the closed door. Silence for a time, then the slamming of a door somewhere outside—car door. Engine cranking up, revving, revving—him doing that on purpose so I'd be sure to hear—and then diminishing, becoming lost in the snow-laden wind that skirled against the walls and windows of my prison.

He was gone.

And I was alone.

THE SECOND DAY

It wasn't until the next morning that I was able to grasp the full enormity of what lay ahead for me, what I would have to face over the days, weeks, maybe months of this kind of imprisonment and isolation.

I woke up with the knowledge, lay in the icy dawn with it swelling inside my head like a malignant tumor. Last night, in those first hours of aloneness, I had managed to block out most of it behind a barrier of hate and frantic activity. I had paced back and forth, back and forth, indulging in a monologue of curses. I had prowled through the provisions, looking for something, anything that I could use as a possible tool for escape. I had done the same with my pockets—wallet, keys, change, handkerchief, nothing, nothing. I had tried yanking again and again on the chain, tried picking the padlock with each one of my keys, opened a can of something and tried to use the lid to dig into the wall around the ringbolt. All senseless, wasted effort that got me nothing but scraped palms and a cut finger, and left me mentally as well as physically exhausted. Sometime long past nightfall I had stretched out on the cot and wrapped myself in the blankets and fallen into a fitful sleep. Woke up once, while it was still dark, with hunger gnawing at me, but I hadn't eaten because my mind wasn't working right and somehow it translated eating into a weakness, a giving in. So I had gotten up, used the toilet, drunk some cold water from the sink tap and splashed a handful over my face, and then gone back to the cot and again swaddled myself in blankets and uneasy sleep.

Now my mind was clear, and the truth was unavoidable: I was a condemned man, just as the whisperer had said, with three or at the most four months to live and very little chance of reprieve or escape. I was in an isolation cell fifteen feet square, with nothing more to occupy my time than old books and magazines, pencils and pens and blank paper, and a radio that probably wouldn't bring in much except static because this was mountain country and winter besides. And I not only had my imminent death to cope with, I had the problem of keeping my sanity throughout the ordeal. Death itself no longer terrified me the way it had at one time, though this kind of death would not be easy to reconcile. But insanity . . . that was something else again. That was a hideous looming specter, a screaming darkness, that filled me with the most primitive loathing and revulsion.

The fear began to seep in again as I lay there. And then to seep out through my pores in a prickly sweat. I kept my eyes shut and lay still while I repaired the internal leaks and restored a dry calm.

This was what I had to guard against, this slow erosion of the dikes my mind had already thrown up against the roiling waters of unreason. Plug each little hole before it grew larger, threatened the entire protective structure. Keep the dark tide from flooding in, from dragging me down into its depths.

No matter how bad it gets, I thought, I can't let that happen. That's my number one priority. And the way to keep it from happening is to live minute to minute, hour to hour, day to day. Don't look ahead; don't think about this afternoon, much less tonight, and never about tomorrow. Don't think about death, or any more about madness. Believe that I will survive this somehow, never stop believing it for a second.

I will survive.

I *will.*

Get up then, get moving. It's what you do every morning, isn't it? This is no different, you can't allow it to be any different. Lying here passive like this invites brooding, invites self-pity—invites cracks in the dike.

I sat up, disentangled myself from the blankets, swung my legs off the cot. There was a furrow of pain along the back of my left calf where the leg iron had somehow bitten into the flesh. I leaned down to rub at the spot, and to see if I could loosen the thing a little. It was tight around the calf but not so tight that I was unable to work it downward half an inch or so. That was far enough. I didn't want it all the way down to my ankle, where the lower edge would ride against my heel and maybe open a sore that would make walking painful.

It was cold in the room—still snowing outside—but not so cold here in my corner, because I had left the space heater on all night. The coils glowed, radiated warmth, made faint ticking sounds. *Better use it sparingly. It's old and the coils might burn out on you.* Well, he was right, goddamn him. If they did burn out, and the temperature dropped far enough below zero, the blankets and my clothing wouldn't be enough to prevent me from freezing to death.

I reached over, switched the thing off. From now on I'd keep it off during the daylight hours. Use it only at night, and not all night unless the weather conditions were bad enough to warrant it. Bundle up in the blankets, drink plenty of hot tea and coffee and soup—keep warm that way.

Up on my feet. A few stretches, a few squats, a few toe touches: the kind of light calisthenics I sometimes indulged in to loosen stiff muscles, get the circulation flowing on cold mornings. Yes, and what if I adopted a regular exercise program, did a series of calisthenics every day? It would be another way of keeping warm, another way of passing time. And by preventing my body from atrophying in these confines, I would be helping to prevent my mind from doing the same.

The exercise put a sharp, spasmodic clenching under my breastbone. How long since I'd eaten anything? Almost thirty-six hours. Almost a day and a half since the dinner at the Rusty Scupper with Kerry and Eberhardt and Bobbie Jean—

Kerry, I thought.

No, I thought, no, not yet.

I put on my sport jacket and overcoat—I had taken them off last night because it had been warm enough to sleep without them—and then went around the card table, dragging my chain like a fat ghost, and plugged in the two-burner hot plate. Took the coffee pot into the bathroom and filled it with water and brought it back out and put it on the stove. Hunted through the canned goods, settled on beef stew. Opened the can, dumped the stew into the saucepan, put the saucepan on the other burner. Spooned a little coffee into the enameled mug, then added a little more because this was my first morning, I didn't need to worry about conserving it just yet. Set out the one bowl and a plastic fork and spoon, opened a package of saltines, opened another package of paper napkins. Did all of that slowly, carefully, establishing a routine.

While I waited for the water to boil and the stew to heat, I picked up the radio and checked to see if he'd put in batteries. He had; the packet in the cardboard carton was a spare set. I flipped the On switch and listened to a steady spewing of static. It was the same from one end of the dial to the other—heavy static, with here and there a murmur of voices or music that I couldn't distinguish. I carried the radio to the window, held it up to the glass, and fiddled with the dial again. Same thing. But the wind was up, whipping and bending the nearby trees, and it was snowing pretty heavily. Maybe I could tune in a station once the storm eased, or when the weather improved.

And maybe I couldn't. It might be impossible to pick up anything from here with an ordinary radio. It might be that this portable was just another little torture device in his war of nerves. . . .

The smell of the stew cooking made my stomach clench again, my mouth water. But it wasn't appetite; it was the need to fill a cavity. I emptied the stew into the bowl, added a handful of crushed crackers, made the coffee, took cup and bowl around to the cot and ate sitting down. The stew was tasteless but I managed to get all of it down. The coffee was a handle on normalcy, part of the same morning habit pattern that had ruled most of my adult life —something that stirred me into facing up to a day's offerings, even the burnt ones.

So I let myself think of Kerry then—not for the first time since I'd been here, but for the first time with any concentration. Was she all right? Yes. He wouldn't bother her; he hadn't lied to me about that. Believe it. His hatred was for *me*, his punishment for whatever it was he thought I'd done to him strictly personal and private. Just him and me. If he'd wanted to include Kerry he could have picked up both of us Friday night when we'd returned to her place. There hadn't been many people on the street at that hour, either; he could have pulled off a double snatch without much trouble. But instead he'd waited for me to come out alone.

Just him and me.

But she would know by now that something had happened to me. She would have at least suspected it sometime yesterday, when I didn't call as I'd promised, or even earlier if she'd noticed that my car was still parked near her building. She'd have gone to my flat, and when she'd found no sign of me there she would have gotten in touch with Eberhardt. By now they had probably contacted one of Eberhardt's cop friends at the Hall of Justice. But in California you have to be unaccounted for for seventy-two hours before a missing persons report can be filed; it would be Tuesday before there was an official investigation.

Kerry would be frantic by then. Eberhardt, too, though he wouldn't let anybody know it. It would only get worse for them as the days passed, as the investigative wheels spun and spun and churned up nothing at all. And those wheels *would* churn up nothing . . . unless someone had seen me abducted, written down the license number of the whisperer's car, and the police were able to track him down and force him to reveal what he'd done with me. Not much chance of that, was there? No. So slim a chance it wasn't even worth considering.

I could feel Kerry's pain, Eberhardt's pain, because it was the same kind that was inside me. And the longer I was chained up here, the more that pain would increase. And what if I died here in three or four months, according to plan? *I have a burial spot all picked out for you. And*

*you mustn't worry—I'll dig your grave deep so the animals
won't disturb you.* My remains would never be found, nor
any trace of what had happened to me. Vanished into thin
air, vanished as completely and mysteriously as Ambrose
Bierce and Judge Crater and Jimmy Hoffa. Poof! Gone.
Missing and presumed dead—that would be the official
nonverdict. But Kerry and Eberhardt would never know
for sure. And they would wonder and they would hurt, at
least a little, for the rest of their lives. . . .

No. Dangerous territory. Off limits, back off. Minute to
minute, remember? Hour to hour, day to day, don't look
ahead, don't speculate, don't let your imagination run
away with you. Kerry's a big girl; she'll be fine. And you
think Eberhardt hasn't handled worse than this? They'll
come out of it all right. Just make sure *you* do too.

I got on my feet, went into the bathroom and washed
out the soup bowl and then brought it back out and set it
on top of the bookshelf. Made another cup of coffee, much
weaker this time—more for warmth than anything else.
Without the heater on, it was chilly in here; I could almost feel the bite of the wind that kept snapping and
howling at the cabin walls outside. I moved around to the
cot, picked up one of the blankets and folded it around my
body.

As I stood sipping my coffee, my gaze came to rest on
the calendar that lay open on the card table. Open to this
week, the first week in December. With my free hand I
flipped through some of the pages. One of those two-year
calendar/daybook things, for this year and next. Today
was . . . what? Sunday? Sunday, December 6. The calendar was there because he wanted me to know what day
it was, to count how many had gone by and how many lay
ahead. But I could turn that knowledge into an advantage

by using it to maintain my orientation, my sense of order and normalcy. One thing that would surely weaken your grip on sanity would be losing track of days of the week, dates, time itself. That would put you in a shadow world, a kind of deadly limbo, and it was a short fall from there into madness.

Using one of the pencils I drew an × through the box for Saturday, the fifth, my first day here, and another × through the box for today. This would become another part of my morning routine.

I started to put the pencil down. Didn't do it because I found myself looking at the pads of yellow ruled paper— and remembering what he'd said yesterday, in his sly way, about my writing my memoirs. Well, maybe that wasn't such a bad idea. But not in the way he'd meant it. Suppose I made a record of what had happened to me since Friday night, every detail I could remember, every impression? It might help me figure out who he was, what his motive was.

It would keep me busy too, keep my mind occupied for long periods of time. And once it was done I could go on to something else—a sort of journal, a damning chronicle of my ordeal. Put down whatever came into my head. Make writing a daily activity, to go along with an exercise program and the routine I established. I had done enough client reports in my time; I had a pretty fair grasp of English. It wouldn't be difficult work, and it was the kind I could lose myself in once I got started.

The idea energized me a little, enough so that I caught up one of the pads and sat down with it in my lap. And before long I began to write.

THE THIRD DAY

It's all down on paper, everything that happened during the twenty-four hours between Friday night and Saturday night. Twenty-nine pages using both sides of a sheet to conserve paper. I spent most of yesterday working on it and half of today. My fingers are stiff—writer's cramp. But the important thing is that I've included *all* the details, even the smallest one. You can't forget something that might be vital when you've got it down in black and white. Or black and yellow.

I wonder if anyone else will ever read it.

It won't be him. I'll make sure of that.

I still don't have an inkling of who he is. Men like me, men who have been in law enforcement work for better than three decades, touch thousands of lives directly and indirectly. We have a profound effect on some of those lives; we inflict pain on some, in most cases because they deserve it but, in a few unavoidable instances, even when they don't. You can't help that, no matter how hard you try, how many precautions you take. So he has to be someone I hurt once, intentionally or by accident, deservedly or otherwise . . . but that narrows it down not at all. He could be any one of a hundred or two hundred people out of my past.

What do I know about him? So damned little. He's intelligent, well-spoken—white collar rather than blue. Average height, slim build. Caucasian. Age? Hard to tell from either his mannerisms or the disguised voice; say somewhere between thirty and forty-five. Drives an American-made car, make and model undetermined. Carries a snub-nosed revolver. Dresses unobtrusively. Owns or has rented or at least has access to a deserted mountain cabin, location undetermined, that he expects to remain unvisited for a minimum of four months. What else?

Nothing else.

He could be almost anybody.

The snowfall has finally quit. Not much wind now—it's late afternoon—and the overcast doesn't hang quite as low.

I tried the radio again a while ago. Mostly static, but I did find one station that comes through for ten or fifteen seconds at a time before it fades out again. That's encouraging, even though it took me five minutes to bring it in the first time, almost twice as long to bring it back the second time. Country and western station, the honky-tonk variety. But even honky-tonk stations do news broadcasts now and then, don't they?

Reception should be better when the clouds lift and the wind dies down. Tonight, maybe. Or tomorrow morning. I'll keep fiddling with the dial until I can hold the signal for longer periods.

Soup for dinner. Split pea. And half a can of fruit cocktail.

While I was heating the soup, it occurred to me that I might be able to use the hot plate for another purpose. I could take some of the napkins and paper towels, roll them into a tight cylinder, and then set the cylinder on fire with the hot plate—make a kind of torch. Then I could try to burn or char the wall around the ringbolt. With enough burning or charring of the wood, maybe I could work the bolt loose.

But I didn't consider the idea for more than a few seconds. It's no good. In the first place, the wall is made of thick, smooth-sanded pine logs; there's almost no chance that I could do much damage to a log like that even with repeated attempts. And in the second place, there's the danger of accidentally starting a fire I couldn't control. It could happen, no matter how careful I was. And what chance would I have of putting out a fire, chained up like this, the bathroom at a distance and nothing larger to carry water in than a saucepan? No. The possibility of being burned alive is even more frightening than the prospect of death by starvation.

There has to be another way.

Men have escaped from prisons for as long as there have been prisons. Escaped from fortresses, from isolation cells smaller and more barren than this one—from every kind of lockup there is or ever was. Whatever one man can think up, another man can find a way to circumvent. That's the nature of the beasts we are.

I'm as bright, as clever, as resourceful as he is, damn him. There has to be a way out, something he overlooked, some little crack in this escape-proof prison that I can squeeze through. And I'm going to find it.

Sooner or later I am going to find it.

THE FOURTH DAY

Why thirteen weeks?

Why not twelve—three full months, a more conventional number? Why *thirteen?*

The possible importance of this didn't occur to me until this morning, while I was exercising. I checked the written record I made and I'd put down more or less verbatim what the whisperer said on Saturday night: *There is enough food on those shelves to last thirteen weeks.*

There must be some significance in the number, some reason for him to pick it as the optimum number of weeks for my survival. Is he someone I helped send to prison who served a total of thirteen years? This little corner resembles nothing so much as a jail cell; everything in it has a prisonlike function. He could be trying to replicate for me, in a thirteen-week microcosm, what he was forced to endure for thirteen years—with death being *my* release. But I can think of only one man who went to prison on my testimony and served exactly thirteen years; he was in his mid-fifties when he got out of San Quentin and he died three years later of natural causes.

Something that happened thirteen years ago, then? I've tried to think back, remember what I did, the cases I had, thirteen years ago, but it isn't easy. Time distorts memory, and memory distorts time. There are a few things I'm sure took place just that many years back; others might have been thirteen or twelve or fourteen or fifteen. And of the ones I'm sure of, I can't pick out any one person that he might be, any motive strong enough for this kind of revenge.

What else could thirteen represent, if not years? An occurrence on the thirteenth of the month—the thirteenth of December, maybe? If he'd snatched me on the thirteenth of this month, then yes, that might be it. But he hadn't. He'd made his grab on December 4—Friday, December 4. Some sort of correlation between four and thirteen? No, that's reaching too far.

Look at it another way: Why *did* he pick December 4? Why not December 3, or December 5 or any other damn day? Could have been nothing more than random selection—the day he was ready, when all his preparations were made. But it could also be that there's an underlying meaning to the date too. Something that happened on December 4 thirteen years ago? Possible. But if I can't be sure entire cases took place in a given year, how the hell can I remember something that might have happened on a specific date that long ago?

Thirteen. Thirteen. A superstitious symbol, an unlucky number for some and lucky one for others. Suppose it's a lucky one for him? The thirteen weeks might not have any meaning beyond that. I might be trying to make too much out of it, stumbling around in a blind alley. . . .

Let it go for now. The thirteen weeks means something or it doesn't, and if it does I'll figure it out eventually. That's the way my mind has always worked. Let it alone, let it simmer on a back burner and one day it all comes boiling up to the surface.

Gnawing in my belly—it's time to eat. Spam. I used to hate Spam when I was a kid; I haven't eaten it in twenty years or more. But I looked at a can while I was making coffee this morning, and it started my mouth watering. Funny.

Why should I crave Spam after all these years, in a place and a situation like this?

THE FIFTH DAY

Good weather this morning. Blue sky, sunlight slanting in through the window at an oblique angle. I stood at the window for a long time, watching the sun sparkle on the snowdrifts and the snow-heavy tree branches and the icicles hanging from the near eaves of the shed roof. Snow looks so clean and fresh with the sun on it; everything looks clean and fresh, untouched, unsullied, and it gives you hope. Not that I'm losing hope. No. But with the day bright like this, so clean-looking, the loneliness is a little easier to handle and I don't have to work so hard to keep my spirits up, to keep on believing.

I fiddled with the radio again while I was at the window and had better luck. The honky-tonk station came in for a visit and hasn't left yet, at least not for more than a few minutes at a time. It's staticky and it keeps fluctuating, but it's audible enough.

Station KHOT, out of Stockton. That gives me some idea of where I am. A Stockton country station doesn't figure to have all that much range, so that puts this cabin somewhere in the Sierras to the east of Stockton. Yosemite's to the southeast; so are clusters of little Mother Lode towns and ski resorts. Doesn't figure he'd have taken me down that far. More likely, this place is in Amador or Calaveras or Alpine county; lots of wilderness in that section of the Sierra foothills, not too many towns, and a sparse population in winter. And the traveling time would be just about right, if my memory hasn't distorted those long, painful hours on the road.

All right: the Sierra foothills east or northeast of Stockton. That isn't much, but it's something. Not having *any* idea of where you are is like existing in limbo, as if you were already dead.

So I've been listening to KHOT and its honky-tonk music. One of the songs they played was "You Picked a Fine Time to Leave Me, Lucille," and for some reason it brought a sudden, vivid image of Kerry. The hurt got so bad so quickly I had to move the dial to get away from it. I found another station, somebody talking, but it was so static-riddled that I could only make out random words and sentence fragments—not enough to understand much of what was being said. When I switched back to KHOT I caught most of a news broadcast. All sorts of things happening on the international and national and local scenes, but no mention of me. That's not surprising, though. I'm yesterday's news by now.

The radio is still on, still playing country music. "Silver Threads and Golden Needles." Very spritely, even though the lyrics themselves aren't too cheerful. It's good to hear the sound of another human voice, even a singer's over a staticky radio. The silence was beginning to get to me a little. Much more of it and I might have started talking to myself just to relieve it.

Music, and the sun shining off clean snow outside. This day won't be too difficult to get through. Not too difficult.

* * *

There are forty-three books in the carton of paperbacks
—forty-two different titles. Eleven mysteries, four by Aga-
tha Christie, including two dog-eared copies of *Sleeping
Murder.* Two spy novels. Five adult Westerns and four
traditional Westerns and one pioneer-family saga. Two
science fiction novels. Six historical romances. Three Har-
lequin romances. Two sex-in-the-big-city novels. Two
show-business biographies. One book on organic gardening. One fad diet book. One history of jazz. And one book
on how to avoid stress.

In the carton of old magazines there are a total of
thirty-seven issues and seven different titles. Five issues of
Vogue, all from the late seventies. Six issues of *Sports Il-
lustrated* from 1985 and 1986. Twelve issues of *Time,* random over a five-year period beginning in 1976. Two issues
of *The Yachtsman,* dated June and July of 1981. Eight
issues of *Arizona Highways,* six from the late seventies and
two from 1980. Three issues of *Redbook,* dated March,
May, and August of 1986. And one issue of *Better Homes
and Gardens,* dated January 1985.

I've put all of the them, books and magazines, into little
separate piles along the wall next to the cot. No reason for
that—I can't reach most of them easily without sitting or
lying on the cot—or for cataloguing them as I have, other
than to pass the time. The first couple of days, I didn't
read anything. I tried once, the second day, but I couldn't
concentrate, could not sit still. Monday morning I forced
myself to page slowly through an issue of *Sports Illus-
trated.* And Monday evening I looked at a couple of issues
of *Arizona Highways,* until the photographs of wide-open
spaces caused the loneliness and the trapped feeling to
well up and I had to stop.

On Tuesday I picked out a traditional Western novel called *Gunsmoke Galoot*. Silly title, but it was originally published in 1940 and that was the sort of title they put on Westerns back then. I managed to get through one chapter in the morning, another in the afternoon, and still another before I went to sleep. Yesterday I was able to sit still long enough to read two chapters at a time until I finished it. I remember very little about the plot or characters—just that the writing had a nice pulpy flavor that was comforting, almost soothing.

I've never read Westerns much, books or pulps, though I don't have the attitude of some people that they're childish and inferior to most other kinds of fiction. Of the more than six thousand pulp magazines I've collected over the years—

My pulps. What will happen to them if I don't get out of here? What will Kerry do with them? Sell them off? Put them in storage? And the rest of the things in my flat . . . books, clothing, furniture, the accumulated detritus of a man's life? And the flat itself, what about that? The rent is paid until the first of the year; my landlord is a generous sort, he won't start pressing for back rent until February, but what then, when he does start pressing? Will Kerry pay the rent, on the slim hope that I'll be found alive or return on my own? or will she—

No, dammit, it's not going to work out that way. Stop trying to look ahead! Today is what matters. The here and now.

Of the 6,000 pulps in my collection, only about 50 or so are Westerns. *Dime Western, Star Western, .44 Western, Western Story.* All are issues from the thirties and forties, most with stories by writers who also wrote detective stories: Frederick Brown, Norbert Davis, William R. Cox. A

few have stories by Jim Bohannon, a writer who used to
contribute Western detective stories to *Adventure*. I met
him at a pulp convention in San Francisco a few years ago
—the same convention at which I met Kerry and her
parents, Cybil and Ivan, both former pulp writers themselves. Cybil wrote hard-boiled private-eye stories under
the male pseudonym Samuel Leatherman; Ivan wrote
horror stories—still writes them at novel length. It's an
appropriate field for him because he's something of a horror himself. He hates me because he thinks I'm not good
enough for Kerry, and too old for her besides; I hate him
because he's a grade-A asshole and how did I get off on
Ivan Wade? The subject here is Westerns, for Christ's
sake.

I used to like Western films and serials when I was a
kid. Every Saturday my ma would give me a quarter and
send me off to the neighborhood movie theater, alone or
with friends. That way, I wouldn't be home when my old
man . . . the hell with my old man, I'm not going to
write about *him*. I liked the crime films best, the serials
about detectives like Dick Tracy, superheroes like the Spi-
der and Captain Marvel, but I would sit just as engrossed
through a Gene Autry or Roy Rogers or Three Mes-
quiteers film, or chapters of Western serials. I remember
one serial, I think it was called *Adventures of Red Ryder*.
It had an Indian boy in it—Little Beaver. I envied that kid
as much as I envied the pulp private eyes when I got
older. I wanted to *be* Little Beaver, run around having
exciting adventures, wear a headband with a feather in it,
Jesus that film made an impression on me. I must have
been eight at the time, maybe nine. Little Beaver . . .

Now I seem to have drifted into childhood reminis-
cences. What the hell is the point in that? Or in wasting

any more paper on the subject of Westerns? It may pass the time but it doesn't seem to be doing me much good otherwise. Besides, my fingers are starting to cramp up.

Station KHOT has faded out again and I should try to tune it back in. Then something to eat, and a chapter or two of another paperback, and then maybe I'll wash out my shirt and underwear. They're starting to smell, and with the sun out it's not as cold in here as it has been; I can wrap myself in one of the blankets while the clothing dries in front of the heater.

I wish I could shave, too. My beard is growing out and it itches. But there's nothing I can use for a razor, except maybe a can lid and that would cut hell out of my skin. I'll just have to endure the discomfort until my facial hair gets long enough and the itching stops.

Tuna, crackers, and some Oreo cookies for lunch—a regular feast. But I've been on short rations from the first, and I've got to stay on them just in case. I've even taken to reusing one tea bag three and four times, and making coffee with just half a teaspoonful of instant.

Clouds in the sky now. The sun is hidden and it won't be long before it sets. There are long shadows, night shadows, on the drifted snow outside. I can see other shadows in the trees—crouching in the trees like animals, predators hiding there waiting for nightfall.

Cold in here again. And wouldn't you know it, my shirt and underwear still aren't dry.

THE SIXTH DAY

No more sun. Heavy clouds instead, gunmetal gray and veined with a kind of gangrenous black. Ugly clouds. Fat, bloated clouds full of rain. Break open pretty soon, dump rain like gray piss on the rest of the day.

I can't keep still. Cold in here, the air smells of rain even in here, I need to move around. I'm not going to write any more, pointless to keep writing crap like this.

Gray piss all over the rest of the day.

THE SEVENTH DAY

Yesterday was bad, the worst since I've been here, and today doesn't look much better. More dark clouds, more rain—it hasn't stopped raining since yesterday noon.

I'm still edgy, depressed. It's getting to me, all of it, the weather, the chain and the leg iron, the short rations, the staticky radio, *all* of it, and I can't seem to break the mood. Dangerous frame of mind, I *know* it is, I know I've got to snap out of it, but how? How? I did an hour's worth of nonstop exercises this morning, then paced and paced and paced until I was fatigued, but the workout didn't seem to have any effect on me mentally. I don't even want to eat. My belly is screaming for food but the thought of food makes my throat close up. I've *got* to eat, though. Got to keep my strength up.

Frigging weather. Why doesn't it stop raining?

I keep wondering if he'll be back.

Nearly a week now since he left. And he said he wouldn't come again until he was sure I was dead. But will he be able to stay away that long? The whole purpose of this prison is to make me suffer, right? A man who hates that deeply, who craves revenge that much— wouldn't he want to keep tabs on his victim, get a first- hand look at some of the suffering? Seems likely he would. He'd have to have tremendous will power not to. And wouldn't he want to make sure I hadn't found some way to get free, no matter how escape-proof he thinks this place is? If I were him I wouldn't be able to sleep night after night for as long as four months if there was even the remotest chance of my prisoner getting loose, coming af- ter me.

But I could never be a man like him, so how can I know what goes on in a mind like his? Maybe he's completely satisfied that there's no way for me to escape. And maybe just the *thought* of my suffering is enough for him.

Still. Still, there's a chance he'll come back. I *want* him to, because then I might be able to gull him into believing I'm sick, catch him off guard that way. He wasn't careless before, but that doesn't mean he can't be maneuvered into making a mistake. Oh yes, I want him to come back, I want him to make a mistake, I want to get my hands on him.

I want to kill him.

Only one other person I've felt that way about. Man named Emerson who hired a gunman to take out Eberhardt a few years ago. I happened to be with Eb at his house when the gunman showed up and both of us got shot, Eberhardt so seriously that he almost died. I tracked Emerson down with every intention of canceling his ticket —only he was dead when I caught up with him, dead of a freak accident, and it came as a relief because I didn't have to put myself to the test after all, find out if I really was capable of cold-blooded murder when the moment of truth arrived. Now, looking back on that time, I *know* I would not have been able to kill Emerson. All my life I've lived and worked within the law. And I've seen too much torn and bleeding flesh, too much death and dying, to want to inflict that kind of indecency on another human being.

But this is different. What the whisperer has done to me isn't human; *he* isn't human. He's a dangerous animal, a mad dog. And I *can* kill a mad dog—I know that just as surely as I know I wouldn't have been able to destroy Emerson.

Every man has his price in murder, just as he has his price in wealth or power or love. When the mad dog locked me in these chains we both found mine.

THE TENTH DAY

My daily routine is well established now, some of it by choice and some of it dictated by the contents and con- fines of my cell.

Wake up around seven, get up immediately. To the win-

dow first, for a look at the new day. Passable weather this
morning: high, broken overcast, streaks and wedges of
blue here and there. The sun hasn't appeared yet; I keep
hoping it will before the day ends. But at least there
haven't been any more rainstorms. The one over the
weekend lasted two full days, broke at last on Sunday
afternoon—and the worst of my depression broke with it.
Odd how the weather can affect your mood so pro-
foundly. I can tolerate overcast and snow flurries, I've
discovered, but I dread long periods of rain. And I yearn
for the sun. In a way I've become a sun-worshiper: I need
it to help me survive.

Back near the cot for my morning exercises. Sit-ups
first; I can do a set of fifty now, where I could do only
twenty-five when I started. Then leg pulls and stretches,
easy enough with my right leg, damned difficult with my
left because of the leg iron and the chain. Then push-ups,
twenty or so, then on my feet for knee bends, toe touches,
several other twists and stretches and jerks that I can't
name because I've more or less made them up myself. I
can do an hour's worth of exercises now without fatigue.
Tomorrow I'll increase the time by fifteen minutes. And
keep increasing it in fifteen-minute increments whenever I
feel I'm ready. Eventually, I should be able to use up most
of the morning in exercising, and that will be good because your mind shuts down when you're making physical
demands on your body. Sweat and strain equal a period of
relative peace.

Drag the chain into the bathroom, use the toilet, then
strip to the waist, brush my teeth and wash my face, and
take a quick sponge bath with the dampened cloth. Avoid
looking into the cracked mirror over the sink; I've only
glanced at my reflection once, two days ago, and that was

plenty. The face itself is unpleasant enough, with its coating of straggly gray whiskers and its haggard aspect. But the eyes . . . I'm afraid to look into my own eyes, for fear of what I might see reflected there.

Put on shirt and coats, go get the coffeepot and fill it with water and then take it back out and put it on the hot plate. Plug in the hot plate. Spoon coffee into the mug (coffee in the morning, tea in the afternoon, tea at night). Draw an ✕ through the day's date on the calendar. Switch on the heater, just for a few minutes, to take some of the chill out of the room: I'll be feeling cold again because my body has cooled after the morning workout. Find something on the shelves to eat for breakfast; open the can and set it aside. By this time the water should be boiling. Make the coffee, take the cup to the cot and sit down with it. Turn on the radio, try to bring in KHOT— the only station I seem to get on the radio. The last few days it hasn't come in for more than thirty seconds at a time, but this morning I got one twenty-minute stretch of golden oldies like "Orange Blossom Special" and "Your Cheatin' Heart," songs I'm beginning to like in spite of myself, and several other stretches of five to ten minutes each. Plus part of a news broadcast that told me a bunch of things, none of which I particularly wanted to hear (and nothing about me, of course). I've always been an ostrich when it comes to the daily news. For too long my life has been overrun with pain and suffering and ugliness; I don't need any more of it in black and white, or in bright colors with some newscaster speaking solemnly in a voice-over—the same newscaster who will be joking it up with a weatherman or a sportscaster two minutes later. So I didn't listen to much of the radio newscast, paid the most attention to a sports update that told me the Forty-niners won last Sunday. Let's hear it for the Forty-niners.

When I've finished the coffee, return to the hot plate and make another half cup. Then pour my breakfast into the saucepan and heat that. Eat breakfast on the cot, washed down with my second cup of coffee. Wash out the saucepan and the plate afterward, put them back on the top shelf next to the hotplate.

Pace for a while, twenty minutes to half an hour, as long as I can stand it.

Sit or lie on the cot and read a chapter or two or three of one of the paperbacks. I'm partway through an unauthorized biography of Frank Sinatra now, as a change of pace from the fiction. Lurid stuff, plenty of sex, lots of glitter and glamour and big money, all sorts of innuendo on a variety of fronts. All I knew about Sinatra before I started this book was that he was a crooner and a decent actor and a paisan who may or may not have a few underworld connections. Now I know enough to make me care even less about him than I did before.

Write a little, as I'm doing now. If I happen to feel like writing, that is. I haven't the past two days, so I didn't bother; there was just nothing I cared to set down on paper. Today I felt like picking up a pen again and I seem to be going on at some length. Not for any therapeutic reason . . . or maybe it *is* therapy, in a way, the kind that helps you keep things in perspective by confronting your thoughts, writing them out. But I don't want to force it. Does it matter if I keep a record of every single day I'm here? I don't see how it can.

Work on the wall for a while. I started doing that four days ago, during the rainstorm—bent and flattened one of the soup cans at the top and in the middle to fit my hand, so that it resembles a kind of scraping tool, and then gouged and rubbed and scraped at the wood around the ringbolt. I've been doing that every day since, for an hour or so at a time, even though it hasn't done much damage to the log and I really don't expect to get out of here that way. This is a kind of therapy, too, a way of reinforcing my resolve not to give up.

Pace some more, back and forth, forth and back, dragging that goddamn chain (I don't listen any more to the slithering, clanking sound it makes—I've found I can shut my ears to it if I try hard enough). Do that until I feel tired enough to sleep for an hour or two. Afternoon naps are good for you, particularly when you get up around my age. Ask any doctor, ask Dear Abby, that's what they all say.

After the nap, read another chapter or two in the current paperback. I might also read a chapter or two *before* I fall asleep, if that's what it takes to clear my mind and make me drowsy.

Get up, put fresh water on the hot plate, make a cup of tea. No afternoon meal; just two meals a day, morning and evening, to conserve provisions.

Drink the tea while thumbing through one of the magazines, spot-reading when something catches my eye—the ads, mostly. Modern magazine advertisements can be interesting sometimes, though not as interesting as the ones in the pulps. You can find ads for the damnedest things in thirties and forties issues of *Popular Detective, Flynn's, Complete Detective, Strange Detective Mysteries,* a host of others. Ads for trusses, false teeth, lonely hearts clubs, sex manuals, anatomical charts, nose adjusters to alter the shape of your schnozz, home study courses in taxidermy and how to be a detective or a secret service operative.

Cures for tobacco addiction, alcohol addiction, epilepsy, rheumatism, piles, pimples, warts, stomach gas, and kidney problems. Booklets on how to patent your invention, how to stop stammering, how to analyze handwriting, how to make love potions, how to "become dangerous" and lick bullies twice your size, how to raise giant frogs for fun and profit. Hundreds more just as improbable. Somebody ought to do a book of pulp-magazine ads, reproduce the screwiest ones in their entirety. For my generation it would be more than a collection of high-camp hucksterism; it would provide instant nostalgia with each and every page.

Wash out the tea cup, put it back on the shelf. Maybe try to bring KHOT in again, maybe pace a while longer or do a few more exercises, maybe look out the window if the weather is decent, maybe work a little more on these misery pages, these burnt offerings, this indictment. Improv time. Don't want to establish *too* rigid a routine here. Got to leave a little room for spontaneity, right?

By this time it should be late afternoon, getting on toward dusk. Switch on the lamp, if it isn't on already. Switch on the heater, if *it* isn't on already, because once darkness settles, no matter what the weather is like, it gets chilly in here.

Almost time for supper. Make preparations—and take time doing it, there's no hurry, let the belly do a little begging for its evening meal. What'll it be tonight? Corned beef hash? Very good choice, sir, very nourishing. Corned beef hash, crackers, tea, and—let's see—how about some nice Fig Newtons for dessert? I haven't had Fig Newtons since I was a kid, and when I was a kid I hated them. If I told my ma once I told her fifty times how much I hated Fig Newtons, and still she bought them, still she put them in my school lunch pail or on my dessert plate at home. I gave up eventually and ate them, every last one, instead of ignoring them or throwing them away. Mothers are good at making you give up, making you eat or do things they think are good for you. It's a subtle form of mind control that, if practiced properly— and my ma was an expert at it—retains its hold on you no matter how long you live. I still hate Fig Newtons, so tonight I'm going to eat Fig Newtons, and not just because I can't afford to waste food. If I were confronted with a package of Fig Newtons somewhere else, at any time, I would probably eat the damned things then too. The only reason I haven't eaten them in thirty-five years is that I've somehow managed to avoid being confronted with them.

Eat supper while paging through another magazine. Wash the plate and cup and saucepan, put them away on the top shelf.

Read another chapter or two, sitting or lying on the cot.

Do another twenty minutes or so of exercises.

Wash my hands and face in the bathroom sink. Strip down to my underwear (if it's not too cold to sleep in just underwear). Turn off the heater and the lamp. Wrap myself in the two blankets and lie down and will myself to sleep immediately so that I won't lie there in the dark and think and maybe brood. I remember seeing a movie once, one of those old Topper comedies with Roland Young, and one of the players asked Eddie "Rochester" Anderson if he was afraid of the dark. He said no, he wasn't afraid of the dark; he was afraid of what was *in* the dark. I laughed at the time; I'm not laughing now. I'm afraid of what's in the dark, too—the dark recesses of my mind.

And that's my day. This day, and with minor variations, all my yesterdays and all my tomorrows until I find a way out of here. On the one hand, the regular routine creates the sense of normalcy I need and acts as a kind of mind-numbing drug for most of my waking hours. On the other hand, the monotony and the crushing loneliness can't help but have negative long-range effects.

Now I know exactly how hard-core convicts feel, men in solitary confinement, prisoners on death row. And yet most of them can look forward to their release; even the ones on death row have a mathematically better chance of survival than I do—lawyers working for new trials, commutations, stays. And those prisoners aren't forced to wear leg irons and chains, not anymore. And they have other prisoners to talk to, friends and relatives who come to visit them. I have no one. No friend or loved one who has any idea of where I am, no way anyone can work effectively for my release. There is only me. My world has shrunk to this corner, fifteen feet by fifteen feet, and I am its only inhabitant. For all I know, what I hear on the radio may be nothing more than a tape playing in an empty studio, and the entire human race has been eradicated and I am the last man in the world, trapped here in *my* little world.

But that makes no difference in how I get through my days. I haven't lost my will to survive, nor will I lose it, and so I go on. Minute to minute, hour to hour, day to day. Living on three things other than the meager rations of food.

Hope.

And my love for Kerry.

And my hatred of the mad dog who put me here.

THE TWELFTH DAY

Christmas songs on the radio. The one playing right now is an oldie called "Silver Bells."

Soon it will be Christmas Day . . .

Hazy sky and pale sunlight this morning, as though the sun were shining through milk, and KHOT's signal is stronger than it has been on any day since my imprisonment. The song that was playing when I first switched on was "Rudolph, the Red-nosed Reindeer." There have been half a dozen others since: carols and old favorites by Merle Haggard and Johnny Cash and Tammy Wynette, novelty items like "I Saw Mommy Kissing Santa Claus" and "Grandma Got Run Over by a Reindeer."

This isn't the first day the station has put on Christmas songs, but it's the first day I've paid any real heed to them. First day I've let myself think about Christmas, how close it is. And now that the thought is in my head, I can't seem to get it out again.

Today is December 16—Wednesday, December 16.

Friday of next week is Christmas.

Only nine more shopping days left.

Usually I put Christmas shopping off to the last minute, but this year I vowed to buy my presents at least one week and preferably two weeks early. I hate crowds. And no matter where you go in the Bay Area one or two days before Christmas, the crowds are unbelievable—holiday commercialism at its most demented. So I wasn't going to put myself through any more of that last-minute lunacy, not *this* year. I even had what I was going to buy people pretty much worked out. That way I wouldn't have to wander around looking for something suitable. I could just walk into this or that store and buy the gift and walk right out again.

For Kerry I was going to get a videotape of *Gone With the Wind,* one of her favorite old movies. And a pair of white jade earrings she'd admired in a jewelry store window last month. And a Norwegian ski sweater, blue and white with a reindeer design, that I saw in a Saks ad and figured would look good on her. The only things I hadn't chosen yet were her joke gift and her card. We've exchanged joke gifts at Christmas every year we've been together. Once she gave me a huge plastic jar full of popcorn; last year I gave her a gorilla mask, because she'd once confessed to a secret desire to own a gorilla suit so she could scare hell out of people who came knocking at her door. That kind of nonsense thing. As for her card, I have to be careful in what I select because she doesn't care for the fancy or traditional or sentimental variety. She prefers something simple, or better yet, something humorous.

For Eberhardt, the only other person I regularly buy presents for, I had a new briar pipe and some decent tobacco in mind. His old pipes stink and so does the tobacco he uses, a foul black mixture he gets somewhere that looks and smells like burning horseshit.

This week Kerry and I would have gone to one of the neighborhood lots and picked out a tree. We've done that the last couple of years and it's always been a special occasion. Then we'd take it back to her apartment and trim it and sit around afterward watching the tree lights and feeling Christmassy. Last year we got to feeling more than that and ended up making love on the carpet, so exuberantly that one or both of us knocked off a couple of ornaments and broke one. First time I've ever had *that* under my tree, she said.

Next week there's her office party. I don't like parties much but she insisted that I go last year, so I gave in reluctantly and went expecting to have a lousy time—and had as good a time as anybody else who was reasonably sober and didn't try to grope one of the agency secretaries behind the water cooler.

And a couple of days before Christmas, we'd drive around the city and look at the decorations people put up —the flocked and tinseled trees, the manger scenes and cardboard sleighs and Santas and strings of colored lights around windows and doors and in shrubs. You can still see that kind of traditional Christmas spirit in San Francisco's neighborhoods. It always puts the spirit in me, too, makes me think of when I was a kid and Christmas had a special aura and a special meaning . . . one that goes away when you grow up and that you can never recapture. Innocence is part of it; so is wonder. As an adult you can remember what it was like, you can feel nostalgia for it, but you can't really *feel* it anymore. It's like trying to touch a ghost: all vague outline and no substance.

And on Christmas Eve Kerry would cook a special dinner—she's a very good chef—and then we'd open some of our presents. Not all of them, we always save a couple for Christmas morning. And then we'd go to bed and make love, we always make love on Christmas Eve, and when we woke up it would be Christmas and we'd open the other presents and then have breakfast and later on we'd go over to Eberhardt's and share a holiday drink with

him, exchange presents, and then we then we I don't want
to go on with this it isn't doing me any good I can't go on
with this.

It hurts to remember, it hurts to think about Christmas
and Kerry and the way things used to be and won't be this
year. No more of it. No more Christmas music, either,
shut the radio off and keep it off.

It *hurts* too much.

THE SIXTEENTH DAY

I'm losing weight.

I came in here at about 245, belt stretched all the way
out to the last hole, gut starting to bulge over all around.
A couple of years ago I dropped 25 pounds eating salads
and eggs and yogurt, healthy stuff like that. Got down to
about 215, felt good, looked pretty good, managed to keep
the weight off for almost a year. But I like beer—correc-
tion, I *used* to like beer—and I used to like to eat and I've
always had sloppy habits, my food intake being no excep-
tion. So I put the 25 pounds back on over the past year,
plus another 5 for bad measure. Porky Pig, that was me
when I got taken out of the real world and transplanted
into this one.

Now, though, the weight is coming off again. My pants
are loose at the waist and I've taken the belt in one notch
already, with another not far off. Short rations, the en-
forced two-meager-meals-a-day diet—that's one reason.
Exercise is another. I work out an hour and a half each

morning now, another half hour each evening. If I keep
up that kind of escalating program, I'll be in tip-top shape
at the end of three months. Down to about 210, muscles
where all the flab used to be . . . maybe I'll be strong
enough to rip that goddamn ringbolt right out of the wall.

Sure. And maybe I can also huff and puff and blow the
wall down.

Yessir, tip-top shape at the end of three months. Best
I've looked in more than thirty years, since my tour in the
military. Of course, I won't look so good once the food
starts running out. It won't be muscles bulging then; it'll
be ribs and bones. And the gut won't be flat, it'll be con-
cave. By the time I die of starvation, I might even be all
the way down to 195 or so . . . first time in my adult life
I've weighed less than 200 pounds.

The whisperer won't even know me when he comes to
bury my corpse.

THE SEVENTEENTH DAY

What was it he said that last afternoon, after he made his
grisly little joke about cutting off my leg with one of the
can lids? Something about it being the equivalent of an
animal chewing off a limb caught in a trap?

Well, here's an interesting little problem in self-analysis:
Suppose I had an axe or a hatchet. And suppose there
isn't any other way out of this prison. Would I be able to
chop off my own leg in order to escape?

Never mind the fact that this cabin is isolated—more

than a mile from its nearest neighbor, he said—and that I don't know anything about tying off severed arteries. Never mind that I would surely bleed to death before I could crawl more than a couple of hundred yards. Let's say help is close by. Let's say that if I were able to chop my leg off, it would guarantee my survival. Would I be able to do it then? Would I have the guts and will of a fox or a wolf in the same situation?

I wonder.

I wonder just how many people *would* have an animal's courage if they were confronted with that decision.

THE TWENTIETH DAY

'Twas the night before Christmas and all through the cabin, not a creature was stirring except the poor miserable bastard trapped here in chains.

THE TWENTY-FIRST DAY

Christmas Day.

And it's snowing outside, it has been snowing most of the night. What we have here is a white Christmas. Outside the window it's all picture-postcard stuff, snow falling, snow mantling the trees, the overcast high so that you

can see everything in sharp relief. Any minute now, Bing
Crosby will come strolling out of the woods singing
"White Christmas." Or he would if he wasn't dead.

Now, now, let's be cheerful here. It's Christmas Day,
it's a white Christmas, let's have a little good cheer.

Deck the halls with boughs of holly, fa la la la la, la la
la la. 'Tis the season to be jolly, fa la la la la, la la la la.

All right, that's enough for now. A man can only take
so much good cheer at one time. Too big a jolt and I
might OD. Spread it out, make it last, there's a long long
day of celebration ahead.

Long day ahead for Kerry, too. How will she spend it?
Sitting home alone, wondering, remembering how it was
with us on Christmases past? Over at Eberhardt's—he'd
have invited her, the circumstances being what they are—
or with one of her lady friends?

With Jim Carpenter?

Good-looking guy, Carpenter, suave, sophisticated,
very successful in the ad business, eight or nine years
closer to her age than I am, wears $800 suits and still has
the trim body of an athlete. Besides which, he's one of her
bosses—Bates and Carpenter, San Francisco's fastest rising ad agency. Maybe he's been consoling her during the
past three weeks, out of the office as well as in. Providing
the strong male shoulder, the reassuring words in her time
of need. How soon before she goes to bed with him, if she
hasn't already? Tonight, tomorrow night, some night next
week—

Hey, hey, hold it right there.

Suppose she does go to bed with Jim Carpenter? So
what? You stupid jealous schmuck, why shouldn't she
crawl into the sack with him or anybody else if she needs
it badly enough? You expect her to keep the home fires

burning forever, on blind faith? Stay celibate until she's a
crone? For all she knows you're dead, pal, dead and buried somewhere—she doesn't know *anything* about what
happened to you, for Christ's sake. She's hurting too, you
think you're the only one? Don't start condemning her,
blaming *her* for anything.

Don't doubt her, not even for one second.

Don't stop loving her.

Heigh-ho, better lighten the mood again. Jingle bells,
jingle bells, jingle all the way. Oh what fun it is to ride a
one-horse open sleigh. There, that's better. That's the old
spirit.

Wonder how Eberhardt and Bobbie Jean are getting
along? Has he slept with her yet? Popped the marriage
question yet? No, it's too early for him to be thinking
seriously about tying the knot, too soon after the Mysteri-
ous Disappearance of His Partner. Got to observe a decent interval of mourning, after all. But it'd be nice if they
do get together eventually. She'd be good for him; Kerry
was right about that. He needs a woman with both feet on
the ground and something in her mind besides sex and a
collection of cobwebs and dust bunnies.

Snowing harder now. Where's old Bing? Or don't they
dream of white Christmases where he is now?

Frosty, the snowman, was a hap-hap-happy soul, dee
dee dee dee, dee dee dee dee, dee dee dee dee dee dee.

Well, what have we here? Can it be a parade of all my
Christmases past, like ghosts lining up for review? Yes,
indeed. Let's see, these were joyous, and these were not so
joyous, and this little group over here sucked out loud.
None even close to *this* one, though. No presents on this
Christmas; no fancy dinner, no wassail, no lovemaking,
no caroling, no candlelight services at Mission Dolores to

celebrate the birth of the Saviour. Instead we have tea and canned beef stew and canned spinach and Triscuits, we have snow and a Christmas-card view through a rimed window (who needs cards when you've got the real thing), we have unrelieved static in place of traditional music, and we have chains in lieu of colored lights and tinsel. But hey, it's still Christmas, right? Sure it is. It's still the greatest holiday of them all.

Merry Christmas, Kerry.

Merry Christmas, Eb.

Merry Christmas, Bobbie Jean.

Merry Christmas, you whispering mad dog son of a bitch.

Peace on earth, good will to men.

THE TWENTY-FIFTH DAY

I've been sick the past three days. Bad cold or flu, maybe even a touch of pneumonia. Fever, chills, aching in all my joints, weakness, nausea. I couldn't do much of anything except lie on the cot, swaddled in my overcoat and both blankets, the heater turned all the way up, and drift in and out of sleep and a kind of delirium. Made myself get up once the first day to use the bathroom, fell down on the way back and couldn't stand up, could not stand up, and had to crawl the rest of the way to the cot. Vomited on the floor later on because I was too weak even to try for the bathroom. Didn't eat anything the first day, took a little soup and some tea the second morning that I threw back up, took more soup and tea the second night that stayed down. Yesterday I managed to hold solid food in my stomach again—about half a can of macaroni and cheese.

Once, during the worst of it, I dreamed that I was outside the cabin, running through the snowdrifts, laughing, free, and woke up feeling so shattered to find myself still shackled that I had to fight to keep from breaking down. Dreamed another time that Kerry and I were in bed, her bed, lying with our arms around each other after making love, and then she got up and went away and didn't come back, didn't come back, didn't come back, and I searched everywhere for her but she was gone and I knew I would never see her again. That dream nearly unmanned me too.

Bad, very bad, those three days. The worst so far.

But whatever virus had hold of me, it seems to have weakened and let go. I woke up drenched in sweat and feeling that heavy, different kind of body ache that tells you a fever has finally broken and your body is rebuilding its defenses. Woke up feeling hungry, too, always a good sign. I was able to get up and move around, go through most of my morning routine—everything but the exercises —without too much difficulty. I ate a whole can of Chef Boyardee ravioli, a whole can of corn, a whole can of peaches in heavy syrup. No sense in conserving rations today or tomorrow. I've got to regain my strength, guard against a relapse. Another viral bout like this one, at my age and with poor nourishment and no medication of any kind, and I might not survive it.

I've got to make a decision about the heater. Keep it on most of today, and run the risk of those old coils burning out from overuse? Or shut it off and keep it off until after dark, when the cold gets even worse, and run the risk of more sickness? It'll be bitter cold in here without it; snowing again today, and the temperature must be well below freezing outside. But those coils have begun to ping loudly every now and then, as if in protest, and I'm afraid they won't last with continuous use. Twice yesterday I shut the thing off for ten to fifteen minutes when the pinging got loud, and the coils seemed all right again when I switched it back on. The periods between the loud pings are decreasing, though . . . starting to do it again right now. It could give out any time.

All right, then, I *have* to shut it down for at least part of today. The risk of pneumonia isn't as great as the risk of freezing to death, which could happen to me if the heater quits working. The coats and blankets, the hot coffee and tea just aren't enough protection.

This afternoon I read over the pages I wrote on Christmas Eve and Christmas Day. And they made me uneasy, they scared me more than a little.

Rambling stuff, only half coherent, like the scribblings of a borderline lunatic. I've been trying to tell myself it was the virus already at work inside me, creating a sort of waking delirium, but that won't wash. The truth is, I *was* a little crazy those two days. No longer in complete control.

There's an explanation for it. The loneliness, the pain, missing Kerry, missing normalcy, a buildup of self-pity— all of that magnified by the holidays. That's why, statistically, there are more suicides during the Christmas season than at any other time of the year. Still, I can't use that as an excuse. I am not a statistic, I am not just anyone—I'm me. If I give in to the pressure I'll lose control again, and if that happens I might not be able to regain it. And then I *wouldn't* be me any longer, would I?

THE TWENTY-NINTH DAY

I saw a deer this morning while I was standing at the window looking at the new day—the first living thing I've seen in four weeks.

It came down out of the trees higher up—just movement at first, flashes of dark brown and white until it reached level ground. Then, slowly, it ventured out into the open, and I saw that it was a big, white-tailed, six-point buck. His eye had picked out a patch of grass near the shed, where the thin snowpack has melted away. The weather has been sunny the past two days, and warm enough to turn the snow slushy, to reveal patches of earth in places where there is no shade.

I watched the buck nibble at the grass. Every now and then he would raise his head, keen the air, as if aware that he was being watched. Once he seemed to look straight at me and I stood very still, even though I was pretty sure he couldn't see me behind the window glass. He couldn't smell me, in any case, so he wasn't afraid. He stayed there feeding for fifteen minutes or so, and I stood motionless all that time, watching him.

God, he was a beautiful animal. How can anyone kill an animal like that, shoot it down for sport? I don't care what arguments hunters use, it isn't right to take an innocent life like that, *any* innocent life, unless there is no other choice—and then it should be done with the most profound regret. Life, most life, is too precious. That deer's was so precious to me this morning that I felt an aching sense of loss when he finally finished feeding, turned, bounded away into the trees, and was gone from *my* life, probably forever.

But he left me with something, too: fresh hope. For one thing, he is a symbol of freedom. For another thing, he came on the second day of the new year, and what is a new year but a new beginning?

An omen, then. A symbol and an omen.

I am going to survive this winter just as that deer will survive it. I *know* that now. I have no doubt of it.

THE THIRTY-FIRST DAY

The radio has quit working. No sound, not even a hum, when I switched it on this morning. I thought it was the batteries at first and put in the replacement set, but it still doesn't work. Must be a blown transistor or tube or something.

It's not as much of a loss as it might have been two or three weeks ago. I can get by without it now. If I need conversation or music in here, I'll create it myself.

After all, don't psychologists say that talking to yourself is one way of validating your own existence, reassuring yourself that you're still alive and kicking?

THE THIRTY-FOURTH DAY

Thought for the day:

For weeks before all of this happened, ever since that ugly case involving the Purcell family, I contemplated retirement. Talked it over with Kerry, and she was all for it —provided, she said, I was sure I wouldn't grow bored and discontented. Not me, I said. Detective work is no longer the be-all and end-all of my life, I said. I can find plenty of things to do, I said, plenty of ways to occupy my time. Bored? Discontented? No way.

Well, bullshit.

What is *this* if not a kind of forced retirement? This filling up of my days with endless routine, marking time until the Grim Reaper shows up? No purpose in my existence here other than survival; no purpose in retirement, either, other than survival of a somewhat less painful variety. I'm miserable now, confined to this room by chains I can see, feel, hear slithering along the floor whenever I move. If I were home, retired, rattling around my empty flat all day, wouldn't I be just as miserable in the long run? And just as chained? Invisible chains, sure, much longer than this one and allowing me much more freedom of movement, but still confining in their own way?

I'm a detective, dammit. That is not only what I am, it's *who* I am. I hate the business, I hate the things I see, the people I have to deal with, the actions I'm sometimes forced to take. But hey, who says you have to love your job to be good at it, to take satisfaction from it, to need it to give meaning and fulfillment to your life? I'd wither up

and die in the chains of retirement, just as I'll wither up
and die if I don't escape from *these* chains. I know that
now. I should have known it all along.

When I get out of here, I am not going to retire. I am
going straight back into harness. Find the mad dog first,
and then resume my duties at the agency and keep right
on working until, God willing, I die in bed at the age of
ninety after successfully completing one last case.

Retirement is hell, so to hell with retirement.

THE THIRTY-SIXTH DAY

The stench in here is bad and getting worse by the day.
Garbage is part of it, but the worst part of it is me.

I've filled up two of the cardboard cartons with empty
cans and cookie and cracker wrappers. At first I didn't
bother to rinse out the cans before I dumped them into
the cartons; but then the food remnants began to rot and
smell, and I had to spend part of a day cleaning them out
with soapy water. Now I rinse each can thoroughly as I
use it. Still, the accumulation of them and of the micro-
scopic food particles that I wasn't able to wash away have
gradually built up a sour odor. The odor in one of the
cartons got so bad that I pushed it out into the middle of
the room, to the full extension of the chain, and then
skidded it over to the far side of the room. If this were
spring or summer, I would have ants and maybe mice and
rats to deal with on top of everything else.

But the real problem is my body odor and my clothing

and the two blankets. Washing out my shirt and underwear and socks once a week, using nothing but a bar of
hand soap, doesn't do much to get rid of the soaked-in
sweat smell. Sponge baths don't do much to cleanse my
body, either. I'm afraid to wash my hair, matted and
greasy as it is, because of the threat of another bad cold, of
pneumonia. And there's nothing I can do about the blankets or the cot or my coats or my trousers.

All of this is as much an indignity as the rest of it. I've
been turned into a filthy, rank-smelling bum—I have been
made unclean.

I hate him for that, too. As if I needed any more fuel to
keep the hate burning high and hot, like a fire on the edge
of my soul.

THE THIRTY-NINTH DAY

I've given up scraping at the wall around the ringbolt with
flattened cans and the edges of can lids. It's wasted effort,
pointless and frustrating and psychologically debilitating.
I am not going to escape that way. In all this time I've
managed to scrape a circular furrow around the bolt no
more than an eighth of an inch deep. At this rate it would
take me a year, maybe two, to work through the log to the
outside. And I'm more convinced than ever that I would
need to work all the way through in order to free the bolt.
He didn't just imbed it in the log; no, he drilled a hole
straight through to the outside, fitted the bolt into the

hole, and then fastened it in place with a locking plate of some kind. I've never doubted his intelligence, his cunning, his thoroughness. It would be a mistake to doubt them now.

What I can and still do doubt is his ability to foresee and effectively block every conceivable method of escape. There is something he overlooked, something *I'm* overlooking. There has to be. I've believed that all along and I'll keep believing it until I find the weak link in the chain . . . metaphorically if not literally.

THE FORTY-THIRD DAY

Funny, but old memories seem to come bobbing up to the surface lately. Things I haven't thought about in years, that were lodged and forgotten in the depths of my mind, most of them from my youth—and I don't understand why, here and now, after all the days in this place.

The house where I grew up, for instance. It was in the Outer Mission, in a little Italian working-class enclave near the Daly City line. Big rambling thing, built in the twenties, part wood frame and part stucco, with a fenced-in rear yard that had a walnut tree in its exact center. I used to climb the tree when I was a kid, sometimes to pick walnuts when they were in season, sometimes just to sit and think or read. Drove my ma crazy until she decided I was old enough not to break a leg climbing in or out; then she quit yelling at me to put my feet on the ground and keep them there.

That memory of my ma, and others too. She was a big, sweet-faced woman, hiding a load of pain and sadness under a jovial exterior. My old man was one reason for the pain and sadness. My sister Nina was another: Nina died of rheumatic fever at the age of five. I don't remember much about her, except that she had black hair and black eyes and she was very thin; I was only eight when she died. Ma couldn't have any other children and so she lavished all her maternal love on me. I was lucky in that respect. If she'd been anything like my old man, the whole shape of my life might have been different.

She loved to cook, as did most Italian women of her generation. She would spend hours in the kitchen, making Ligurian dishes from her native Genoa. Focaccia alla salvia, torta pasqualina, trenette col pesto, trippa con il sugo di tocco, burrida, tomaxelle, cima alla Genovese, dozens more. Lord, the aromas that would fill the house from her kitchen! Garlic, spices, simmering sauces, frying meats, baking breads and cakes and gnocchi e canditti. I can close my eyes now, even here in this place, and it's as if I'm back in that big house surrounded by all those succulent smells.

There was one Sunday when I was twelve or thirteen— a feast to celebrate the wedding of one of my cousins. It was a warm day and we ate in the backyard, on tables covered with white linen cloths, and there was accordion music—Ma's brother was a professional accordion player —and dancing, and homemade dago red and grappa from another brother's ranch in Novato. It was a special occasion so I was allowed to drink a glass of strong red wine with the meal, and combined with the sun's heat it made me woozy. Some of the guests and relatives laughed, my old man loudest of all, but Ma wasn't one of them. She never laughed at me. She never laughed at anyone.

She never laughed much at all.

Big woman from Genoa. Big sad loving woman who traded the old world for a new one, and made the best of a life she didn't deserve. She was exactly as I remember her —not a saint, no, but good. Down deep where it counts, as good as anyone God ever made.

THE FORTY-FIFTH DAY

He was here last night!

He came back, he was here, *he was right here in this room watching me while I slept!*

When I woke up and saw one of the doors across the room standing partway open, saw in front of it the straight-backed chair he'd sat in that first night, I thought I was hallucinating. I came up off the cot with chills racking me, scrubbing at my eyes, staring. But the chair stayed where it was, the door stayed open, the son of a bitch was here.

Rage boiled up, a black savage rage, and I lost control for a time . . . I don't know how long. I shouted curses, I ripped at the chain until my hands started to bleed. I hurled empty cans from the garbage carton at the chair and the open door. Then, all at once, the wildness was gone and I was down on all fours, spent, my breath rasping out in little puffs of vapor like smoke from the fire inside.

When I could stand again I went to the window, looked out. But it was an act of reflex: I knew there would be nothing to see, nothing to alter the same old view. And there wasn't: He was long gone.

He must have come in the small hours, when he could be reasonably sure that I would be asleep. Left his car some distance down the road so the sound of the engine wouldn't carry and wake me up. Picked last night because the weather was clear and there was a full moon, bright and silvery—it was the last thing I saw through the window before I slept. Made his way around on the other side of the cabin, all stealth and cunning, and let himself in through a window or another outside door. Eased that inner door open, eased the chair through, stood or sat there watching me sleep, the moonlight spilling in and making every detail clear to him. Enjoying what he saw . . . oh, he enjoyed every fucking minute of it, you can bet on that.

I *knew* he couldn't stay away. Knew he'd come back at least once to check up on his handiwork. And I should have known it would be this way, skulking around in the night, watching me in the night and then making sure I'd realize it when I woke up and he was already gone. Far more satisfaction for him that way than facing me, talking to me, giving me even a few minutes of human contact. And far more torment for me.

How long was he here? Five minutes, ten, twenty, thirty? Over there in the dark, watching, something evil in the dark watching and smiling and feeding on what he saw like some kind of vampire . . . Jesus, every time I think of it it makes my skin crawl, it adds fresh fuel to my hatred and my longing to destroy him. I've never felt this

kind of bloodlust before, nothing even remotely like it. It's
an ugly and frightening thing, like an alien substance alive
and growing in my body. And yet it's also sustaining
somehow—a force I can use to help shore up my faith and
my resolve.

Setting all this down on paper has calmed me, put me
back in control. But I don't think I can write much
longer. The palm of my right hand is cut and abraded
from the chain, and holding the pen, pressing down with
the point, is painful. There's pain in my left heel, too,
where the goddamn leg iron slipped down during my
frenzy and dug into the flesh.

Enough for now. I better wash out all the cuts as a
precaution against infection.

The leg iron.
The leg iron!

THE FORTY-SIXTH DAY

I've found the flaw in his plan, the weak spot in his "es-
capeproof" prison. There's a way out of here, just as I
believed all along—and all along it has been right here in
front of me, I have been staring at it day after day, I have
been carrying it with me every time I move.

The leg iron.

It was when I went into the bathroom yesterday to
wash out the cuts that the realization came to me. I was

sitting on the floor, working on the gouge in my heel with
the wet washcloth, pushing the leg iron up out of the way
with my left hand . . . and then I saw, really *saw,* what I
was doing.

The leg iron had slipped down off my calf. In the beginning it had been tight around the calf, then a little less
tight, and a little less tight, and yesterday, for the first
time, it had slipped all the way down. I must have lost at
least 20 pounds in the past six weeks, maybe as much as
25. And I'd been heavy when he brought me here, 245 or
better—Kerry had been after me to start dieting again. I
must be down around 220 now. My pants are baggy, my
shirt hangs on me like a scarecrow's: flattening gut, tight-
ening thighs, thinning calves. I always did have big legs,
and when I put on weight the fat tends to deposit there as
well as around my middle. Go on a lengthy diet and one
of the first places the weight loss is visible is in my legs.

Sitting there on the floor I straightened out my left leg
and foot so that the heel pulled back in against the ankle;
then I worked the iron down as far as it would go. Got the
lower edge over the gouge in my heel, over the heel itself
by a fraction of an inch until the upper edge of the iron bit
hard into the flesh of my instep. A little of the wildness
came back into me then, and I had to fight myself to keep
from trying to force the iron any farther. The worse thing
I can do right now is to cut up my foot; cuts might get
infected, the foot might swell.

I thought then of slicking it with soap, to make the
metal slide more easily over the flesh. But it didn't help,
not yet anyway: I still couldn't get the iron down any
farther on my instep.

I've got to be patient. I can afford to be patient now

that I've found the means of escape. I'll lose more weight; with the amount of food I'm eating and the daily exercise program, I can't help but lose more weight. All I need is another fraction of an inch off my foot. People don't think of losing weight off their feet but it happens. Shed enough poundage, you'll see the difference on just about every part of your body, feet included. I know, I've been there— fat and not fat, fat and not fat, a vicious cycle all my adult life.

Another month to six weeks should do it. Six weeks maximum. The remaining provisions will hold out that long, I'll see to that. And I'll hold out too if I'm careful, don't overdo anything, don't cut up my foot, don't catch pneumonia. Patient and careful. The day will come. That's the only way to look at it.

The day will come when I'll be free again.

THE FIFTY-SECOND DAY

Two hours of calisthenics in the morning, one hour in the afternoon, another hour before I go to sleep at night. If I'd tried to keep up that kind of schedule before my world shrank to this stinking prison, I would have put a killing strain on my heart. But I've eased into it gradually, and I pace myself through each session, and with the absence of close to thirty pounds (it must be close to thirty by now), there doesn't seem to be much strain at all. I'm plenty tired by the time I crawl under the blankets, and I sleep quickly and deeply, but it isn't the sleep of exhaustion.

The muscles in my arms, shoulders, and legs have become visible; my belly is almost flat. I'm turning into . . . what's the expression these days? Hunk? That's it: I'm turning into a hunk. Wait until Kerry sees me. She won't recognize me.

I won't recognize myself, either. Because I still haven't looked in that cracked mirror in the bathroom. And I won't—I will not look in a mirror again until I get out of this place. I wouldn't know the gaunt, bearded stranger in the glass, and I don't want to know him. He isn't me; he's a stand-in, a surrogate, an impostor. The real me is waiting down inside—he hasn't gone anywhere, he's just in a temporary state of suspended animation—and once I'm away from here he'll come out again. And when I finally do look in a mirror I'll see *him,* not the stranger with the beard and the terrible eyes.

Does that make any sense? I don't know. I don't care much right now.

Using soap for grease, I can work the iron the tiniest bit farther over my heel and down along my instep. And that's all that matters.

THE FIFTY-NINTH DAY

Another tiny bit closer to freedom. Almost half the leg iron will slip over my heel now before the lower edge binds hard into the instep.

I have to force myself to eat two full meals a day; have

had to for the past week. There is a part of me, a kind of imp of the perverse that lives in all of us, that keeps insisting I eat tiny portions or nothing at all, because that way I'll lose weight even faster. Yes, I keep telling the imp, and maybe then I'd die of malnutrition before I could get the iron all the way off. Or at least make myself too weak and sick to walk away from this cabin once I get free of the shackles. It's still winter outside, there are still occasional snow flurries, and there is snow on the ground and it is still damned cold. I can't travel on foot in freezing weather with only a topcoat for warmth and protection. I'd collapse before I made half a mile; I would probably die of exposure.

No, I must eat regular good-sized meals to keep my strength up. The weight is coming off slowly, naturally; there's no sense in trying to accelerate the process. Patience. Patience and care.

What I have to concentrate on now is the future, what happens *after* I get out of here and out of these mountains. For the first time since he chained me here, I have to start looking ahead, start making plans.

I need to concentrate on *him,* too. How can I find him unless I have some clue to who he is, where he might be? And the key to that may well be the thirteen weeks' supply of provisions.

Why thirteen? I've got to keep asking myself that question until I come up with the answer.

What is the significance of thirteen?

THE SIXTY-FIFTH DAY

More old memories crowding up to the surface, unbidden and this time unwanted. Unpleasant memories of my old man, of the way he lived and the way he died.

I hated him, growing up, with as much intensity as I loved my ma. And after his death I forgot him, shut him out of my mind and my life so completely that now, forty years later, I can't dredge up even the slightest image of him. Just vague impressions—gestures, random actions, shouted words. And all of those distasteful.

I was seventeen when he died. Once he was buried I said good-bye to Ma and I joined the army and went away to fight in the South Pacific, in another of this century's collection of wars. When I came home again, after four long hard years, no scars on my body but the first of many on my psyche, Ma and I never once talked about him, not to each other and not in each other's hearing. Neither of us mentioned his name until the day Ma died, five years after my return. Then, on her deathbed, she said with some of her last words, "Try to forgive him," and I said I would, for her sake, but I couldn't. And I never have.

He was a drunk, my old man. That was his worst sin because it was the root of all his others. He was all right when he was sober: a little gruff, a little cold and distant, but you could deal with him on a more or less reasonable basis. It was a different story when he had liquor in him. He became abusive, he slapped Ma around and he slapped me around until I got old enough and big enough to put a stop to it. He gambled heavily—low-ball poker, horses, boxing matches. He lost job after job—he worked on the docks, mostly, and was in the middle of the "Bloody Thursday" clash between police and striking longshoremen in 1934—until finally no one would hire him anymore, not even relatives. He still brought home money now and then, sometimes in large amounts, but he wouldn't say where he'd got it, and when that happened he and Ma would fight and then he would start drinking and storm out of the house and stay away for two or three days. I found out later that he was mixed up in some sort of waterfront black-market operation. But I didn't tell anyone, least of all Ma; it would have hurt her even more, put even more lines in her round Italian face and even more pounds on her round Italian body. (He drank to excess; she ate to excess for solace and escape. When she died, prematurely, at the age of fifty-seven, she weighed 247 pounds.) I should have confronted the old man about his black-market ties, but I didn't do that either. I wish I had. Sitting here thinking about him now, after all these years, with the bitterness undiminished by time, I wish to Christ I'd stood right in his face and told him what a son of a bitch he was.

It was the booze that killed him. He was drinking a fifth and more of whiskey a day in the last couple of years of his life, and it ate like acid through his liver and put him in the hospital and killed him within a week of his admission. I went to see him at San Francisco General just once, at Ma's insistence. The impression I have of him then is of someone small and wasted and old, even though he was only fifty. I didn't say anything to him—he was partially sedated at the time—and I only stayed a minute or so. Ma

stayed a long time. She went every day and stayed a long
time and then came home and fixed huge meals and ate
most of the food herself. There wasn't anything I could do
for her. I spent most of that week, that deathwatch, in my
room reading pulp magazines and army enlistment bro-
chures and vowing to myself that I would not be like my
old man, I would not, I would not drink whiskey and I
would not steal and cheat and I would not hurt the people
who were close to me.

I've lived up to those vows the best way I know how. I
don't drink whiskey, I'm reasonably honest, I don't willingly inflict pain on those I care about or on any decent
human being. Whatever else I am, whatever my shortcomings, I am not my old man's son.

Sudden insight, one I've never had before: He made me
the way I am today. In his own uncaring, selfish, drunken
way, my old man made me exactly the kind of person I
grew up to be.

THE SEVENTY-FIRST DAY

The heater died this morning.

I turned it on to low as I always do, to let it warm up
slowly, and right away it started to make a series of loud
pinging and thumping noises. I watched it for a few seconds, went to shut it down again—and there was a banging, a flash with sparks in it, and the thing died. I
switched it off, let it cool for an hour, and switched it back
on. Nothing. Dead as hell.

And outside it's snowing again and the temperature must be ten below zero. Exercising kept me warm for a while, but once my body cooled down I had to fold myself up in one of the blankets and drink cup after cup of hot coffee until it was time for the next set of exercises. I'll have to keep wearing the blanket and drinking too much coffee and tea every day from now until I'm free. Eat more and exercise more, too, to maintain my body heat. The threat of pneumonia, of freezing to death, is twice as severe now, with all the life gone out of the heater and its corpse lying over there bent and broken against the fireplace, where I hurled it in a moment of rage and frustration.

But it *can't* be much longer until I'm able to work that leg iron all the way over my heel and off. Another couple of weeks at the outside. I can stay healthy that long . . . I've got to stay healthy that long. I won't let that frigging heater finish me when I'm this close to freedom.

THE SEVENTY-FIFTH DAY

Five straight days of snow and chill moaning winds. Drifts piling up outside, deep enough to cover the lower third of the shed. Meat-locker cold in here—so intense three nights ago that I had to flatten out one of the cardboard cartons and wrap it around my body under my clothing. The instant coffee is almost gone, and there is only half a package of tea bags left. At least I don't have to worry about the pipes freezing and cutting off my water supply: If that were possible it would have happened by now. Whoever plumbed this place must have used copper piping.

Sniffles in the morning, chronic runny nose, but no major symptoms of illness. So far.

I can get the leg iron, now, to within half an inch of coming off. Frustrating, that last agonizing half inch, but I just don't dare try to force it any farther. I must have lost nearly thirty-five pounds but I still need to shed another five or so. God, how long to do that? Another ten days to two weeks at the most. I don't think I can stand the waiting any longer than that.

THE EIGHTIETH DAY

Sunshine, the first in more than two weeks. And the temperature has climbed a good fifteen degrees in the past twenty-four hours.

Thank Christ.

THE EIGHTY-FOURTH DAY

Out of coffee. Out of crackers and cookies and most other things. Enough provisions left to last about three more weeks—more than the thirteen he planned.

Thirteen, thirteen. That damned number haunts me, and yet its meaning continues to elude me.

But I'll be gone from here before the food runs out. Long before. Soon. Any day now. Every time I sit down to try removing the leg iron again, I start to sweat and tremble with anticipation. Still can't quite do it. Almost, but not quite yet.

THE EIGHTY-SEVENTH DAY

So close . . .

THE EIGHTY-NINTH DAY

It isn't thirteen years or thirteen weeks, it's thirteen *days.* That's the significance in the number, that has to be what this is all about. Why didn't I realize it before this? Blocked out the details, that's why, the same way I blocked out the image of my old man.

Thirteen days in April, in the year of our Lord nineteen hundred and seventy-two. Thirteen long, difficult days. But if that's it—and it must be because I just don't see how it can be anything else—I still don't know who he is. Or the exact nature of his motive. Or why he would wait all this time, nearly sixteen years, to take his revenge.

He wasn't someone directly connected with what happened back then; I'd remember him now if he was. And yet I must have met him, we must have had some kind of contact, else why the disguising of his voice, why the ski mask to keep me from seeing his face? A relative or friend of Jackie Timmons, as crazy as that possibility is?

A relative or friend of the sixteen-year-old boy I killed?

THE NINETIETH DAY

FREE!

Part Two
SALVATION

THE FIRST DAY

It came off with almost no effort. All the long days of waiting, all the struggle and frustration of trying to work it free, and on this last day, this *first* day, it came off with the same ridiculous ease as removing a shoe.

I dragged the chain into the bathroom, I sat on the floor and took off my left shoe and sock, I greased my ankle with a mixture of soap and a little fat from the last can of Spam, I eased the leg iron over the heel and pushed it down the instep. And there was a moment of binding and resistance, just a moment, and then it slid right off, all the way off, and I was sitting there looking at it—an empty pair of locked iron jaws held in both my hands, shining a little from the grease, like a skinny obscene gray doughnut with a huge hole in the middle. I must have stared at it stupidly for a few seconds before I reacted. Then I yelled out loud and hurled the thing away from me, couldn't bear to be touching it any longer, and half-crawled, half-stumbled out of the bathroom.

The next several minutes were an emotional blur. I laughed a little, cried a little, grabbed up a pen and wrote the word FREE! in big block letters on the journal pad. Found myself at the cabin's front entrance, pawing at the door knob, and it was unlocked and I threw the door open and lurched outside and stood there in a patch of old snow with my face upturned, dragging in the cold mountain air, free air. The wind, chill and blustery out of a dirty gray sky, and the snow cold-burning my bare foot, eventually started me shivering and drove me back inside. And when I shut the door and leaned against it I was all right again, back in control again.

My naked foot was numb in places, tingling in others; I returned to the bathroom, sat on the floor to pull on my sock and shoe. There was a shrieking urge in me, then, to gather up some things and get out of here for good. I refused to give in to it; summoned logic to keep it at bay. Things to do first, several things. And it was already past noon. I'd be a fool to leave now, with only a few hours of daylight left and snowdrifts on the ground and no clear idea of where I was or how far I would have to walk. I could stand the rest of today and one more night in this place, now that I was free of the chain and the leg iron. Couldn't I? Not much choice in the matter: I had to, so I would.

I took a couple of breaths and made myself walk slowly across the room. I was conscious now of my unshackled leg and it felt odd to be walking normally, without the restricting weight of the chain. When I got to the chair he'd hauled out and sat in on his night prowl I had another impulse, gave in to this one, and kicked at the chair, sent it clattering against the front wall. One of its legs broke; I laughed when I saw that. It felt good to laugh again. It had been so long that the sound came out cracked and rusty.

I stopped in front of the door that was standing ajar, pushed it wide open with the tips of my fingers. Bedroom, empty except for a roll-away bed topped with a pillow and two blankets and a comforter—the bed he must have slept in the night he brought me here. I went in, opened a closet door, found the interior empty except for an accumulation of dust: Nobody had lived here in a long time, possibly as long as a year or eighteen months. I left that room, went through the second door in the same wall. Another bedroom, this one without furniture of any kind and an equally barren and dusty closet.

The door in the inner wall next to the fireplace led into a smallish kitchen. Gas stove, unplugged refrigerator, corner table with two chairs, nothing much else. I opened the cupboards, drawers, the storage area under the sink. All empty. A screen door gave on a rear porch; I moved out there. Clutter of discarded things in one corner—a ginger jar lamp with a water-stained shade, some folding chairs, an old mattress, bundles of old magazines, an easy chair with its backrest bleeding white stuffing. Grouped in another corner, a narrow stall shower and a laundry sink and a twenty-gallon water heater. And against the inside wall, a small stack of cordwood and kindling festooned with spiderwebs.

Another cupboard hung crookedly above the laundry sink; I opened that and found more emptiness. There didn't seem to be anything in the cabin to tell me who owned it, where I might find him—at least not on this first look-through. Later I'd go through it again, much more carefully. I had plenty of time. Time had almost run out on me but now I had a fresh supply: Freedom buys time, freedom equals time, freedom is time.

I gathered an armload of wood and kindling, took it back into the main room, and laid it out in the fireplace. No matches on the premises but that wasn't a problem. I tore up some of the magazines the whisperer had provided, stuffed them under the logs with the kindling, then switched on the hot plate and twisted pages from another magazine together to form a paper torch and lit that off

the burner. In minutes I had a fine hot blaze going. I sat
on the floor in front of it, close, letting the heat radiate
over me and penetrate deep, bone-deep, to melt away
three months of chill.

The flames had a hypnotic effect; the more I stared into
them, the more everything around me seemed to recede,
to take on the quality of images in smoke or thick mist. I
saw Kerry's face in the flames, and the hurt started again,
but it was tempered now by a thin yearning, an even thinner joy. I tried to hang on to the yearning and the joy, to
make them grow into something strong and sustaining,
but they were caught under a layer of hate like a fibrous
membrane you could see through but couldn't tear loose.
And pretty soon it wasn't her face I was seeing, it was his
masked one. I imagined him cooking there in the fire,
screaming while his skin blistered and crackled and
burned away from his skull, and for a time the illusion
gave me much more pleasure than the prospect of seeing
Kerry again.

Somewhere inside me, a small voice seemed to be mur-
muring, "You're not all right, you're a long way from
being all right." I heard it, but I paid no attention to it. It
was just a voice in a crowded place.

The heat itself broke the spell, became so intense that it
forced me back away from the flames. I got up—and
found myself staring at the corner that had been my home
for the past three months. It seemed strange from this
aspect, unreal, unfamiliar, as if it were part of a hallucina-
tion or delusion under which I had been laboring for a
long time. I put my back to it, walked into the first bedroom and rolled the bed with its pile of bedding out in
front of the fireplace. That was where I would sleep to-

night. For one thing, it didn't stink of my own sweat. For another, it would be softer, warmer than the cot.

Something drew me to the side window—the shed, I realized after a few moments. Was there anything in it I could use? I was warm enough now in my clothing and the blanket I had tied around my body under the overcoat; I went outside, slogged through snowdrifts and the icy wind, and managed to dislodge the seal of frozen snow on the lower third of the shed door, then to drag the door open. All that the shed contained were some rusty tools and a crippled wheelbarrow and a pair of old snowshoes hanging on one wall.

I started back out, stopped, and went ahead to the showshoes. One of them had a cracked frame, and some of the gut stringing on the second was frayed and loose, but they both looked serviceable enough. There might be deep drifts somewhere along the road or roads I would have to follow tomorrow, if I could even make out where the roads were: There had been a steady and sometimes heavy snowfall over the past few days. The road that led up here was invisible as far as I could see downslope to misty stands of spruce and a hillock even higher than the one on which the cabin had been built. At least, I judged that that was where the road must be; there were trees everywhere else.

So I might need showshoes at some point. I had never been on a pair in my life, but how difficult could it be to learn to walk on them? Nothing seemed very difficult anymore, after what I had been through.

Back in the cabin, I propped the snowshoes against the wall inside the door. The fire was still burning hot and the room had warmed considerably. Mountain cabin on a winter afternoon: very cozy, very rustic. I laughed again and went out to the rear porch for more wood. I made four trips and built a stack of logs alongside the hearth, where they would be within easy reach whenever the fire began to die down. I wanted it warm in here tonight, all night. That would make it a little easier to face the cold tomorrow morning.

Now I was ready for another search of the place, a slow and methodical one this time. I started with the first bedroom, as I had before, looking for something, anything, that would give me a lead to the identity and whereabouts of the whisperer. And I found something, out on the rear porch—the last area I searched. It wasn't anything definite, but it was more than I had expected to find. And I had started past investigations with much less.

Studded on the front of the water heater, just above the control panel, was a little metal plate with words stamped into it: RITE-WAY PLUMBING AND HEATING, 187 SLUICEBOX LANE, SONORA, CA. The heater didn't look to be more than seven or eight years old; plumbing contractors usually keep records dating back that far. If Rite-Way Plumbing and Heating was still in business—big if, these days—the people there could probably tell me who owned the cabin, or at least who had owned it when the water heater was installed.

The plate gave me something else, too: confirmation of my guess about the general location of this place. Sonora was a town in the central Mother Lode, east of Stockton. Too low in the Sierra foothills to be getting this much snow, which meant that the cabin was situated at a higher elevation; but it still had to be close enough to Sonora to warrant a contractor from there being called in to do its plumbing. Somewhere off Highway 108, maybe . . . no, too populated up that way, too many ski resorts, until you got up as far as Pinecrest. There was another state road, I couldn't remember the number, to the north of Sonora, out of Angels Camp; its upper reaches were closed in the winter, but the lower sections around Murphys and Arnold ought to be passable except when the snowfall was unusually heavy. And that area was sparsely populated at this time of year.

It was near dusk by this time and I realized I was hungry. An hour ago, the thought of food would have made me gag; now I craved something to eat. I made myself go back into the cell, open cans, put water on to heat, mix the last of the Spam with a can of spaghetti and put that on to heat. When the food was ready I took it and a cup of tea over to the bed, put another log on the fire, and sat in the heat to sip and chew and swallow. Before I was finished, darkness closed around the cabin, blackout-thick. The fireglow created weird, restive shadows in the room that made me think of demons and hungry things creeping, made me edgy enough to get up and turn on the lamp. Afraid of the dark, afraid of firelight. Just two of the things he'd done to me . . . two of the more minor things.

After a while I took off coat, blanket, filthy sport jacket, and cardboard insulation, and lay down on the bed with the comforter over me. I wasn't sleepy; the edginess was still inside me. I lay watching the fire, with thoughts running around and around in my head, running into each other and caroming off until a pressure built up and started a pounding in my temples. I got up and paced for a while. Remembered I hadn't done my nightly exercises —no sense abandoning the program now—and went through an hour's worth of calisthenics, working up a good sweat in the heat from the fire. I felt better then, calmer, calm enough to turn off the lamp before I got back into the bed.

My thoughts were sharper now, less chaotic. Some of them: What if he decides to come back again tonight? Not much chance of it, with the weather being what it is and all the snow on the ground . . . but suppose he managed it? He'd see the fireglow, he'd know I was free—would he come in after me or would he run? And if he ran, suppose it was far enough so that I might never find him? No, he couldn't run that far. I'll find him no matter where he is, where he goes. Let him come tonight. Let him come to-morrow night or any other night between now and the day I find him, let him discover I've escaped. Better that way, much better. Let him know I'm free, let him know I'm after him, let *him* live with fear for a while . . .

Eventually I tried to direct my mind away from him, to focus on Kerry and Eberhardt and going home again, but he kept getting in the way. He was like a parasite growing inside me, some kind of poisonous fungus that had to be destroyed before I could even begin to think about resuming my old way of life.

First things first. Tomorrow first, escape first. I wasn't out of the woods yet . . . ha! I wasn't, for a fact. It was probably better than a mile to the nearest neighbor, more miles to the nearest town, and at that I couldn't just walk up to somebody's door, looking and smelling as I did. I'd be turned away, or somebody would insist on calling a doctor or the authorities. Contact with a law-enforcement agency was the last thing I wanted right now—word to get out that I was alive and of my ordeal. Avoid people, except in case of an emergency, until I got myself cleaned up and presentable again—that was a priority item. There would be a way to manage it. There are ways to do just about anything if you're determined enough.

And after the outside of me was spruced up so that I didn't frighten women and little children? Visit the neighbors then, find out if any of them knew anything? No. It would take too much time, and chances were it wouldn't get me anywhere. Most mountain cabins are deserted in winter; and people who do choose to live in one year-round like their privacy and aren't always acquainted with their neighbors, especially if the neighbors are summer residents and haven't occupied a place in more than a year. Even if somebody could supply a name it was doubtful he'd have a current address to go with it, or any idea of where the owner could be found.

Rite-Way Plumbing and Heating was my best bet, at least for starters. If it turned out to be a dead end, then I could come back up here, wherever *here* actually was, and begin canvassing other homes in the area.

One way or another, I would find out who the whisperer was and then I would find him.

And then I would kill him.

Bad night.

Dreams, ugly and distorted and mercifully unclear. I woke up once sweating and believing I was still shackled to the wall, and something like a wail came out of me before I groped at my left ankle, felt nothing there, separated illusion from reality. Another time I came awake thinking I had heard something, thinking he'd come back, he was there in the cabin with me. I jumped out of bed and caught up a piece of cordwood and prowled the rooms for ten minutes, listening to night sounds and the cry of the wind. Nobody here but me. I ached when I finally accepted that: I couldn't put an end to it here and now, in the very same execution chamber he had built for me.

Bad night, yes, but I had had so many bad nights. And it didn't really matter anyway.

All that mattered was that I was free.

THE SECOND DAY

Eight-thirty A.M.

Cold and gray again today. More snow had fallen during the night—there was a layer of fresh, ice-filmed powder over everything—and there would probably be more flurries before the day was finished. Dry out there now, though, and not much wind.

I turned away from the window, restless and impatient to be on my way, to put distance between myself and this place. But there were preparations to be made first. And I wanted the temperature to rise a little higher, to take the knife edge off the chill of night and early morning.

I put water on to boil for tea, opened the last two cans of chili and emptied them into the saucepan, and set that on the other burner to heat. I had no appetite but it would be foolish to go out into that snowy wilderness without fueling up beforehand.

The snowshoes caught my eye. I went and got them, sat on the bed to see how they fitted on my feet—something I should have done yesterday. The foot straps on both were all right, but on one the things that evidently fastened around the ankles were badly frayed; one good tug and they would break. Was there something among the clutter on the rear porch that I could use to replace or reinforce them?

Yes: some twine that had been used to tie up a bundle of old issues of *Life* and *Look*. It was thin twine but when I worked it off the magazines and tested it, it seemed sturdy enough. I carried it back in, broke it into smaller pieces, doubled the pieces and tied knots in them at intervals to strengthen them even more, then tied each together with a thong to bridge the frayed spots.

The chili and the water were boiling by then. I made a cup of strong tea, gagged it down with the food. The need to get out of there was urgent in me now, almost a physical hurt. I held it down by force of will. If I left without taking precautions I might well regret it later.

One corner of the pillow casing had a tear in it, revealing the foam-rubber entrails. I widened the tear, ripped the casing in half and then into strips; took off my shoes, tore up some pieces of cardboard, and bound those around my socks with the strips for added protection against the cold. Then I wrapped both blankets around my body, over my regular clothing, and buttoned and tightly belted my overcoat to hold them in place. I had lost so much weight that even with the two blankets I did not quite fill out the coat. In the bathroom I tied the larger of the hand towels over my head and under my chin, like a babushka. Not much protection against wind and snow, but I had no other kind of headgear and I needed to wear something.

Almost ready.

There was a package of Fig Newtons left, the only remaining item of food that wasn't canned; I stuffed it into one overcoat pocket. Into the other one I put the journal pages, all of them, torn off their cardboard backings and folded in half. I didn't want the whisperer to find them if he came prowling before I caught up with him. They were for my eyes only. No one, I had decided, would ever read them except me.

That was the last thing; now I was ready. I caught up the snowshoes, went to the door, and walked out into the chill morning.

Whiteness carpeted everything within range of my vision. Downhill to my left, an avenuelike break in the spruce forest marked the probable course of the access road. After I had gone forty yards or so I stopped and turned to look back at the cabin, to fix in my memory its exterior design and its exact location. I hoped to Christ I would never have to come back here; but if I did I wanted to be able to recognize it easily from a distance.

The snowpack was slippery but the drifts didn't become a problem until I was in among the trees, where there was a series of little ridges and hollows. In the low places the drifts were calf-high and it was like trying to wade through a dense mixture of water and sand. When I came onto a section of higher ground where the snow was only a couple of inches deep I strapped on the snowshoes and tied the thongs around my ankles. It took me a couple of minutes, and a near fall, to get the hang of walking on them. You had to keep your legs wide apart to prevent stepping on one snowshoe with the other, and you had to swing your legs in a kind of waddling gait to maintain balance. Otherwise, snowshoeing wasn't much different from normal walking.

Once I got used to them I made good time, following the winding break through the spruce forest. The wind

had picked up and I was conscious of its steady whine and
rattle in the stiff tree branches; but it was behind me and it
didn't penetrate the warm layers of fabric around my
body. Because I had no gloves, I kept my hands bunched
down deep in the overcoat pockets. The cold got to them
anyway, and seeped under and through the tied towel to
numb my ears, but there was no pain or discomfort yet.
On the contrary the cold gave me a muted sense of exhila-
ration. It was different from the cold I had felt inside the
cabin all those weeks, refreshing, invigorating—a reaffir-
mation of the freedom that was mine again.

The long downslope ended in another hollow, this one
much wider and flat-bottomed and deep-drifted. The second hillock, steeper than the one I'd just descended, rose
on the far side. The trees thinned out ahead and most of
the upslope was bare, so that I couldn't be sure of where
the road continued up and over. I made a guess and
started up.

Snowshoeing was more difficult on an incline; I began
to get tired before I had reached the halfway point. I tried
moving in a zigzag pattern and that made the going a little
easier. Near the top and directly ahead of the course I had
set, dwarf fir and the tips of jagged ice-rimmed rocks
poked up out of the snowpack. This couldn't be where the
road was, then. I veered away from the rocks, diagonally
to my right.

I was forty or fifty yards from the top when a hidden
outcrop snagged my right snowshoe and pitched me off
balance. Reflexively I thrust the other shoe forward to
catch my weight but it slipped on the icy surface of another rock, angled down through the drift and into what
must have been a cavity between the rocks. There was a

sharp snapping sound and I went down sideways into
deep snow that billowed up and half buried me.

In frantic movements I jerked my right leg free and
struggled around onto my buttocks, spitting snow and
wiping it out of my eyes. When I tried to get up there
seemed to be nothing beneath me to put my weight on. I
rolled over, shivering; particles of snow had gotten under
the collar of my coat, gone slithering down my back and
chest. I still couldn't get up and I had to fight off a thrust
of panic as I floundered around again until I was facing
downhill, my legs spraddled out below me. I could feel the
ground, then, with my hands and hips. I managed to get
both palms down flat, then pushed and twisted upward. It
took two tries before I was able to heave myself erect.

But the frame on my right showshoe had snapped in
two places; when I tried to put my weight on it it folded
up around my ankle and threw me back down into the
drift. The panic jabbed at me again, the same kind of
panic a poor swimmer must feel in deep water. I rolled
again, coughing snow out of my mouth and throat, blowing it out of my nose. I couldn't see; everything had become a misty white blur. Once more I flailed over onto my
buttocks, twisted upward. Finally managed to stand her-
onlike on one leg, sawing the air with both arms until I
had my balance.

I stood there wobbling, feeling crippled and anxious
because I was out of my element, in a survival situation
that I didn't understand or quite know how to cope with.
Maybe the right shoe would take a little weight, if I was
careful . . . but when I tested it my right foot sank and I
couldn't free the left shoe to slide it forward, and I almost
fell again.

Calm, stay calm. Think it through. Don't do anything else without thinking it through.

I cleared my eyes, took deep breaths until the apprehensive feeling eased and some of the tenseness went out of me. All right. The first thing I had better do was to get rid of the snowshoes; the right one was too badly damaged and that made the other one just as useless. I untied the thongs, pulled off the right shoe and let that leg down as far into the churned up snow as it would go—thigh-deep. Then I took the other shoe off and got that leg down so that I was standing on both feet.

Walking was something else again. The first step I took, with my right foot, I sank to my hip on the left side. I tried it again and again, slowly and deliberately, and found a way to move forward and upward without losing my equilibrium, but each step netted me no more than eighteen inches of progress. The effort of moving, burrowing forward at this snail's pace, was so great that I had to stop before I had gone more than ten yards.

I rested for a time, looking up at the crest of the hill. Maybe the drifts weren't as deep along its flattish top, over on the other side; at least the going would be easier downhill. And if there was another steep hillock on the far side? One obstacle at a time. Get up to the top of this one first.

I struggled upward again, one short slogging step after another. It was slow, exhausting work and I had to stop twice more to rest my aching legs before I was able to cover the last few yards to the crown.

The snowpack *was* shallower up there. There were only a few spruce trees, nothing much else, and the wind had thinned the drifts down to a depth of less than a foot, exposed patches of bare ground along the far lip. Ahead and below, where the downslope flattened out into a long, wide, treeless snowfield, the drifts were unbroken and looked deep. But it wasn't the drifts that caught and held my attention.

There was a road down there.

It ran along the far edge of the snowfield, where the terrain rose sharply into steep red-earth cutbanks and tree-clad hillsides. Its surface was mostly covered with a thin crust of snow, except for streaky areas where the wind had scoured it away and the asphalt showed through. But it was the high windrows flanking it on both sides that clearly identified it as a road, and gave me a small measure of relief. A snowplow had made those windrows; and no county sends out snowplow crews to clear mountain roads unless there is enough traffic to warrant it.

The road was maybe 300 yards from where I stood atop the hill—300 yards of wind-smoothed virgin snow. No telling from here just how deep the drifts were; I would find that out when I started wading through them. If I'd still had the use of the snowshoes, I could cover the distance in a few minutes. As it was . . .

I started downslope, keeping to the cleared patches wherever I could, and the first seventy-five yards or so weren't bad. Then the drifts began to deepen, and before I was three-quarters of the way downhill the snow was hip-high and getting deeper. Flakes of frozen powder got into my clothing, burned where they touched bare flesh. My hands were stiff and numb inside the coat pockets. The wind was still up and it hammered at me, chilled my neck, sent tremors through my body.

The depth of the drifts leveled out to just above my waist. But the snow was packed solidly down close to the

ground, and I couldn't make more than six to eight inches
with each lifting, thrusting forward step. It wasn't long
before the muscles in my hips and thighs began to cramp
from the strain.

Near the bottom of the slope, I put a foot forward and
down and there was no ground under it. I plunged into a
depression of some kind, and for an instant my head was
submerged and I was struggling wildly in freezing whiteness. Snow particles stung my eyes, poured inside the collar of my coat, caked in my nostrils. I fought upward,
thrashing with my legs—and one foot found purchase,
then the other, and I came heaving up through the surface
blowing and gasping. Slapped clumps of icy wetness off
my face and out of my eyes and stood for a time, racked
with cold spasms, to get my breath and my composure
back before I pushed onward.

It took me something better than an hour to cross the
last 150 yards of the snowfield. Twice the drifts deepened
to armpit level; both times I veered away, half flounder-
ing, until I found a shallower course. I was so fatigued by
the time I churned out onto the roadbed, where the snow
was only a few inches deep, my legs wouldn't support me
and I fell to my knees. Knelt there shaking, swaying like a
sapling in the wind, until I was able to summon enough
reserve strength to boost myself upright and keep my
wobbly legs under me.

Which way, left or right? I seemed to recall, dimly, that
the last turn the whisperer had made that night three long
months ago had been to the left: left turn and then we'd
climbed up and down the hillocks and eventually stopped
near the cabin. I wasn't sure I could trust my memory
after all this time, but I had to go one way or another; and
to the right the road ran in a gradual downhill curve. To

the right, then. And hope to God I reached some kind of
uninhabited shelter before anyone came along or I collapsed from the cold and the dragging tiredness.

Before I started walking I remembered the package of
Fig Newtons I'd put into my overcoat. Mostly sugar,
those things: fast energy. I fumbled in the pocket, and the
package was still there; I pulled it out, managed to tear
the cellophane wrapping with my teeth. I choked down
three bars, and three more as I set off, and three more at
intervals until I had eaten all of them.

I had to move in a slow, shuffling gait because of the
weakness in my legs and because the asphalt was ice-slick
beneath its patchy skin of snow. The three or four inches
on the road had to be yesterday's and last night's snowfall,
I thought, which meant that the snowplow crew had been
here sometime within the past twenty-four hours. Would
they come again today? Probably not. Not enough new
snowfall, and this wasn't a major road; its patched and
eroded condition told me that. Had to be other cabins
around here somewhere, though. And people living in
them. I listened for engine sounds as I walked. If any
vehicle came along I would have to get off the road, take
cover behind a tree or rock or bush close by. My tracks
might give me away, though the wind seemed to be ob-
scuring most of the ones I was leaving on the road. Still, I
would have to try.

Only it didn't come to that. There was nothing to hear
but the steady throbbing plaint of the wind, the steady
throbbing plaint of my breath as I shuffled and shivered
my way downhill. Nothing to see but the swaying
branches of the trees. The sky had taken on a restless look
and seemed to have lowered, so that its grayness partially
obscured the tops of the hills that rose on my left. The

chill in the air seemed to have more bite in it, too. It was going to snow again before long.

I had gone maybe a quarter of a mile before I saw the first sign of habitation. The road straightened out after a long leftward bend, and off to my right, above the tops of a thick stand of blue spruce, a thin spiral of smoke—chimney smoke—lifted into the low-hanging grayness above. The cabin itself was invisible behind the trees, and that was good because it was no place for me. I kept going, even more cautiously now, and pretty soon I came to the access drive. From there, through the trees, I could see part of the cabin—a big A-frame with a Ford Bronco parked under a lean-to to one side. The Ford had been there all night because the surface snow on the drive was smooth, unbroken. There was nobody out and about, nobody to observe me as I moved past and out of sight.

The first flakes of snow began to flutter down, then increased to a thin flurry almost at once. Just what I needed—Christ! I kept my head pulled down into the collar of my coat as I walked, eyelids half-lowered; but even so the wind-flung crystals stung my cheeks and made my eyes tear.

After a time I saw the shape of another cabin materialize among the trees ahead. No smoke coming out of this one, or at least none that I could make out, but it was just as inhabited as the previous one. The snow skin on its lane had been rutted by thick tires, probably sometime earlier today.

I got past there, too, without anybody coming out to ask who I was and why I was traveling on foot in a mountain snowstorm. The fall got even thicker, coming down now in shifting patterns that obscured most of what lay outside a hundred-yard radius. Some of the flakes adhered to the skin of my face, forming a crust and turning my eyebrows into little ridges of ice. The shiver spasms grew more violent, and my legs grew weaker, and the understanding crawled into my head that if I didn't find shelter soon I would crumple into an inert mass and never get up again.

Shuffle-step, shuffle-step, shuffle-step. Another fifty yards, and another leftward jog in the road, and another twenty-five yards—

—and another access drive opening up to my left. Unmarked snow on this one; I might have missed it entirely if it weren't for a break in the trees and a closed and icebound bargate across its entrance. I stopped, squinting through the swirl of flakes, but I couldn't make out anything except the wind-tossed shapes of spruce and fir.

Chance it: I had no other choice, now. Even if the home was occupied I would have to bang on the door, take the risk of being admitted. I turned in toward the gate, sank immediately into drifts up to my knees. Plowed ahead a few painful inches at a time, angling around the gate and then over into the trees where the drifts were a little shallower. I was moving then in half-light and shadow, both externally and internally: My mind seemed to have gone as fuzzy and indistinct as my surroundings.

Minutes lived and died—I had no perception of how many—and suddenly I found myself peering at a small A-frame cabin half hidden by trees and snowfall. There was a quality of illusion about it, as if it might be two-dimensional. But I wasn't imagining it because it stayed where it was, didn't shimmer or fade like a mirage, and after several seconds I pushed ahead. Went from tree to tree, leaning against one frozen trunk after another; if I hadn't had their support I would have fallen. The

A-frame got closer, seemed to take on more substance. I scraped at my eyes to bring it into clearer focus. Shutters on the windows, snow piled up over the porch. Closed up for the winter? Yes. It had that empty, waiting aspect deserted dwellings take on.

There were thirty or forty yards of deep-drifted open ground along the front; it might as well have been a thousand yards. But the trees ran in close to the right-hand wall toward the rear, with no more than a few yards of drift to cross back there. I kept moving from tree to tree, jelly-kneed now, almost grateful for the drifts because they held me upright. More lost minutes, and then I was back near the cabin's rear corner. Somehow I tunneled legs and body through ten feet of thigh-deep snow, then leaned hard against the corner to rest and take stock of the back wall. Midway along, steps rose to a platform porch, some of them hidden, the three that I could see thickly crusted. I groped my way along the wall, fell against the steps; couldn't get my legs under me, and crawled up the three steps and onto the porch.

Screen door. I leaned up on my knees and managed to take a grip on the handle with fingers that were stiff and had almost no feeling left. Damn thing was locked on the inside. I yanked, yanked again, yanked a third time in a kind of dull frenzy. The hook-and-eye fastening ripped loose and the door came shimmying open in my hand. I batted it aside, got my body between it and the inside door. That was locked, too, but it had a pane of glass in its center. I clawed up the screen door until I was standing, but my left leg buckled when I tried to put weight on it and I nearly went down again. Balanced on one foot, hanging on to the screen door with my left hand, I used my right elbow to break the glass and punch out shards.

Reached in, found the locking bolt, threw it. And twisted
the knob and tried to walk in and sprawled through on
hands and knees instead.

The wind made a whimpering noise, or maybe it was
me. I crawled around in a half-circle, managed to shove
the door shut again. Flakes of wind-hurled snow whipped
in through the broken window, swirling past me into a
shadowed areaway that opened into what appeared to be a
kitchen. I lifted onto my knees, got my back against one
of the areaway walls, and used my shoulders and my right
leg to stand erect. The left leg still wouldn't work; I had to
drag it, hobbling on the right one and clutching the wall,
to get into the kitchen.

Not much light in there, because the windows over the
sink were shuttered. But I could make out a small refrigerator, a table and chairs, a propane stove, some cupboards and a standing cabinet, a dark alcove that was
probably used as a larder. An open doorway on the far
side led to the other rooms: a big living area with dust
covers over the furniture, so that they had a lumpish
ghostly look in the gloom, and a single bedroom and bath.
That was all. The place smelled of winter cold and damp
but not of must or decay. Closed up for a while, but not
much longer than late last fall. Somebody's warm-weather
retreat.

I sank onto a couch-shaped piece of furniture in the
main room by necessity, not by choice. I just could not
stand up any longer. Little shivers and slivers of chill
worked through me, and my hands burned and quivered,
and my throat was so sore I could barely swallow. Sick.
Exhausted. Badly used. But still alive. Can't kill me, by
God, not *this* way either.

I didn't sit there long—just long enough for a little

feeling and strength to seep back into my limbs. The icy wetness of my clothing, the chill in the room, and the overhanging threat of pneumonia prodded me up again. Get out of these wet things, get into something dry and warm, and do it quickly.

My left leg gave out again halfway across the room. I cursed it and hammered at it with my fists, dragged it under me, dragged myself up. And this time it supported enough of my weight so that I could hobble through into the bedroom.

The double bed had been stripped bare, but when I opened a big oak wardrobe I found blankets, sheets, pillows on an upper shelf. Some items of clothing also hung in there, both a man's and a woman's. I gave a heavy plaid lumberman's shirt a quick inspection; it seemed large enough to fit me. On the floor in there were half a dozen pairs of shoes and boots, and a pair of men's slipper-socks. I took out the slipper-socks and the heaviest of the blankets, carried them into the bathroom.

Dark in there . . . and it stayed that way, because when I flipped the light switch nothing happened. Electricity must have been turned off for the winter. I fumbled out of my damp, smelly wrappings, dried myself with a towel hanging from one of the racks. Kept rubbing my body until the skin began to prickle. Then I encased myself in the dry blanket. But still tremors racked me, set my teeth to clacking like old bones being shaken in a box.

It wasn't until I started to put on the slipper-socks that I realized two toes on my left foot had no feeling. Neither did the tip of the little finger on my left hand. Frostbite? I hurried into the bedroom, over to the window, and opened one of the shutters partway to let in some light. Tiny dead-white patches on the finger and both toes, each

surrounded by painful reddened areas. Fine, great. I
seemed to remember that the best thing for frostbite was
to soak the affected parts in hot water. That sent me back
into the bathroom. But when I twisted the hot water tap,
not a drop came out of it. The cold water tap was just as
dry. The owners must have shut the water off for the
winter too.

Was the propane stove in the kitchen hooked up? If so I
could melt a pan full of snow, get hot water that way. But
it would mean getting dressed, going out in the storm
again to collect the snow, and I just wasn't up to that. I
was afraid to reexpose myself to that freezing cold.

I opened the medicine cabinet above the sink, pawed
through its contents looking for burn ointment. There
wasn't any, and it was just as well, because now I remembered that you weren't supposed to put that kind of stuff
on frostbite. Keep the bitten areas warm, that was the
next best thing to soaking in hot water. The cabinet did
yield two other items I needed, though: a bottle of aspirin
and a bottle of Dristan cold capsules.

I pulled on the slipper-socks. In the bedroom I rummaged through bureau drawers looking for a pair of
gloves that would fit me. Didn't find any there, but there
were some old fur-lined ones in a drawer inside the wardrobe. The glove fit snugly on my left hand but not so
snugly that I couldn't bend the fingers.

I glanced over at the nightstand, where I'd set the bot-
tles of aspirin and cold capsules. I couldn't swallow any of
the medicine dry; even chewed up it would lodge against
the fiery constriction in my throat. Maybe there was
something to drink in the main room or in the kitchen
. . . preferably something alcoholic. I hated the taste of
whiskey, thanks to my old man, but two or three stiff jolts

would help warm me. And whiskey was also good for
frostbite, because it dilated the blood vessels.

Out to the main room—walking better now, the left leg
responding stiffly. No wet bar or liquor cabinet or wheeled
bar cart; I even lifted up some of the dust covers to make
sure. A tall, shallow redwood cabinet on one wall caught
my eye, and not because I thought there might be liquor
in it. I moved over to tug at its doors. Locked. Check it
later, tomorrow. No time for that kind of work now.

The kitchen again. The cold back there, the wind and
random flakes skirling in through the broken window and
along the areaway, raised goosebumps on my skin, set up
a fresh series of tremors. I drew on the right glove, then
made a rapid search of cupboards, the standing cabinet,
the refrigerator. Nothing to drink in any of them. I shuffled into the larder, probed among a thin supply of cans
and cartons and jars. On a shelf near the bottom, my hand
closed around a bottle with a familiar shape . . . wine? I
took it out to where I could see it more clearly. Wine, all
right—a heavy Sonoma County red. Not as good as whiskey but it would have to do.

I got the foil wrapping off the neck. Screw top. Good. I
took a tumbler from one of the cupboards, transported it
and the wine to the bedroom. Poured the glass full,
choked down a third of it with four aspirin and four Dristan capsules, drank the rest in quick little gulps. The heat
of it spread immediately, took away some of the chill and
eased the trembling. The alcohol went straight to my
head: Within seconds I was woozy and I had to sit on the
bed.

Lie down, I thought. You're dead on your feet, it won't
be long before you pass out.

I got up long enough to toss sheets, pillows, other blankets from the wardrobe to the bed, then crawled under the pile, still wearing the slipper-socks and the gloves. Poured wine, drank it, then tugged sheets and blankets around and under me until I was completely covered, wrapped up like a bug in a cocoon. Pretty soon I didn't feel the cold anymore. The last of the chill gradually went away and then the shaking quit altogether. And at last the warmth and the wine and the medicine combined with exhaustion to drag me down toward unconsciousness.

I didn't fight it; I was safe enough here. The snowfall would have obliterated most of my tracks by now, and without them to make somebody curious, no one but the owners would have any reason to come here; and why would they show up in the middle of a near blizzard? Sleep was what I needed most right now—the rest of today and tonight, a dozen hours at least. With that much rest, with the self-doctoring I had done and would keep doing, I should be well enough to travel again tomorrow morning. . . .

THE THIRD DAY

I didn't go anywhere in the morning. Or at any time during that day. I was not even able to get out of bed for more than a couple of minutes until late afternoon, almost twenty-four hours after I first lay down.

The first time I woke up, it was pitch dark outside and I was sweaty, feverish, so weak and achy that I could barely lift up to pour more wine, shake out more aspirin and cold

capsules; and swallowing was a torment. The second time
I woke up, morning light had seeped in through the window shutters and I felt marginally better: still sweaty and
feverish, with a headache from the wine, but my throat
was less sore and I wasn't quite as weak or stiff. I got up
to use the toilet, and thought about staying up, getting
dressed, but I didn't try to do it. The storm had blown
itself out during the night, and the sun had put in an
appearance; but it was still cold and windy. Going out
into that wind and wading through the snowdrifts in my
condition would have been suicidal. So I took more medicine, with just enough wine to wash it down, and rewrap-
ped myself in the blankets and slept again, fitfully and
with jumbled dreams. And when I woke up the third time
I was drenched in sweat, the headache was gone, there
was that broken-fever feel in my body when I moved, and
I was wolf-hungry.

Yesterday's battle with the elements hadn't damaged
my watch; the time was 3:35. I lay there for a minute or
so, listening to the wind beat at the cabin walls, watching
my breath come out in round white puffs. Then I sat up,
took the glove off my left hand to examine the little finger.
The tiny patch of frostbite was still there but it hadn't
spread and the skin around it looked less inflamed; and
when I touched the tip I had feeling in it again. I put the
glove back on, drew the slipper-sock off my left foot. The
two frostbitten toes looked better, too, though the top
edge of one was still numb.

I swallowed two more aspirin and two more Dristan
with the last of the wine. Swung out of bed, stood up on
legs that creaked and ached dully but seemed to work well
enough. The wardrobe provided a thin turtleneck sweater,
the lumberman's shirt, and a pair of faded and patched

Levi's. Tight fit on all of them, but not so tight that my movements were restricted.

My own clothes, the ones I had worn for more than three months, were bunched up on the floor where I'd dropped them. I remembered the journal pages and bent to the overcoat, reached a hand into the pocket. They were still there, damp and crumpled. I pulled them out, saw that the writing was still legible, if a little smeary, and spread them out individually on the floor to dry. The only other thing I wanted from those clothes was my wallet and keys. He'd let me keep those, and why not? He'd expected to bury them along with my corpse. I had no idea how much money the wallet contained, so I counted it. Sixty-nine dollars. Not much, but enough to get me by if I was careful. I ought to be able to use my credit cards for most things I would need, without anyone recognizing my name. My disappearance had likely been publicized statewide, because of its bizarre nature, but there wouldn't have been any media mention for at least a couple of months, and people have short memories.

I set the wallet on the bureau, threw a blanket around my shoulders for added warmth, and went out into the kitchen. The wind wasn't as sharp today, blowing in along the areaway, and it wasn't bringing in any snow. But it had brought in plenty during the past twenty-four hours: There was a long white carpet on most of the areaway floor and halfway across the kitchen.

The propane stove wasn't hooked up, and there was no way to hook it up; it didn't contain a tank, nor was there a tank in the larder or anywhere else that I looked. Cold food, then. The larder yielded two cans of sardines, a can of mixed vegetables, another of peaches, and a second bottle of red wine. I found a can opener in one of the drawers, took it and the other stuff into the bedroom, and sat on the bed to fill the hole in my belly.

When I was done I opened the shutters over the bathroom window to let some light in there. The cabin had been virtually invisible from the road, so there didn't seem to be any risk in that. It took me a while—two minutes or so—to work up enough courage to face myself in the mirror, but it had to be done and so I did it.

Christ! Wild tangle of beard and hair, both gone grayer than I remembered, almost white in spots; unhealthy grayish pallor, sunken eyes with things shining in them that I didn't want to see, refused to focus on. The whole of the face had a partially collapsed aspect from all the weight I'd lost, as if some of the skull structure itself had eroded away. It struck me that I could reach up and take a handful of my features, bunch them up in my fingers the way you can grasp and bunch up an animal's fur.

I clutched at the sink, staring at the face in the glass, and the hate welled up in me until I was bloated with it. I had to turn away before long. I felt that if I didn't turn away I would continue to swell until the hate burst out of me like pus out of an overripe boil.

I stood with my back to the glass until I had myself under control again, my emotions screwed down under a tight lid. Then I opened the medicine cabinet and took out the cuticle scissors and safety razor I had seen in there yesterday. I made myself look in the mirror again—at the beard and hair this time, only those. I couldn't leave here with either one as wild as it was. And because it would be painful to try to do a complete shave without water, my only choice with the beard was to trim it to a respectable size and shape. Keeping the facial hair was probably a good idea anyway. Combined with how leaned down I was, it made an effective disguise. For all I knew a disguise would be beneficial when I went a-hunting.

The beard trim took me ten minutes. I spent another couple scraping off edge-stubble with the razor to even it out. There was a comb in the wardrobe, and I used that to work the snarls out of my hair. Then I trimmed it as best I could. There was nothing I could do about its filthiness, except to cover my head with a cap or hat when I left here. There had to be some kind of headgear in the cabin.

When I was finished I looked . . . what? Less frightening, less like a man who had suffered through ninety days of hell. Reasonably normal as long as you didn't look closely at the eyes. But there was nothing I could do about them, either, not externally.

The afternoon light was beginning to thin and fade. I closed the shutters against a battalion of shadows creeping among the white-clad trees outside. My legs had begun to ache again, and the scratchiness was back in my throat, and I was starting to feel the cold through all the things I wore. Almost time to get back into bed, drink a little more wine, sleep for another few hours. But not quite yet. There was still something I wanted to do first.

Among the utensils in one of the kitchen drawers was a big, thick-bladed butcher knife; I got that and took it into the main room, to the redwood cabinet I had noticed yesterday. The lock on the cabinet doors was the kind you could loid with a credit card. Using the knife I had it sprung and the doors open in fifteen seconds. Gun cabinet, just as I had thought. Enough rack space for four rifles or shotguns, but the only weapon of that type it contained was a Kodiak bolt-action center-fire rifle. On the shelf at the bottom were three boxes of ammunition, two for the rifle and one for a .22 handgun. The piece that the .22 cartridges fitted was on the shelf too, wrapped in chamois cloth: a High-Standard Sentinel revolver, short-barreled, lightweight, with a nine-round cylinder capacity. Not much of a weapon, really, except at close range—and even then it wouldn't have much stopping power. I broke it open, spun the empty cylinder, checked the sights and the hammer and trigger action, peered inside the barrel. At least it was clean and seemed to be in smooth working order.

I hesitated for a moment, with the gun balanced in the palm of my hand. But only for a moment. I had to have a weapon and this one was available—and deadly enough. What difference did it make if I added the theft of a hand-gun to the theft of food and clothing, to breaking and entering and unlawful occupation of a premises? There had been a time, not so very long ago, when any sort of illegal activity had gone against my grain. But it didn't seem to matter much now. Principles, ethics, were for men whose lives had not been turned upside down, who had not spent three months chained to the wall of a mountain cabin.

I took the revolver and the box of cartridges into the bedroom, and loaded each chamber before I undressed and got back into bed. The thought of the .22 there on the nightstand, loaded, ready, waiting, was another kind of medicine to help me sleep and make me well again.

THE FOURTH DAY

MORNING

It was a few minutes past nine when I finished writing the note, the last thing I had to do before leaving.

I anchored it down on the kitchen table with a can of creamed corn, so it wouldn't blow off and maybe get overlooked. Six lines written on a torn-off piece of paper sack with a marking pen I'd found, addressed to the A-frame's owners, Tom and Elsie Carder, whose names and Stockton address I'd gotten from an old letter in the pocket of a woman's Windbreaker. Six lines that apologized anonymously for breaking in, for the damage I'd done and the things I'd taken; that promised I would make restitution before the end of the summer. Six lines that meant what they said.

I wrote them because I had been wrong yesterday, when I'd said to myself that breaking the law no longer mattered to me, that principles and ethics were for men whose lives had not been turned upside down. The truth was, I hadn't lost any of my respect for the law, nor any of the principles by which I had always lived. The ordeal I had been through hadn't done that to me, and what I intended to do in the name of justice wouldn't do it to me either. There was a fine line here, such a fine line: You could kill someone who had wronged you terribly, you could compromise your principles that much and still be able to live with yourself; but if you compromised them completely, if you threw *all* your beliefs and ideals out the window, then you also threw out your humanity and you were no better than the man who had wronged you or all the outlaws you had done battle with over the years.

This understanding came to me earlier today, when I gathered up the journal pages and my eye fell on one of those I'd written about my old man: . . . *vowing to myself that I would not be like my old man, I would not, I would not drink whiskey and I would not steal and cheat . . . I'm reasonably honest, I don't willingly inflict pain on those I care about or on any decent human being. Whatever else I am, whatever my shortcomings, I am not my old man's son.*

And I'm not. The words gave me a jolt for that reason. I will soon take the law into my own hands, yes; I believe I have a right to do that under the circumstances. But at the same time I still do not believe in stealing and cheating and willingly inflicting pain on anyone except a mortal enemy, and I never will, and I must never do any of those things except under extreme duress and then only if I'm prepared to pay the price.

I am not my old man's son.

I went down the areaway, out through the rear doors onto the snow-crusted platform porch. The sky was mostly clear today, mottled here and there with pale puffs and streaks of cloud, and the wind was little more than a murmur. Sunlight glittered off the snow surfaces, made a prism of an icicle hanging from one of the pitched eaves. The temperature had warmed considerably, but the air still had a wintry bite. I had bundled myself up like a child from head to foot: woolen cap pulled down over my ears, woolen muffler, the fur-lined gloves, turtleneck sweater and lumberman's shirt and faded Levi's, a padded bush jacket that came down to thigh level, three pairs of socks, and a pair of heavy, high-top hiking boots. My wallet and the journal pages were in pants pockets; the .22 Sentinel revolver was in the zippered right pocket of the bush jacket.

I still wasn't feeling all that well, but I thought I could travel all right as long as I didn't tumble into any more snowbanks and the weather stayed clear. I had spent too many days cooped up inside the cabin walls to want to endure another one here. I needed movement, I needed to get out of these mountains and back to the kind of environment I understood. I needed to begin the hunt.

Getting through the snowpack from the porch to the woods was slow, hard work. Once I was in among the trees, though, the drifts weren't as deep and I could make better time. Even so, it took me twenty minutes to reach the road, angling away from the A-frame so I could come out of the trees where they made a thick border close to the road. That way my tracks would be less conspicuous.

A snowplow crew hadn't been along here recently; there were a couple of inches of slushy, tire-rutted snow on the road surface. I managed to jump out into one of the near ruts and stayed in one or another as I set off downhill, slapping clinging particles of snow off my pants and jacket. Anyone who cared to look closely could see where I'd come from, but maybe nobody would care. In any case, if I encountered anybody I had a story worked out to explain what I was doing tramping around this wilderness on foot.

The wet snow in the ruts was slippery and I had to keep my head down and pick my way along. Just as well, because the sun hurt my eyes whenever its glare penetrated the tree branches and reflected off snow. The morning had a hushed, crackling quality, so that each little sound seemed magnified. But I had gone about a third of a mile, past two more snow-blocked access drives, before I heard the one sound I was listening for.

It came as a low whine at first, some distance behind me. I tensed, and my heart began to beat faster—but I stayed where I was. No point in trying to avoid contact now. I had to deal with people again sooner or later, and maybe I could wangle a ride to the nearest town.

The engine sound got progressively louder until I could hear the change in tempo as the driver geared down for each curve. By the time the vehicle came in sight, I had moved to the edge of the road and was standing there waiting for it. It was a black Ford Bronco with oversized snow tires, the two rear ones wearing chains—the same Bronco, probably, that I had seen parked near the occupied cabin two days ago. The driver slowed when he saw me and as soon as he did I started waving one arm over my head, signaling for him to stop. But I didn't step out into the Bronco's path, and a good thing, too: It rolled right on past me in low gear. Only then the driver must have changed his mind, because the brake lights flashed and the big squat vehicle skewed to a halt thirty yards away on my side of the road.

I moved toward it, hurrying a little, trying to make myself look purposeful and yet harmless. The side windows were smoke-tinted so that you couldn't look in from outside; but the driver had to be looking out at me, all right, sizing me up. When I halted alongside his door I stood motionless for a few seconds, fighting the tension, letting him take a good look. I must have passed muster because the window finally began to wind down, and in a few seconds I was face-to-face with the man behind the wheel—the first human being I had seen in ninety-three days.

He was about forty, heavyset, bandit-mustached, wearing a cowboy hat and a fleece-lined sheepskin coat. The macho outdoors type. The only expression on his face and in his eyes was a wary curiosity. He wasn't alone in the car; the other occupant stood on the backseat peering over the guy's shoulder with six inches of spit-slick red tongue lolling out. Big German shepherd, the kind with hard yellow eyes and teeth like spikes—the kind you'd walk a block out of your way to avoid if you saw it unleashed on a street corner.

The dog built even more edginess in me. I can get along with most dogs but I've had run-ins with this variety before. My hands were down flat against my sides and I could feel the hard outline of the .22 against my right wrist; but that wasn't the way to deal with this guy or his dog, or anybody else if I could help it, except one man. I lifted my arms away from my body, put my eyes on the guy in the driver's seat and kept them there, hoping the tension didn't show.

"Morning. Thanks for—" The words came out in a rusty croak, and I had to break off and clear my throat before I could go on. How long since I had last used my voice? "Thanks for stopping."

He didn't acknowledge that. He said, "Problem?"

"You can say that again."

"I didn't see your car along the road."

"That's because I haven't got it anymore."

"What does that mean?"

"Well, it's like this. My name's Canino, Art Canino," I lied. "My wife and I been staying at the Carders' place . . . Tom and Elsie, you know them?"

"No."

"Well, they weren't using it this time of year so they let us come up for a few days. We been having trouble, the wife and me, marriage trouble . . . you know how it is. So I suggested we get away, off by ourselves, try to work things out. Stupidest goddamn idea I ever had."

"That so?"

"All we did was fight. All we ever do these days is fight. Last night we had a hell of a row and when I went to the can she took the keys and drove off with the fugging car."

"You mean she never came back?"

"That's what I mean. Stranded me up here, no phone in the cabin, no transportation out. Can you believe a woman who'd do a thing like that?"

He thought about it and decided he could. I watched his face relax, a tight little smile form on his mouth. He'd also decided to be amused. I was good for his ego, I was; he could feel superior to a poor schmuck like me. Some people are like that, the macho types in particular: They need the misfortune of others to make them feel good about themselves.

"My wife ever did something like that," this asshole said, "I'd break a few of her teeth for her."

"Yeah. Well, I'm through with mine—this is the last straw. Soon as I get back to Stockton, I'm hiring a lawyer to file for divorce."

"That where you're from? Stockton?"

"Now it is. Moved there five months ago, from up north. Eureka. Hell, I don't even know anybody well enough I can call to come pick me up. How am I going to get home?"

"Don't look at me," the guy said.

"No, no. But there must be a bus or something . . . what's the nearest town I could catch a bus to Stockton?"

He shrugged, smiling his smug little smile. "I never been on a bus in my life."

"Sonora? Maybe I could get one in Sonora."

"Maybe."

"That's not too far from here, is it?"

"Far enough."

"I don't suppose you're going anywhere near there . . . ?"

"Not me. Deer Run's as far as I'm going."

Deer Run. That was a wide place on a secondary mountain road ten miles or so north of Murphys; I'd passed through it once, a long time ago, and I remembered a handful of buildings—hardly enough to justify the place being called a hamlet, much less a town. It was where I'd estimated my location, and maybe thirty miles from Sonora.

I said, "I'd be glad to pay you if you'd take me as far as Sonora."

"Yeah? How much?" But he wasn't really interested; I could tell by the tone of his voice.

"Forty dollars?"

"Nah. I got things to do this morning."

"Fifty."

"Can't do it, pal," he said, and paused, and then said, "Could be Mary Alice'd know somebody who will."

"Mary Alice?"

"She runs the store in Deer Run."

"That where you're going, her store?"

"Among other places."

"Well, would you mind giving me a lift there? I'd appreciate it; I'm tired of walking."

I put a pleading note in my voice, hating myself for doing it, and it made him laugh. He said, "Sure, why not? I won't even charge you nothing."

"Thanks. Thanks a lot."

"Come on, get in."

I went on the passenger side, opened the door. He must have said something to the dog; it was sitting all the way back on the rear seat, not drawn up but not relaxed either, watching me with those hard yellow eyes. I could feel the eyes on me as I slid inside and they made my skin crawl, ran the edginess right down into my hands so that I had to clasp them together in my lap to keep them from shaking.

"Dog make you nervous, pal?"

"Well . . . a little."

"Makes a lot of people nervous," the asshole said meaningfully, but with the amusement still in his voice. "That's because he's attack-trained. Never know what kind of trouble you'll run into these days, even way up here."

"No. No, you sure don't."

Neither of us had anything else to say on the drive into Deer Run. It wasn't much of a drive—less than ten minutes and no more than a mile. The hamlet lay tucked up in a hollow surrounded by timbered hillocks, maybe a dozen buildings, and half a hundred junked cars and trucks poking up out of the snow. It had a primitive aspect, as if the past fifty years or so had passed it by. Only three of the buildings were business establishments: a general store and post office, a service station, and an out-of-business, boarded-up "antique" store. Those three buildings were located just beyond where the road we were on intersected with another county road. That one must have been the through road to Murphys in one direction, to

Highway 49 and San Andreas in the other: It had been cleared by a snowplow crew that was working now at one end of the hollow—two big snowblowers and half a dozen yellow-clad men—and it ran like a snaky black vein through all the sunlight white.

There was a road sign at the intersection, and when the guy braked there I had a quick look at the wooden arrow pointing back up the way we'd come. It read: Indian Hill Road. Okay. Now I knew exactly where my former prison was situated.

We pulled over into a cleared area in front of the store. It was a weathered building made of clapboard and corrugated iron siding, with pitched roof lines to prevent snow from piling up on top. It didn't have a name, or if it did there was no sign announcing it that I could see. We got out, all three of us, and the guy let the dog nuzzle around my legs as we tramped inside. He liked what it did to me; he laughed in my face, a barking sound like the German shepherd might have made. I thought: *Easy, easy, he's not important, none of this is important,* to keep myself from doing something foolish, like knocking the laugh back down his throat.

The interior of the store looked and smelled like country groceries everywhere: weak lighting, closely set aisles, rough-hewn floor; mingled odors of damp and dust, brewing coffee, refrigerated meats and overripe cheese and stale bread. A woman sat behind a long counter area, half of it a meat and deli case and the other half a checkout counter, along the right-hand wall. She was in her sixties, grossly fat and encased in a bulging dress much too small for her. A cigarette in a black holder slanted from one corner of her mouth.

The guy said, "Mary Alice, who you think I got here?"

She gave me an impersonal glance, the kind you'd give a side of beef to see how much fat there was on it. "Never saw him before."

"His name's Canino, been staying at one of the cabins up on Indian Hill. His wife run off with his car last night and stranded him."

"Stranded him, eh?"

"Can you beat that?"

"Known it to happen," Mary Alice said, and shrugged. The aftertremors of the shrug ran down her layers of fat like an earthquake's along a fault line.

"He lives in Stockton but he don't know how to get home," the guy said. "Thinks maybe he can get a bus from Sonora."

"Suppose he can."

"Offered me fifty bucks to drive him but I can't do it. You know somebody?"

"Jed, maybe. Fifty bucks, you say?"

I was getting tired of the two of them talking about me as if I weren't there. And that damned dog was still poking my legs with his slobbery muzzle. I said to Mary Alice, "Fifty dollars, that's right. It's all I've got to spare so I won't haggle." Then I said to the guy, "You mind calling your dog away from me?"

"What for? He won't do nothing to you unless I tell him."

"Get him away from me."

"Now listen, pal—"

"Get him away from me."

There was something in my voice or my face that wiped away his amused expression, stiffened him a little. He scowled, seemed to think about taking offense, looked at me in a new way, and then moved a shoulder and said,

"What the hell," and called the dog over to where he was standing.

The fat woman was looking at me in a new way, too, as if she were seeing me for the first time. She probably was. And it was as if the guy's amusement had lodged in her after it left him, because a faint smile kept tugging at one corner of her mouth. I had the impression then that she didn't like the asshole any more than I did.

She said to me, "I'll ring up Jed, see if he can take you. You want anything before I do?"

"I could use some hot coffee."

The guy said he could use some too, and she went and poured two cups from an urn behind the deli case. She gave me mine first. I drank it standing at the counter; he drank his wandering up and down the aisles, throwing things into a grocery basket, the shepherd following him like a shadow. He caught my eye once but he didn't hold it. Whatever else he thought of me now, he'd changed his mind about one thing: He didn't think I was such a schmuck anymore.

AFTERNOON

It was not somebody called Jed who drove me to Sonora; it was a gnarly old geezer named Earl Perkins. Jed was out somewhere, two other people Mary Alice called couldn't or wouldn't do the job, even for fifty dollars, and it was almost one o'clock before she rounded up this Perkins character. The asshole and his dog were long gone by then. I was so impatient to get to Sonora, ask my questions at Rite-Way Plumbing and Heating before it closed for the day, that I paced the store aisles to work off some of the nervous tension. Only then I found my thoughts turning to Kerry, to how much I wanted to hear her voice and know that she was all right, and the telephone began to draw my attention, and this just wasn't the time or place to make that kind of call. So I took myself outside and paced the parking area instead, trying not to think about anything at all.

Perkins showed up in a newish Jeep Cherokee that had snow tires on it but no chains. He was an easy seventy, small and gristled and tough-looking, like a piece of old steak. He looked me up and down, said to my face that I was a damned fool for letting a woman screw me instead of vice versa (Mary Alice laughed at that), and demanded the fifty dollars in advance. I gave him two twenties and two fives. Mary Alice had charged me a dollar for two coffees and a blueberry muffin, so that left me with eighteen dollars cash.

Perkins was a fast driver, even on snow-slick roads; he was also a damned good driver, and once I accepted that, I was grateful for the speed. The impatience was still in me; I sat forward on my seat and touched the .22 in my jacket pocket and thought again about Rite-Way Plumbing and Heating and what I would find out there. A name I would recognize or one I wouldn't? A lead or a dead end? Either way, I would know soon.

Once we passed through Murphys, the stark winter landscape began to disappear. What had been snowfields and snow-laden spruce and fir became, in these lower elevations, a mosaic of patchy white, dry brown, the dark green of oak as well as evergreen, and hints of spring verdure. When we turned onto Highway 49 at Angels Camp, Perkins drove even faster. There weren't many cars on the road and he zoomed around most of the ones

we came up behind, as if he were trying to win some kind
of high-speed rally. It put a little of the edginess back into
me then because I was worried about us getting stopped
by a county cop or a highway patrolman, of my having to
show ID. But I didn't say anything to him. He would
have resented it and probably driven even faster.

It was two-fifteen when we came into the outskirts of
Sonora. I knew the town a little, or had a few years ago,
but my memories of it weren't pleasant. An old friend
named Harry Burroughs used to live near there and he
had hired me to do a job for him and it had turned out
badly, very badly. That had been my last visit to this area.
It had been summer then and the town had been teeming
with tourists come to gawk at "an authentic Mother Lode
gold town." Now, in early March, it was all but deserted
—oddly so, I thought. A few cars creeping along the main
drag, no pedestrians on the steep sidewalks, most of the
stores wearing Closed signs. It might have been dying—a
venerable relic rescued and born again for the tourist
trade, now enfeebled once more and ready to take its place
beside all the other ghosts of the California Gold Rush.

I said as much to Perkins: "Looks like a ghost town."

"Well?" he growled. He wasn't much of a talker—he
hadn't spoken a dozen words to me on the drive—and he
seemed to resent my wanting to start a conversation now
that we had arrived. "Why shouldn't it be?"

"I don't know. I was just commenting."

"What'd you expect on a weekend this time of year? A
parade?"

"Weekend?"

"Well?"

"What day is this?"

He gave me a sideways glare, as if he thought I might

be joking. When he saw that I wasn't, the look changed shape, as if now he thought maybe I wasn't quite right in the head. "Mean to tell me you don't know?"

"No. What day is it?"

"Sunday. What day'd you think it was?"

Sunday! The guy in the Bronco hadn't mentioned the fact; neither had Mary Alice nor any of her customers. And it had been so many days since I'd looked at the calendar, I had lost track of which day it was. I'd done all that pacing in and around the Deer Run store, I'd been sitting on the edge of the seat all the way here . . . and it was Sunday, and most places were closed and Rite-Way Plumbing and Heating was sure to be one of them. Two-fifteen now—eighteen or nineteen hours before I could ask my questions, maybe learn some of the right answers. . . .

"Say," Perkins said, "what's the matter with you? You havin' some kind of seizure?"

"No, no, I'm all right."

"Don't look it to me."

Sunday, Sunday. It was almost funny in a crazy way and I wanted to laugh, but I didn't do it. I was afraid that if I let the laughter come out I wouldn't be able to stop it.

Perkins said, "Well?"

"Well what?"

"Where you want me to let you off? Bus station's closed on Sundays, or didn't you know that either?"

". . . A motel, I guess."

"Which one?"

"I don't know any motels here. The first one you see."

Perkins shook his head. "Mister," he said in his irascible way, "you got fog in your head, you know that? How do you get along in this world, anyhow? How'd you live so many years?"

Eighteen or nineteen hours . . .

EVENING

I sat in my room at the Pine Rest Motel on Highway 49 near the fairgrounds, staring at the TV without really seeing it. The only reason I'd put it on was for noise. A while ago, after twenty minutes under a steamy shower, I had gone down to the restaurant adjoining the motel and eaten an early steak dinner with all the trimmings. I had put away all of it, though it might have been Spam and canned fruit cocktail for all I'd tasted and enjoyed it, and I had been full when I came back up here. I was still full, but I was also empty. Full and empty at the same time. The impatience had drained out of me, leaving a temporary emotional cavity. Tomorrow it would fill up again. Tomorrow, when the hunt officially began.

Every now and then I would catch myself glancing over at the telephone on the bedside table. The very first thing I'd done when I took this room was to pick up the phone and dial Kerry's number. And the line had rung and rung and kept right on ringing until I replaced the receiver. I'd tried twice more, once before and once after dinner, and there was no answer those times either.

It didn't have to mean anything. She was out somewhere, that was all; she would be home later. Besides, it wasn't as if I was going to talk to her, tell her I was alive and safe and that pretty soon I would be coming home. I only wanted to hear her voice, to know that *she* was alive and safe. Then I would hang up.

It was a selfish thing, to want to relieve my mind and not hers. Nor Eberhardt's; I had no intention of calling him. How could I talk to either of them, with the hate festering inside me and my life still in a kind of limbo? What could I say to them? Could I confide that I intended to kill the man who had abducted me and made my life a hell for the past three months? Try to explain that I couldn't rest, couldn't begin to pick up the pieces of a normal existence, until I had done this thing? No, of course not. They would only try to talk me out of it, and that would do none of us any good. Or instead of telling them the truth, could I just say I was alive and well, I would be home soon, don't worry, and then hang up? That would make it even harder for them, not having any of the answers; it would open wounds that must be just now starting to heal, and keep them open for days or even weeks until I finally showed up.

Better this way. Better for all of us if I let them go on knowing nothing for a while longer. Then, when I did get in touch with them, it would be all over and they would never have to know the whole truth. I could bury the final chapter along with the whisperer's corpse, just as he had planned to do after my death, and nobody would ever have to know the whole truth except me.

I stared at the TV, listened to the noise . . . waited. It was warm in the room but I was still cold; I would probably be cold for months to come. After a time I got up and ran a hot bath—I still felt unclean, too—and soaked in it for half an hour. The patches of frostbite on my toes and finger seemed to be shrinking, and I had regained feeling in all three digits. No more danger there. I seemed to be getting over the other physical effects of exposure, too. The weakness was mostly gone from my arms and legs, I

was no longer plagued by chills, and the sore throat was
gone.

The noise of the TV had become an irritant, and when I
came out of the bathroom I switched it off. The phone
beckoned; I went to it and punched out Kerry's number
and let it ring a dozen times. Still no answer.

Without thinking about it, I dragged out the journal
pages and got into bed with them. I told myself that scan-
ning through them, reliving even a few of those agonizing
days in the cabin, was a form of masochism and would
serve no purpose. But I did it anyway.

*Thirteen days in April, in the year of our Lord nineteen
hundred and seventy-two. Thirteen long, difficult days. But
if that's it—and it must be because I don't see how it can be
anything else—I still don't know who he is. Or the exact
nature of his motive. Or why he would wait all this time,
nearly sixteen years, to take his revenge.*

*He wasn't someone directly connected with what hap-
pened back then; I'd remember him now if he was. And yet
I must have met him, we must have had some kind of
contact, else why the disguising of his voice, why the ski
mask to keep me from seeing his face? A relative or friend
of Jackie Timmons, as crazy as that possibility is?*

A relative or friend of the sixteen-year-old boy I killed?

Jackie Timmons. Car thief, shoplifter, dope runner,
burglar—all those things and more at age sixteen. Hay-
ward street kid, tough and not very bright; if he'd lived he
would surely have ended up in San Quentin after he
reached the age of legal majority. But he hadn't lived,
because his path had crossed mine one dark April night,
on a rainslick street in Emeryville.

A man named Sam McNulty had a wholesale jobber's
warehouse there: TVs, stereo equipment, large and small

appliances that he supplied to small dealers in the East
Bay. It was long gone now—McNulty had died in the
mid-seventies and his relatives had mismanaged the operation into bankruptcy—but it had been thriving in April
of 1969. And McNulty had been having trouble with
thieves. The police couldn't catch them, even with
stepped-up patrols, and the thieves had swiped half a
dozen color TVs from under the nose of a sleeping
nightwatchman. So McNulty had hired me to see what I
could do. I had brought in another private cop, Art
Baker, because a job like that is always better worked in
pairs, and Art and I staked out the warehouse. The fourth
night we were there, Jackie Timmons and two of his pals
showed up in a battered Volkswagen van, cut through a
chain-link fence just as they had twice before, and then
jimmied a warehouse window. Art and I were waiting for
them. They ran, and we chased them, and in the confu-
sion Jackie got separated from the other two; they took off
in the van, the way punks like that will, and left him to
fend for himself. I didn't know that when I slid in behind
the wheel of my car and Art clambered in on the passenger side. And I never saw Jackie come out through the
dark hole in the fence, start to run after the van, because I
was intent on chasing it myself and getting the license
number. One instant there was nobody in front of the car;
the next instant he was there, running, and there was
nothing I could do, there was no time to swerve or brake.
I hit him head-on doing thirty and accelerating.

The impact threw him thirty feet into a construction
company's dumpster. He was still alive when I got to him;
still alive when the emergency ambulance arrived; still
alive for the next twelve days. But he had suffered massive
brain damage as well as internal injuries and he died on

the thirteenth day of his coma, without regaining consciousness.

I was exonerated of any blame, of course—any legal blame. But Jackie Timmons had a mother and she didn't exonerate me. He had a twenty-two-year-old pregnant sister and she didn't exonerate me. He had street friends, neighbors, and they didn't exonerate me. And I didn't exonerate myself, not at first, because no matter what Jackie Timmons was and might have become, he had been sixteen years old and he was dead and his death was on my conscience. It was a long time before I could sleep at night without seeing him lying broken and bloody next to the dumpster on that rain-slick Emeryville street.

His mother screamed at me in the hospital when I went there to check on him a couple of days after it happened; she called me a damn murdering pig and worse. His sister spat in my face. But that had been the end of it. I did not see either of them again; I didn't see any of his friends, either, including the two who had been with him that night, because the van turned out to be stolen and they were never identified, never made to answer for those particular crimes. There were no threats on my life, no attempts at reprisal—no repercussions of any kind. It was just a tragic incident in a profession filled with tragic incidents, buried under layers of scar tissue. You have to forget; you can't go on doing my kind of work unless you learn how to forget.

Only now it looked as though somebody *hadn't* forgotten. After sixteen years, somebody connected with Jackie Timmons not only still hated me enough to want me dead but to put me through the worst kind of torment before I died. It didn't seem possible, this long after the fact—and yet nothing else made sense either. Thirteen days for

Jackie to die . . . thirteen weeks for me to die. And for some reason, a span of sixteen between the two thirteens.

Sixteen. Jackie had been that many years old when he died; was there some kind of correlation between the two? Possibly. But what kind of madman waits sixteen years to avenge the death of a sixteen-year-old kid?

Tomorrow, I thought. Tomorrow I start to find out.

Part Three
HUNT

THE FIRST DAY

MORNING

Sluicebox Lane turned out to be a short, carelessly paved street a third of a mile from the Pine Rest Motel. Rite-Way Plumbing and Heating took up most of the second block on the north side—a good-sized combination of pipe yard, warehouse, showroom, and business office. It was twenty of nine when I walked into the office and showroom at the front.

Water heaters, sinks, and small color-coordinated mock-ups of a bathroom and a kitchen took up two-thirds of the interior; the other third was the office, with a couple of desks arranged behind a low counter. Only one of the desks was occupied, by a plump middle-aged woman with streaky, dyed blond hair and a demeanor that just missed being bovine. She stood when I approached the counter, smoothed out the tweed skirt she was wearing, and showed me teeth any dentist would have been proud of, real or not. "May I help you?"

"I hope so. I need some information?"

"Yes?"

"About a customer of yours six to eight years ago. The owner of a cabin up near Deer Run."

Wrinkles appeared in her forehead, creating a V that pointed down the length of her nose. "I don't understand . . ."

"I'd like the person's name."

"You don't know his name?"

"No, Ma'am. That's why I'm here."

"Why do you want to know his name?"

The impatience came crawling back; I could feel the muscles in my stomach draw tight. All right, then, I thought. Tell her who you are, show her the license. If she read or heard about the disappearance and makes the right connection, bluff it through.

I said, "I'm a private detective. Working on an investigation." I got my wallet out and flipped it open to the photostat of my California PI license.

She said, "Oh," with a small amount of surprise and nothing else in her voice, and looked at the license just about long enough to identify the state seal. And if she noticed that I was clean-shaven in the photograph she didn't comment on it. One of these placid types, born without much imagination or curiosity. "Well, I'm afraid I can't help you."

"Why not?"

"We don't give out information about our customers."

"It's very important—"

"Besides," she said, "all our work orders and invoices are filed alphabetically. Without the customer's name, I couldn't very well . . . oh, Mr. Hennessey. Could you come over here a second?"

There was a door to the warehouse back beyond her desk and a silver-haired guy in his fifties, wearing a pair of overalls and duck-billed cap, had come through it. He angled over to the counter, smiled and nodded at me—I smiled and nodded back at him—and said to the woman, "What's up, Wilma?"

"This man wants to know the name of one of our customers. He's a private detective."

The guy's craggy face lit up at that, as if she'd told him
I was somebody important or famous. He gave me a
closer, appraising look and an even broader smile. "No
kidding?" he said. "A private eye?"

"That's right."

"Like Magnum, huh? Mike Hammer, Spenser?"

"No," I said, "not like them."

"What, no fast cars and hot broads?"

"No."

"Mean to tell me real private eyes aren't like what you
see on TV?"

"Not hardly. I'm just doing a job, the same as you."

It was the truth and he liked it; it put him on my side.
"Yeah, that's what I figured. All that bang-bang, sexy
stuff is so much crap, right?"

"Right."

"Sure. It's like I told my wife: Private eyes don't get
seduced any more than plumbers. I been in this business
thirty years and I never had a customer try to get in my
pants. Man *or* woman." He laughed as though he'd made
a joke, and winked at Wilma. She smiled dutifully, but
without either humor or appreciation; the expression in
her eyes said that as far as she was concerned, all men
were little boys and sometimes it was a chore putting up
with them.

I managed a small chuckle for his benefit. He liked that
too. He said, "I'm Bert Hennessey, I own the place," and
poked a callused hand across the counter at me. I took it,
gave him my right name—just the last one, in case he
wanted to look at my license. But he didn't. And the name
didn't seem to mean anything to him, any more than it

had to Wilma. "So why do you want the name of one of
my customers?"

"A case I'm working on."

"What kind of case?"

"A confidential one."

"Oh, sure. He live here in Sonora?"

"I don't know. All I know is that he owns a mountain
cabin up near Deer Run, on Indian Hill Road—or he did
six to eight years ago. You installed a water heater for
him, maybe ran some copper piping and did some other
work on the place."

"How'd you find that out?"

"The water heater's got your tag on it."

"Ah. Deer Run, you say?"

"On Indian Hill Road. Six to eight years ago."

"Deer Run, Deer Run . . . oh, yeah, I remember. I
don't get many jobs up that way. Only reason I got the
one you mean, the customer called three or four shops for
estimates and I gave him a low one, even with all the
travel time, on account of it was a slow spring and I
needed the work."

"Do you recall his name?"

"Well, I'm not sure." He frowned, thinking about it.
"Seems to me it was a sports name."

"The same as an athlete's, you mean?"

"Yeah. Baseball or basketball player . . . no, both.
White guy used to play for the Giants. And a black guy
played in the NBA, does those Lite Beer commercials you
see on TV. The guy with the big feet; you know, they keep
making jokes about his big feet."

Talk, talk, talk. The impatience had built a jangling
inside me; I clenched my hands tight to keep them still.
Hennessey was enjoying himself, playing a little riddle

game with me, and the only thing to do was to play along with him. If I pushed him he might decide I wasn't such an interesting specimen after all and close up on me. You either encourage people like him or you leave them be and let them get it out in their own sweet time.

I shook my head and shrugged and smiled and said, "Guess I don't watch enough sports on TV."

"My wife says I watch too much," Hennessey said. "She says sports on TV breaks up more marriages than nookie. Not that *she* knows much about nookie," and he winked at Wilma again.

She smiled her dutiful smile. I waited.

"Lanier," he said finally, as if he were answering a big-prize question on a TV game show. Proud of himself, because he knew something a private eye didn't. "Hal Lanier, pretty good infielder with the Giants once, manages the Astros now. Bob Lanier, the black basketball player with the big feet."

"Lanier," I said. It was a letdown because the name meant nothing to me. "You're sure that was his name?"

"Pretty sure."

"What was his first name?"

"That I don't remember."

"Did he live in the cabin year-round? Or did he give you another address?"

"Don't remember that either," Hennessey said. He glanced at the woman. "Look it up, Wilma, will you? Lanier. Must have been 'eighty-one. That was the year we had the slow spring."

"Those files are in the storeroom," she said. There was mild disapproval in her voice. But she was too placid to argue; and when he said, "Won't take a minute, you know

where they are," she released a small sighing breath and
went through the door into the warehouse.

I asked, "What did this Lanier look like?"

"Look like? Well, I don't have much of a memory for
faces . . ."

"It's important, Mr. Hennessey."

"Important case, huh?"

"Yes."

"He do something crooked, this Lanier?"

"He might have."

"Up at the cabin in Deer Run? Some kind of crime
happen up there?"

"Yes," I said, "some kind of crime."

"Can't say what it is, huh?"

"I'd rather not."

"Sure, I understand. Well, let's see. I think he was bald
. . . yeah, that's right, bald as an egg."

"Big man? Medium? Small?"

"Kind of medium, I guess."

"Was there anything unusual about him? Scars, moles,
mannerisms, the way he talked?"

"Not that I can remember."

"How old was he?"

"Oh . . . around our age."

"You're sure? In his fifties?"

"He was no spring chicken, that's for sure."

Not my man, then. If this Lanier had been in his fifties
seven years ago, he would be close to or some past sixty
now. The whisperer hadn't been anywhere near that old;
there had been a quality of relative youth about him, of
that I was certain.

"What else can you tell me about Lanier?"

"That's about all. Hell, it's been so long . . ."

Wilma came back in from the warehouse, carrying a slender file folder in one hand. "Here it is," she said in her placidly disapproving way. "James Lanier."

"James, that's right," Hennessey said. "James Lanier."

I asked Wilma, "What address did he give?"

She consulted the file. "Spruce Cabin, Indian Hill Road, Deer Run."

"Is that the only one?"

"No. There's another here. But it's not local."

Jesus, these people! "What is it, please?"

"It's in Carmichael," she said. "Two-one-nine-six-three Roseville Avenue, Carmichael."

I repeated it, committing it to memory: "Two-one-nine-six-three Roseville Avenue, Carmichael."

"That's right."

"Did he give a telephone number?"

"Yes, I think so . . ."

She found it and read it out, and I repeated it, too, so I wouldn't forget it.

When I thanked the two of them for their help, Hennessey said, "Any time. Wait'll I tell the wife we helped out a private eye. She'll wet her pants." He winked at me, winked at Wilma, and said, "She might even give me a little tonight."

Wilma sighed, pursed her lips, and sat down at her desk. Hennessey grinned. And I went away from both of them.

AFTERNOON

There were no rental car agencies in Sonora; I had learned that last night, from the desk clerk when I checked into

the motel. So after I left Rite-Way Plumbing and Heating,
I found my way to the bus station. The next bus to Sacramento wasn't until tomorrow morning, but there was a
one o'clock coach to Stockton. I spent nearly ten of my
remaining dollars on a one-way ticket. Stockton was some
sixty miles south and a little west of Carmichael, a sprawling northern suburb of Sacramento; it was also about the
same distance from Sonora. I could rent a car there this
afternoon and be in Carmichael sometime early this evening. The sooner I had a car and the freedom of mobility
it provided, the better off I would be.

From a phone booth I called Sacramento County information and asked for a Carmichael listing for James
Lanier. I half expected to be told that there wasn't one,
after seven years, but the operator punched in his com-
puter without comment and an electronic voice gave the
same number Wilma had read to me. So Lanier was likely
still at the same Roseville Avenue address. I could confirm
that by checking the local directory when I got to Carmichael.

I had gotten several quarters and I used those to call
Bates and Carpenter in San Francisco. I had tried dialing
Kerry's home number twice more last night, the last time
at a quarter to eleven, and she still hadn't answered.
Nothing ominous in that, or even significant, but it preyed
on my mind just the same.

When the call went through I said to the woman on the
switchboard, "Kerry Wade, please." There was a click,
another ringing sound, and then another click and Kerry's secretary, Ellen Stilwell, said cheerfully, "Ms. Wade's
office."

She knew my voice, Ellen did—I had called Kerry

often enough at the agency—so I deepened and roughened it when I asked, "Is Ms. Wade in?"

"May I ask who's calling?"

"Then she *is* in?"

"Yes, she is. Your name, please, sir?"

Relieved, I tapped the box with the handset, jiggled the cradle at the same time to make it seem as though there was something wrong with the line, and then hung up. All right. Kerry was alive, safe, well enough to be at her job; now I could put my mind at ease at least where she was concerned.

I went to a café not far away and drank coffee and made myself eat a piece of apple pie. Back at the bus station, I bought a newspaper and caught up on the news. Nothing much had changed in three months: political scandals, corporate scandals, religious scandals, small wars like rehearsals for another big one, all sorts of killing on the individual level. Lots of changes taking place everywhere—change is systemic in all walks of life, sometimes subtle and sometimes not so subtle—and yet certain fundamental things never change. I thought of the line from the Peter, Paul, and Mary song: *When will they ever learn?* Rhetorical question; moot point. We'll never learn. We'll never learn our way smack into the middle of Armageddon, and then we'll say, with the last words we'll ever speak, "How could this have happened? How could we have let this happen?"

The bus left on time. I sat in the back and stared out the window and tried not to fidget. The impatience that Wilma and Hennessey had rearoused in me this morning wouldn't go away. Outside the bus there were green trees and hillsides and then long, barren stretches of cattle graze as we came down out of the foothills into the upper reaches of the Central Valley; inside me there was turmoil, and the knowledge that I was no different from the rest of mankind. Each of us likes to believe we're unique, special. But when something profound happens, something like being chained up alone in a mountain cabin for ninety days, you realize the truth—that in you, as in everyone, there is a thing that crawled up out of the primordial slime a hundred million years ago, a thing so savage and elemental that it can, if you let it loose, overwhelm your humanity and reduce you to its level. This is the thing that causes war, that brutalizes and destroys, that keeps us from ever really being civilized creatures. This was the one thing I was about to unleash . . . even though I knew what it was and what it might do to me. I hadn't learned. I thought I had but I hadn't and in a way that was the most terrible truth I had ever had to face about myself.

We arrived in Stockton a little past three-thirty. A cab driver took another three dollars of my money to deliver me to an Avis office, where I rented a Toyota Tercel—the only nonluxury car they had available—that I could drop off at any Avis outlet in northern California. The woman who waited on me examined my driver's license, wrote down my name on the rental agreement, and ran off my MasterCard without a flicker of recognition.

It felt odd to be behind the wheel of a car again after so long a time. And I was not used to driving small foreign cars like this one. It wasn't until I got out of Stockton proper and onto Highway 99 that I began to relax. And once I relaxed, I felt a sense of release. I was in control again. From here on in, until the hunt was finished, I would not have to rely on anybody but myself.

EVENING

I ran into rush hour traffic above Elk Grove and 99 stayed jammed all the way through Sacramento, so that it was six-thirty when I finally reached Carmichael. I stopped at a Union station just off the freeway and went to one of two public telephone booths to look up James Lanier. The directory had been vandalized in that booth, the whole middle section ripped out; and in the other booth there was no book at all. Life in the enlightened eighties. I talked one of the attendants into hunting up the station's private directory, which turned out to be over a year old. Lanier was listed in there, at least, and at the same Roseville Avenue address.

The attendant sold me a Carmichael street map for two of my last five dollars. I sat in the car with it for ten minutes, first locating Roseville Avenue and then tracing a route from where I was. The distance was three or four miles. Just a short hop . . . but it took me half an hour to get there, because I made a wrong turn somewhere and got lost and had to stop and study the map again to retrace and refigure the route. I was sweating and drawn tight when I finally pulled up in front of 21963 Roseville Avenue.

Nobody was home.

The house was dark, no car under the carport to one side; and nobody answered when I went up and rang the bell.

I sat in the car for a time, still hot and tense, and stared at the house. Typical tract rancher, nothing special about it under its night cover except that the front yard was neatly and lushly landscaped. Not the kind of place you'd expect to find a madman living in, or a link to a madman either. Except that madmen and those who nurture them live in the same places sane people do, from any city's Skid Row to the stately homes and expensive flats of Washington, D.C., and McLean, Virginia. You can't always tell a book by its cover; you can't always tell the lunatics of the world by their cover.

Pretty soon I started the car, drove around until I noticed a Denny's, went in there and ate something—I don't remember what—and killed more time over three coffee refills. It was 9:15 when I pulled up in front of the Roseville Avenue house for the second time.

Still dark, still nobody home.

Now what? I could sit here and wait, but there were people in the neighboring houses, lights blazing in the two flanking Lanier's. A man sitting in a strange car in a neighborhood like this would have a cop asking him hard questions inside of half an hour. A better idea was to drive around some more, keep checking back periodically—for a while, anyway. I was already tired, headachy, gritty-eyed: the long day and the constant tension taking their toll. Make eleven o'clock the cutoff, then. If nobody showed up by eleven, go find a motel and try to get some sleep and then come back early in the morning.

So I drove aimlessly, keeping to major thoroughfares so I wouldn't get lost again. And I returned to 21963 Roseville Avenue three more times, the last one at five minutes past eleven. And still nobody was home.

I'd seen a motel near the Denny's where I'd eaten; I went there, took a room. The woman at the desk was fat and middle-aged and friendly, and it was plain that she found me at least a little attractive. She smiled when she handed over my key. I smiled back, turned away—and as

I did that I was conscious of the weight of the .22 in my jacket pocket and I found myself thinking, with a flash of self-hatred: No, you can't always tell a lunatic by his cover.

THE SECOND DAY

EARLY MORNING

Someone was home when I returned to 21963 Roseville Avenue at 8:30 A.M. A ten-year-old Buick stood under the carport, and down on his knees among the flowers and shrubs in the front yard was a man in gardening clothes— a bald man who looked to be in his early sixties.

I parked across the street. It was a warmish, sunny morning and there was a good deal of activity along the block: kids on their way to school, men and women backing cars out of driveways, mothers with toddlers in tow and babies in carriages. By daylight, it had the look of an older, once attractive and solidly middle-class neighborhood that was now starting to slide a little; some homes needed cosmetic and structural repairs, some yards had been allowed to deteriorate into weed patches; even the shade trees that lined its sidewalks had a ragged appearance. The middle class was a rapidly diminishing segment of this country's population; in another ten years, those families that still qualified would have moved elsewhere, upscale or maybe just sidescale, and this neighborhood would be on its way to becoming a suburban slum tract. Another of the Great American Dreams in remission.

Lanier's was the best kept house on the block. It had been repainted and reroofed not long ago, the lawn was a thick healthy green and well barbered, the flower beds were weed-free. The yard of a meticulous person, one who enjoyed gardening enough to be doing it at 8:30 in the morning.

The bald man was transplanting a nursery tray full of small yellow flowers; and he was so engrossed in the task that he didn't seem to hear me as I walked up the brick path toward him. It was only when I stopped a few feet away and said, "Mr. Lanier?" that he straightened on his knees and looked my way.

"Yes?"

No recognition on his face or in his voice; just a small smile and a mild curiosity in mild blue eyes. Everything about him was mild and nondescript: Mr. Average American working in his garden. I reminded myself that you can't judge a man by his cover—but I had the feeling that if he was involved in what had been done to me, it was in the most peripheral of ways.

"You're James Lanier?"

"Yes, that's right?"

"Do you or did you own a summer cabin on Indian Hill Road near Deer Run?"

"Why . . . yes." He put down the trowel he'd been using, got slowly to his feet. There was an odd methodical quality about his movements, as if it wasn't natural to him to move that way; as if he had once been a quick, energetic man who had undergone some kind of physiological or maybe psychological change. "Has something happened?"

"Happened?"

"At the cabin."

"Then you still do own it?"

"Yes, I do. But I haven't been there since . . . in more than three years. Has the new tenant done something to the place?"

"Tenant. Meaning you've rented it to someone?"

"I haven't, no. Richards and Kirk handled the transaction for me, as they always do."

"Who would Richards and Kirk be?"

"My realtors. And you? Who would you be?"

I told him my name. And I showed him the photostat of my investigator's license.

"I don't understand," he said. His curiosity was a little stronger now, but I had the impression that it was superficial—that he didn't really care who I was or why I was here or what might have happened at his Deer Run cabin. "Is the new tenant some sort of criminal?"

"I'm afraid so, Mr. Lanier. That's why I'm trying to find him. I'd appreciate it if you'd tell me his name."

"I don't remember it, I'm sorry. Susan has all the paperwork on the transaction."

"Susan?"

"The woman I deal with at Richards and Kirk. Susan Belford."

"Can you tell me when the cabin was rented?"

"In October, I think it was. No, early November. Susan was very pleased because it was for six months over the winter. That was the first time she was able to rent it over the winter."

"Would you do me a favor, Mr. Lanier?"

"Favor?"

"Call Susan Belford and ask her to give me the name of the man who rented the cabin. His name and address."

Lanier considered that. "All right," he said at length. "If the man is a criminal . . . yes, all right." He started toward the house, stopped after half a dozen steps, and turned to me again. "Is it nine o'clock yet?"

I looked at my watch. "No, not yet. Fifteen minutes."

"Richards and Kirk doesn't open until nine. Would you like to come in and have a cup of coffee while we wait?"

"If it's no trouble."

"Not at all."

He went onto a narrow porch, opened the door, led me into a bright, clean, comfortably furnished living room that had the stamp of an old-fashioned woman on it: antimacassars on the arms of a couch and two chairs, knick-knacks on tables and wall shelves, a framed embroidered wall motto that said: *Dear House, You Are Very Small— Enough Room for Love, That's All.* On an end table was an overlarge photograph of a woman in an ornate silver frame. I glanced at it as we walked by. Smiling, buxom woman of about sixty, as nondescript in her way as Lanier was in his.

I said politely, indicating the photo, "Your wife?"

It stopped him as suddenly as if I had caught his arm and yanked him still. And such an expression of naked pain came over his face that it made me wince. It lasted only a moment or two; then the mildness smoothed his features again, like a veneer over scarred wood. "My wife Clara," he said in his emotionless voice. "She . . . died three years ago last December."

"Oh, I'm sorry."

"Thank you. She was . . ." He broke off, stood rigidly for a few seconds, lost in some brief, sharp memory. Then he smiled his small smile and said, "Please sit down," and went through an archway toward the rear of the house.

I sat on one of the chairs. I could see the wall motto from there: Enough Room for Love, That's All. And I looked elsewhere, because it made me feel Lanier's pain again. There was no impatience in me today, for some reason; it seemed to come and go, like a malarial fever.

Lanier came back with a full coffee service on a silver tray, set in on a coffee table, poured for both of us. I said I would have mine black, and as he handed me my cup he said, "I always load mine with cream and sugar. You learn to do that in the service."

"What branch were you in?"

"Air force. Twenty years. I probably should have stayed in; Clara thought I should have. She never minded the travel . . ." He broke off as he had before, as a memory took hold of his mind. Pretty soon he said, as if there had been no long pause, "But I had a good job offer. Electronics company in Sacramento. Design work, good salary—jobs like that don't come along every day."

"No," I said, "they don't."

He sat down with his coffee. "Bought this place, bought the cabin in Deer Run, sent our daughter to college. Ruth's married now, lives in Menlo Park—her husband teaches history at the junior college there. I tried to give them the cabin after Clara . . . well, I knew I wouldn't go back up there alone. But they didn't want it. Too isolated, Ruth said. She never did like it much and Jim, well, he prefers water to mountains. They have a sailboat, spend most of their free time sailing on the Bay—" Abruptly he quit talking. Blinked, seemed to shake himself, and then said in a different voice, "I'm babbling. Bad habit of mine. I don't know why I do it."

I knew. But I said, "Don't apologize, Mr. Lanier."

"Ruth says I should get out more, see people, do things. She's right, of course. I belong to the Moose Lodge and I go down there two nights a week now, play cards, play chess. Bowl one night a week too. But that's only three nights. Movies once in a while, but what else can I do? Go to seniors dances, try to meet someone else? My God, I—" He stopped again, took a breath. "I'm sorry," he said, "I'm boring you. You don't want to hear my tale of woe."

"I don't mind. I know what it's like for you."

He raised his head. "You've lost someone too? Someone you loved deeply?"

"Not the way you have. Not permanently."

"Cancer," he said with sudden savage anger, "goddamn cancer. I watched her die. I watched her waste away and die and there was nothing I could do. She was always such a strong woman, rosy-cheeked, healthy . . . she weighed ninety-six pounds when she died. Ninety-six pounds." And he began to cry.

There was nothing for me to do or say. I sat there with the coffee cup and saucer in my hands and watched him mourn and thought about Kerry, what she'd been through the past three months, because that is what you do in this kind of situation: You turn a stranger's grief inward, personalize it.

Lanier's breakdown lasted less than a minute. I watched him take control of himself, the way you take hold of something with both hands. When he looked at me again it was with embarrassment. I wanted to tell him not to be embarrassed, there was no shame in weeping over the tragic loss of a loved one; but those words from me would have sounded hollow, and he wouldn't have listened to them anyway because he was already on his feet, moving away from me. He stood facing the empty fireplace, drying his eyes and face with a handkerchief. When he turned back toward me his movements were once more slow and methodical and his expression was a studied blank. The emotion had been dammed up again behind the wall of mildness and disinterest.

"It must be nine o'clock," he said. "I'll try Richards and Kirk now. Susan always comes in at nine, unless she happens to have a showing."

"Thank you."

"Do you want to speak to her yourself?"

"That might be best. If you'll explain who I am first."

He nodded and went to where a telephone sat on a rattan table. Susan Belford *had* come in on schedule, it developed. She gave Lanier an argument when he told her what he wanted and what I wanted, but only a small one: There were maybe two minutes of discussion before he said, "I'll put him on, Susan, thank you," and motioned for me to come take the receiver.

"Ms. Belford?"

"Susan Belford, yes. Mr. Lanier said . . . you're a private detective?"

"Yes, ma'am."

"Well, you know, we . . . it isn't out policy . . . I'm only doing this as a favor to Mr. Lanier." She had a twitchy, middle-aged voice that kept going up and down register so that some words had a shrill intonation, as if they were being goosed out of her.

"Yes, ma'am."

"Yes, well . . . about the man who rented Mr. Lanier's property in Deer Run . . . what did you want to know? I have the file here in front of me."

"His name, first of all."

"Lawrence Jacobs."

Another one that meant nothing to me. "And his address?"

"Forty-seven nineteen K Street, Sacramento."

I repeated it and then asked, "Would you know if that's a private home, an apartment building, a hotel?"

"It's an apartment building."

"So you did call to verify that Lawrence Jacobs lived there?"

"Of course. We . . . it's standard procedure in all our transactions . . ."

"Do you remember who you talked to?"

"The building manager."

"I mean the person's name."

"No, I don't . . . I didn't write it down."

"Man or woman?"

"Man? Yes, a man."

"And he confirmed Jacobs's tenancy?"

"Well, certainly."

"Did you also call Jacobs's employer?"

"No. He said he was self-employed."

"Doing what?"

"Consultancy work."

Yeah, I thought. "Can you describe him for me?"

"Describe him? Well, really, I meet so many people . . ."

"Please try, Ms. Belford."

"Oh, all right. He . . . well, he just wasn't very memorable. Average. Not tall, not short, not fat or thin . . . average."

"Slender build, would you say?"

". . . I suppose so, yes."

"How old?"

"Mid-thirties? Yes, about that."

"What color hair?"

"Brown."

"Dark brown, light brown, reddish highlights?"

"Just . . . brown."

"Curly or straight?"

"Straight."

"Worn long or short?"

"Short."

"What color were his eyes?"

"Blue? Gray? I'm not sure."

"Was there anything distinctive about his voice?"

"Not that I recall."

"Did he have any moles, scars, tattoos?"

"No."

"How was he dressed?"

"In a suit and tie."

"Expensive suit?"

"No. An inexpensive one."

"What kind of car did he drive?"

"I have no idea," she said.

"You never saw it?"

"Yes. I mean no . . . no, I didn't see it."

Based on her answers, the picture of Lawrence Jacobs that had formed in my mind was just as unfamiliar as the name. But he sounded like my man; the age and build were right. I said, "How did he happen to come to you about Mr. Lanier's cabin? Did he just walk in off the street? Was he recommended by someone?"

"He saw our ad in the *Bee.*"

"A specific ad for Mr. Lanier's cabin?"

"No, it . . . there were other rental properties . . ."

"What did he say when he came in?"

She made a breathy sound; she was becoming annoyed by my persistence. "He said he'd noticed the ad. I just *told* you that."

"What else did he say? Please, Ms. Belford, try to remember."

Another sigh. "He . . . let me think a moment . . ." She took ten moments. Then, "He said he was looking for a quiet, isolated mountain cabin because he . . . some sort of project he was working on and he didn't want to be disturbed by anyone. He said he wanted to hole up for the winter . . . those were his exact words."

"Did he want to see the cabin before renting it?"

"No. He asked me several questions . . . I showed him photographs, we always prepare multiple photos of our listings. When I told him the price he said it would do just fine."

"How did he pay?"

"With a cashier's check."

"Went away and got it and came back?"

"Yes."

"Which bank?"

Still another breathy sound. "The Bank of Alex Brown, a branch in downtown Sacramento. Now really, I . . . we're closing on a property later this morning and I have to . . . I can't take any more time to answer questions . . ."

"Just one more. What was the date?"

"Date?"

"That he came in. That he signed the rental agreement."

"November second, last year. Now is that *all*?"

"Yes, ma'am. I appreciate your time—"

"Thank Mr. Lanier," she said, and hung up on me.

I put the receiver down. November second. Almost five weeks before he'd abducted me—plenty of time to buy all the things he would need, make two or three or four trips to the cabin, install the ringbolt and the chain, complete the rest of his preparations. But how long before November second had he got his idea? How long had it been in the planning stages? Not sixteen years, not anywhere near that long, or he'd have acted on it years ago . . . unless he *couldn't* act on it. Suppose he'd been in prison, or some sort of mental facility? That could be it. But then where had he gotten the money for the cabin rental, for all the provisions and the rest of the stuff he'd needed? Had it before he was put away? Borrowed it from friends or relatives? Stole it? Probably didn't matter—but then again, could be it did.

One thing I knew for sure: Lawrence Jacobs wasn't his name. He would not have wanted his real name on the rental agreement in case anything went haywire with his plan. That was one of the reasons he'd paid with a cashier's check. The other was that handing over a large amount of cash might have made Susan Belford curious, if not actively suspicious.

James Lanier and I had little to say to each other. He showed me to the door, and we spent a few seconds wishing each other well before I went across to the car. When I drove away he was walking back to his garden, a slow-moving, solitary figure marking time, trying to find ways to fill up the rest of his days until—faith and hope being what they are—he could be with his Clara again.

LATE MORNING

K Street was one of Sacramento's central thoroughfares, and 4719 was no more than a couple of miles from the capitol building and all the other not-so-hallowed halls of state government. Still, it was a marginal neighborhood of lower income apartment houses and small business establishments. The building I wanted was an old three-story apartment house, narrow and fronted by two of the city's wealth of shade trees, wedged between another apartment house and a cut-rate liquor store. I parked down the block, went up into the vestibule. Six mailboxes, each with a name Dymo-labeled on the front. None of the names was Lawrence Jacobs; none of them was familiar. The one on the box marked with the numeral 1, O. Barnwell, had the letters "Mgr" after it.

I tried the entrance door. Locked. But through its leaded glass panels I could see someone in the dim hallway inside—a man up on an aluminum stepladder next to a flight of stairs, changing a light bulb in a ceiling fixture. I rapped on the door with my knuckles, and when he heard that and leaned down to look my way, I gestured for him to let me in. He didn't do it. He must have been able to see me well enough through the glass to decide I was nobody he knew or particularly cared to deal with: He made a go-away gesture and leaned back up to the ceiling fixture.

I did some more knocking, this time with my fist. And I kept on doing it, harder and louder, until the racket finally brought him down off the ladder and over to the door. He took another, scowling look at me through the glass, yanked the door open, and said angrily, "Chrissake, what's the fuggin idea?"

"You the manager? Mr. Barnwell?"

"Yeah. But we got no vacancies—"

"I'm not looking for an apartment. I'm looking for a man who calls himself Lawrence Jacobs."

"Who?"

"Lawrence Jacobs. He lived here around the first of November last year."

"Never heard of him."

"Were you the manager back then?"

"I said I never heard of him."

He started to push the door closed. I got a shoulder up against it and pushed harder than he did, hard enough to crowd him backward and let me slide in through the opening. The hallway was clean enough but it stank of disinfectant, old wood, somebody's chicken and garlic recipe. It stank of Barnwell, too—sweat and beer and the too-sweet odor of cheap aftershave.

Behind him, down the hall past the ladder, a door to the ground-floor front apartment opened and a skinny blond woman poked her head out. But Barnwell was too busy glaring at me to notice. He was in his late forties, lard-bellied, balding, with a tattoo on one bare forearm— the name Maggie intertwined with blue-stemmed red roses. He had eaten something with ketchup on it in the past few days: There was a streak of dried tomato red across the front of his sleeveless sweatshirt.

"What the hell you think you're doin, pal?"

"Looking for Lawrence Jacobs. I told you that."

"And I already told you—"

"Sure you did. Now tell me the truth."

"Listen—"

"I will, as soon as you start to talk."

"I don't have to fuggin talk to you."

"Don't you?" I said, soft.

We looked at each other for a time. His features soft-
ened first, like wax under a flame; then the anger in his
eyes cooled; and then his gaze slid away and a tic began to
jump on one puffy cheek. He said, "What are you, a cop?"

"Could be. And maybe I'm somebody you want to mess
with even less than a cop. Capisce, mi amico?"

He didn't like that; I had meant it to scare him and it
did. Enough so that there would be no need for me to
show him the .22. He backed up a step, and he must have
seen the woman hanging out of the open doorway because
her jerked his head toward her and snapped, "Goddamn
it, Maggie, get your ass back inside!" She gave him the
finger, but she didn't argue or waste any time pulling her
head in and slamming the door. So much for blue-
stemmed red roses and the sentiment that went with
them.

Barnwell put his eyes back on me, still didn't like what
he saw, and let his gaze slide off sideways again. He was
nervous now; the tic on his cheek had worsened. He lifted
a hand to poke at it, kept the hand there as if it and the
arm were a protective shield between us.

He said, "Lawrence Jacobs, right?"

"That was the name he was using."

"Okay. Okay. But I dunno his real name, I swear it."

"How long was he here?"

"A week or so, that's all."

"Come on, Mr. Barnwell, you don't rent out apartments for a week or so. We both know that."

"He didn't *live* here, he was just stayin here."

"With one of the other tenants?"

"Frank Tucker. He was a pal of Tucker's."

"Tucker isn't one of the names on the mailboxes."

"He moved out back in December."

"Did he? Where to?"

"Vacaville, I think. Yeah, Vacaville."

"Where in Vacaville?"

"I dunno." But then he paused, and something dark and bitter flickered in his expression. "My old lady might," he said. "I can ask her, you want."

"You do that. But not just yet. How well do you know this Frank Tucker?"

"I don't know him. I don't wanna know him."

"Why not?"

"I got reasons."

His old lady being one of them, I thought. Maggie of the blue-stemmed roses. But there was nothing for me in his domestic problems. I asked him, "Frank Tucker his real name?"

"Far as I know."

"What does he look like?"

"Big bastard, must weigh two-fifty, two-sixty. Arms like fuggin cement posts. Black greasy hair, like Presley used to wear his. You know?"

I knew—and I didn't know. The description meant nothing to me. "How old?"

"Forty, forty-five."

"What does he do for a living?"

"Said he was a truck driver."

"But you don't think so?"

"None of my business what he does."

"Talk to me, Mr. Barnwell. What do you think Tucker does for his money, if it isn't driving a truck?"

"Strong-arm stuff, okay? That's what I think."

"What kind of strong-arm stuff?"

"Any kind. Strikebreakin, head-bustin, shit like that."

"What about Lawrence Jacobs? That his line of work too?"

"Nah, not him. Too small, not mean enough."

"What does *he* do for a living, then?"

"He never said and I never asked."

"He just stayed here with Tucker for a week of so. Stayed in Tucker's apartment the whole time?"

"Well, he went out most days."

"With Tucker?"

"Nah, alone. Just crashin with Tucker. Or maybe . . ." Barnwell let the sentence trail away.

"Or maybe what?"

"I always thought there was somethin funny about him. Tucker, too, kind of. Queer, you know?"

"Meaning you think they had a homosexual relationship?"

"Could be. Tucker likes broads too"—the dark and bitter thing touched his face again—"but Jacobs, he looked pure fuggin fag to me."

The gospel according to O. Barnwell, philosopher and sage. But how much truth was in it? I put it away for the time being—until, if, and when I could find somebody more reliable to bear witness.

I said, "Were Jacobs and Tucker old friends or new friends? How did it look to you?"

He thought about it. "Old friends, I guess. Yeah, they knew each other a while."

"From where? Here in Sacramento, someplace else?"

"I dunno. They never said."

"Is Tucker a Sacramento native?"

"He never said that neither."

"How long had he been living here when Jacobs moved in?"

"Few months. He's the kind moves around a lot."

"He tell you beforehand Jacobs was moving in or did Jacobs just show up?"

"He told me. Said he had this buddy needed a place to crash for a week or two, till he found a place of his own. Didn't ask if it was all right, just told me Jacobs was comin. But what the hell, why should I care? I don't own the fuggin building."

"You talk to Jacobs much while he was here?"

"Nah, I don't like fags."

"Then how come you lied for him?"

Barnwell hadn't been looking at me much, had done most of his talking to the floor or to spots to my left and right. But now his gaze slithered back to my face, held there long enough for him to say, "Hah?" and then went roving again.

"You told a woman at a Carmichael real estate firm that Jacobs lived here, had an apartment in this building. You told her he'd been here for some time, paid his rent promptly, had a steady job."

"Oh yeah, that. Sure. But it wasn't no big deal. He give me twenty bucks, so why not?"

"He tell you what his reasons were?"

"So he could get a place he wanted up there. Carmichael. Said the real estate outfit wouldn't rent it to him if they knew he didn't have an address and was out of work."

"If he was out of work, where did he get the money to rent a place?"

"He never said."

"And you didn't ask."

"Why should I? It wasn't none of my business."

"How long after that did Jacobs move out?"

"Couple of days. He must of got the place he wanted in Carmichael, hah?"

Yeah, I thought, he got the place he wanted, but not in Carmichael. "You ever hear from him again?"

"Nossir, never."

"Or from Tucker since he moved?"

"Not me." His mouth turned down at the corners: anger, bitterness, self-pity. "Maybe my old lady heard. You want me to ask her now? Or you want to?"

"You do it, in private." It was easier that way. He could get things out of her that she'd be reluctant to tell a stranger, even a stranger playing the kind of role I was. Besides, if he was alone when he told her about me, he'd build me up into something pretty nasty—use me as a club to punish her for her real or imagined dallying with Frank Tucker. O. Barnwell, loving husband. "I'll wait here," I said. "One thing, though."

"Yeah?"

"Don't call anybody while you're inside. And don't call anybody after I leave."

"I won't. Who would I call?"

"Because if you do," I said, "I'll find out and I'll come back. You wouldn't want that, would you?"

"Nossir," he said to a point three feet on my left. "You don't have to worry, I won't want no trouble. I'm just a guy tryin to get along, that's all."

"Sure you are. Don't be long, Mr. Barnwell."

He went back past the ladder, moving sideways as if he were afraid to put his back to me, and disappeared inside the ground-floor apartment. A little time passed. I leaned against the wall next to the front door and smelled the building's secretions and thought about Lawrence Jacobs and Frank Tucker. Names, just names. And meaningless descriptions that fit dozens of people whose paths had crossed mine at one time or another. Where did Jacobs fit into the short, unpleasant life of Jackie Timmons? And did Tucker fit into it at all?

Voices began to filter out through the wall from Apartment 1—loud voices that kept getting louder. Barnwell shouting, Maggie shouting back. Then there were other voices, something falling over, a yell of pain, a screech that evolved into the words "You stinking *animal*!" and finally, when the door down there opened and Barnwell reappeared, the steady sound of sobbing.

Barnwell looked pleased with himself as he approached me: The fat worm had turned, and in the process had discovered he still had some sting in his tail. He was a sweetheart, he was. People like him . . . what made them that way? But I knew the answer; the answer was simple. Life made them that way. The hard, bad, sad, grinding task of living the lives they had constructed for themselves.

When he got to where I was he looked me straight in the eye. He had beat up on his wife and that had dissolved most of his fear, made him a man again for a little while. He said, "She had Tucker's address, all right. I knocked it right out of her, the two-timing bitch."

"Well?"

"Two-ten Poplar Street."

"In Vacaville?"

"Yeah. He called her with it after he moved. She said it was innocent, he just wanted us to know in case any of his friends come around or mail showed up for him. But that's bullshit. He never had no friends except Jacobs and he never got no mail."

"When did she last hear from Tucker?"

"Right after he moved, she said. Maybe that's bullshit too. She might of seen him yesterday, for all I know."

"One more thing. What kind of car does Tucker drive?"

"Chrysler. New one. I dunno the model."

"What color?"

"Brown."

"I don't suppose you noticed the license number?"

"Nah. Who notices license numbers?"

"All right, Mr. Barnwell. Just remember what I told you about making phone calls."

"I'll remember. Like I said before, I got nobody to call. And I'll see to it she don't call nobody neither, least of all Tucker. Make sure she don't if I have to bust her fuggin arm for her."

O. Barnwell, humanitarian. O. Barnwell, the Christian ideal.

AFTERNOON

Vacaville is a farming and ranching community off Highway 80, some thirty-five miles west of Sacramento. The literal translation of the name is cowtown, which is appropriate enough, but in fact the town was named after the Vacas, a family of Hispanic settlers in the area. A quiet place, Vacaville, plain and old-fashioned in looks and outlook, hot and dusty in the summer—one of those towns with plenty of history and yet no particular historical attraction for the modern tourist. The only reasons you'd go there were to visit friends or relatives, or business, or to see one of the inmates at the California Medical Correctional Facility nearby. On first reflection, you wouldn't think somebody like Frank Tucker would want to live there. But if he was the kind of man Barnwell had painted him—hired muscle, more brawn than brain—it was exactly the type of town he might pick. For one thing, a few ranchers and farm owners still believed in taking a hard line with recalcitrant laborers, the ones who had the gall to fight for better than starvation wages; such bosses weren't above hiring somebody to knock heads when the "wetbacks" and the "greasers" and the "chihuahuas" got out of hand. Another reason for Tucker to pick Vacaville was that the cost of living was relatively low, by California standards these days; and a third was that as long as you didn't mug old ladies on the street or break up bars on Saturday nights, the local law probably wouldn't pay any attention to you. It was also possible that Tucker had some reason—contacts, a close friend—for wanting to be close to the prison facility.

It was just one o'clock when I drove into the smallish downtown area. I stopped at a convenience store to ask directions to Poplar Street. It was a few blocks off the main drag—an older residential neighborhood, the sidewalks shaded by big leafy oaks and elms. The private houses were mostly of pre-World War II vintage, but a few newer homes and small apartment complexes had sprung up here and there, none of them particularly aesthetic: weeds in a mossy old garden. The apartment building at number 210 was a two-story, brown stucco affair that looked more like a cut-rate motel. Eight units, four up and four down, all the doors facing the street, the ones on the second level reachable by outside staircases and a long low-railed balcony along the front.

There was an asphalt parking area, just as you'd find at a motel; no trees, no shrubs, no flowers except for some potted plants next to one of the street-level apartments. I

put the Toyota into a painted parking slot and went looking for mailboxes. No mailboxes. Each apartment bore a
number and each one had a private mail slot. Number 2
downstairs, the one with the potted plants next to it, also
bore a neatly hand-printed card in a brass holder: Manager. There was no doorbell, so I banged on the panel a
couple of times. Nobody came to see what I wanted.

I turned away with the intention of talking to one of the
other residents; there were three cars in the lot besides my
rental. No, make that four: a green, low-slung Firebird
with a woman at the wheel was just turning in off the
street. It skidded into a space next to the Toyota and a
round brown Spanish face topped by piles of shiny black
hair poked out of the window and said in a gravelly voice
with not much accent, "You looking for me?"

"I am if you're the manager."

"Hold on a minute."

She got out of the Firebird in wiggly, puffing movements—a big woman in an orange flowered dress that
made her look even bigger. She leaned back in for a bag of
groceries, then waddled over to where I waited.

"I'm Mrs. Ruiz," she said good-naturedly. "If you're
selling something, I don't want it." She paused for a beat
and then said, "Not that you look much like a salesman."

"I'm not. I'm looking for one of your neighbors."

"Which one?"

"Frank Tucker."

Her mouth got puckery, as if I'd squirted lemon juice
along with the name. "Him," she said. "You a friend of
that bum?"

"No. I just want to talk to him."

"Some kind of cop, right?"

"How did you guess that?"

"Only two kinds want to talk to Frank Tucker—cops and other bums. But you're too late."

"Too late?"

"He's gone. Moved out."

"When?"

"Couple of weeks ago, like a thief in the night."

"Do you know where he went?"

"Straight to hell, I hope."

"No forwarding address?"

"Hah!" Mrs. Ruiz said. "He owed two weeks' rent, the bum. So who do you think takes all the crap from the owner of this place? Me, that's who. Like it's *my* fault Frank Tucker is a bum. My ex-husband warned me, he said 'Don't volunteer to be manager, querida, it's nothing but headaches.' Well, he was right for once, the only time he was ever right about anything. And I didn't listen."

"Can you tell me—"

"The owner's got *some* nerve," she said, still indignant. "I told him in the beginning Frank Tucker was a bum and we shouldn't rent to him. He said rent to him anyway. I told him Tucker was an ex-convict too, as soon as I found out, but he—"

"How did you find out?"

"What, that he's an ex-convict? I heard him talking to one of his friends. He was drunk or he wouldn't have said it so loud."

"Which prison was he in? The medical facility here?"

"No. Folsom."

Folsom was a maximum security prison off Highway 50 east of Sacramento, not as well known outside the state as San Quentin but with the same kind of hard-core inmate population. I had helped send a few men to Folsom over the years . . . Folsom, Folsom. And a slender man in his thirties, with straight brown hair . . .

I said, "Did he say how long he'd been in Folsom?"

"No."

"Or when he got out?"

"No."

"This friend he was talking to—what did he look like?"

"Like a bum," Mrs. Ruiz said, "what else?"

"Could you describe him?"

"Big, no neck, black curly hair. Forty or so."

"You happen to catch his name?"

"Dino. That's an Italian name."

"Yes, I know."

"Well, he *looked* Italian, that bum."

"Any idea where he lives?"

"No. I never saw him before or since."

"Did you ever see Tucker with a man in his thirties, brown hair, average height, slim build?"

"No."

"Did he ever mention the name Lawrence Jacobs?"

"Not to me. He didn't talk to me and I didn't talk to him."

"Can you give me the names of any of Tucker's other friends?"

"He kept to himself, mostly," Mrs. Ruiz said. "I only saw him with one other bum, the day before he moved out."

"What did that one look like?"

"Fat. Fatter than me and that's *fat.*"

I wondered if the fat man had had anything to do with Tucker's decision to pull up stakes. "Do you know what they talked about?"

"No. The fatty showed up in a big car and went up to

Tucker's apartment and Tucker let him in. I never heard him say a word."

"So you don't know his name."

"No."

"How long did he stay?"

"Search me. I went out shopping and when I came back, the fatty was gone."

"The big car he drove—any idea what kind?"

"Cadillac. Cream-colored Seville. 'Eighty-five." I must have looked a little surprised, because she grinned and said, "I know cars. My ex-husband is an auto mechanic."

"You didn't happen to get the license number?"

"No. Now I wish I'd looked."

"You said Tucker kept mostly to himself—"

"That's right, he did."

"—but did he ever talk to any of the other neighbors? Somebody who might give me a line on where he is now?"

"No way," she said positively. "I know everybody here, I get along with everybody, we're always yakking with each other. That bum didn't talk to anybody around here except the bums that came to visit him."

"He drives a Chrysler, is that right?"

"Right. 'Eight-six LeBaron. Tobacco brown."

"License number?"

"Personalized. MR F T. MR BUM would have been better." She shifted the bag of groceries from one arm to the other. "Anything else you want to know? This bag is getting heavy."

"Not unless you can think of something, some little detail, that might help me find him."

She tried. I watched her round face screw up, the heavy flesh around her eyes draw tight and the eyes themselves disappear behind slits so narrow they might have been

incisions. Then her whole face seemed to pop open again,
like some kind of exotic flower, the eyes reappearing wide
and black—an effect that was almost startling—and she
said with genuine regret, "No, nothing. I wish I could,
that bum ought to be back in jail, but I already told you
everything I know."

Dead end.

Now what was I going to do?

I left Mrs. Ruiz to her groceries and her managerial
woes and drove around for a while, aimlessly. Then, because I hadn't eaten yet today, I stopped at a café on
Merchant Street that accepted credit cards and brooded
over coffee and a steak sandwich. Lawrence Jacobs, Frank
Tucker, an Italian guy with no neck named Dino, a fat
man who drives an '85 cream-colored Cadillac Seville
. . . but where were they now? A possible Folsom prison
connection . . . but I didn't have enough information
yet to identify Jacobs or his motives. And no way to get it
soon unless I picked up his or Frank Tucker's trail again.

Three options, as far as I could see. There was a fourth
—go back up to Deer Run and stake out the Indian Hill
cabin—but I wasn't ready to do that yet. Would do it only
as a last resort. It might be another three to four weeks
before Jacobs decided to return to the cabin; I couldn't
live up there anywhere near that long, alone, doing nothing except waiting. It would be almost as much of an
ordeal as the one I had already been through. It would put
me right over the edge.

Three options. One: Canvass the other residents at 210
Poplar Street, even though Mrs. Ruiz had seemed certain
that none of them knew any more than she did about
Frank Tucker and his activities. Two: Return to Sacramento, to 4719 K Street, and find out if Maggie Barnwell

had held anything back from her husband. Three: Run a
DMV check on Tucker's Chrysler LeBaron with the MR
F T license plate, see what address turned up. The first
two choices struck me as a waste of time. And the only
way I could accomplish the third was to contact Harry
Fletcher at the DMV's San Francisco office. I could swear
Harry to secrecy—but he had a big mouth and he might
let something slip, something that would get back to Eberhardt or Kerry or into the news media. Besides, Tucker
had owned the car while he was living in Sacramento,
might have put the K Street address or some other old
address on the registration. And if he moved around as
much as it seemed he did, he wouldn't bother to notify the
DMV each time he changed residences.

One person he probably would notify was his parole
officer . . . *if* he was out on parole. In the old days I
could have gone through channels, got hold of his prison
record, and if he'd been paroled, the name of his parole
officer. But these weren't the old days. I had fewer re-
sources available to me now, and therefore fewer options
than I would have had on a normal investigation—

Susan Belford, I thought.

Something I should have asked Susan Belford and
hadn't.

Her name and the question popped into my head at the
same time, an obvious question that had somehow failed
to occur to me when I spoke to her on the phone. That
wouldn't have happened if I'd been myself—my old self,
the one with the sharply honed professional instincts.
Maybe the answer to the question was no, but if it was
yes . . .

I pushed up from the table, paid my check, and followed the cashier's directions to a public telephone back

by the restrooms. I spent most of my change on a call to
Richards and Kirk in Carmichael. Susan Belford wasn't
in, but the man I spoke to, a Mr. Unger, said she was due
to "check back in around three." It was two-thirty now. I
gave him my name and asked him to tell Ms. Belford that
I'd called, that I was on my way up to see her, and would
she please wait until I got there. He said he would relay
the message.

   It was twenty minutes to four when I finally found my
way to the shopping center where Richards and Kirk had
their offices. Susan Belford wasn't there. Yes, she'd
checked in as expected. Yes, Mr. Unger had given her my
message but she'd chosen not to wait. No, Mr. Unger
would not give me her home address or telephone number
. . . which meant that she'd told him not to. Usually real
estate agents are more than willing to give out their home
numbers, to the point of listing them on their business
cards.

   I drove to a service station and looked in the telephone
directories for Carmichael and several other nearby com-
munities, including Sacramento. If she lived in one of
those places, she was either unlisted or listed under another name. The only Belford in any of the books was
Leon Belford and Son, Manufacturers of Quality Brass
Fittings.

THE THIRD DAY

MORNING

Susan Belford showed up for work at five minutes to ten the next morning. I had been waiting since nine, when Richards and Kirk opened for business, and I was fidgety and trying hard to conceal my irritation when she walked in.

Today I wore a hound's-tooth sports jacket, the loose-fitting kind with deep pockets so I could carry the .22 without any telltale bulges, and a white shirt and a pair of gray slacks—items I had bought the night before at a cut-rate clothing store in this same shopping center. One reason was that the too-tight clothing I'd taken from the Carder A-frame was beginning to both chafe and smell after three days of constant wear; the other reason was that if I was going to convince the uncooperative Ms. Belford to answer another question, I would need to look as well as act like a reputable private investigator. I had thought so last night, anyway. One look at her, and I knew that neither I nor anyone else would ever have to dress up on her account.

La Belford was a frumpy blond in her late forties, sloppily outfitted in a baggy gray skirt and a white sweater with little spots and streaks of cigarette ash on the front of it. She had mannerisms that were as twitchy as her voice, and such a preoccupied air that she almost ran into me before she realized I had moved into the path she was taking from the front entrance. And in almost running into me, she also came within an inch of setting fire to my new sports jacket with the lighted cigarette she was brandishing in one hand.

She was not glad to see me. She scowled when I identified myself, and made a violent waving gesture with the cigarette that sent particles of ash flying. "You again," she said. "Why do you persist in . . . what is it you want *now*?"

"Five minutes of your time, that's all."

"I answered all your questions yesterday—"

"Not quite. There's one other I should have asked."

"Oh, for heaven's sake. I'm a busy woman, I don't have time for this sort of thing . . ."

"One question, Ms. Belford. Please, it may be important."

"Important, it's always important. Well? What is it, then?"

"Did the man who rented Mr. Lanier's cabin supply any personal references?"

"The man who . . . you mean Lawrence Jacobs?"

"Yes, ma'am. Lawrence Jacobs?"

"Don't call me ma'am," she said. "I hate that . . . ma'am is short for madam, don't you know that? Do I look like a madam?"

She did, as a matter of fact. But I said, "No, of course you don't. My apologies. Now about Lawrence Jacobs—"

"Yes, yes, we usually ask for . . . I'm sure he must have given at least one personal reference. Yes, I *know* he did, I saw it in the file yesterday."

"I'd appreciate it if you'd let me have the person's name and address."

She thought that over for maybe ten seconds, sighed, and then made one of her fluttery gestures and turned on her heel and stalked off across the room. I took that for an affirmative and trailed after her, dodging smoke and more ash from her cigarette. She plunked herself down behind a cluttered desk, aimed the remains of the cancer stick at a cut-glass ashtray; it caught the edge and showered sparks, a couple of which fell on a loose pile of papers. She didn't seem to notice, so I reached over and smudged out the sparks before they started a fire. She didn't notice that either; she was already turning toward a metal file cabinet to one side. But in the process she whacked her elbow into an onyx pen set and knocked the whole thing off onto the floor. *That* she noticed, along with everybody else in the office. She muttered something under her breath, and without any hesitation or pretense at decorum she slid off the chair onto her hands and knees, crawled under the desk with her skirt riding up on plump thighs to retrieve one of the pens, gathered up the rest of the set, hauled her pudgy body back into the chair, and threw the pens and base unit onto the desktop without looking at me or any of her co-workers. Then she swiveled around as if nothing had happened, fumbled open one of the file drawers, and began rummaging inside.

If I had a place to sell or rent, I thought, Susan Belford would be the last person I'd let handle the deal. It was even money she would either wreck or set fire to one out of every ten houses she entered.

It didn't take her long to find the proper file. She even managed to get it out of the drawer and back onto her desk without doing any more damage. I watched her riffle through the papers inside, jerk one out with an unintentional flourish, and peer at it myopically for a few seconds before she said, "Here it is. Mmm, yes, now I remember . . . yes."

She didn't seem inclined to continue on her own initiative, so I made a throat-clearing noise to prod her.

". . . Elmer Rix. Odd name, isn't it?"

And just as meaningless as the others. "How do you spell the surname?"

"R-i-x."

"What address?"

"The Catchall Shop, Yuba City."

"No street or number?"

"No."

"Telephone number?"

"Just a . . . yes, here it is."

She read it off to me and I repeated it twice to memorize it. Then I asked, "Do you know the relationship between Lawrence Jacobs and this Elmer Rix?"

"No, I don't."

"Did you call Elmer Rix to check the reference?"

"Well, of course." La Belford knocked over her purse reaching inside it for another cigarette; several items besides a pack of Salems fell out—comb, brush, compact, a Heath bar—but she left them scattered where they lay.

"Do you have any idea what the Catchall Shop is?"

She had fished a cigarette out of the pack and was bringing it to her mouth—but backward, so that it was the tobacco end she put between her lips. I thought she was going to light the filter, but she realized the mistake in time and reversed the thing. The flame on her lighter was turned up too high: She almost singed her bangs firing up the weed.

"Ms. Belford."

"What?"

"I asked if you have any idea what the Catchall Shop is."

"None whatsoever." She scowled and blew smoke in my face—obliviously, not intentionally. I batted it away with my hand. "One question, you said . . . a dozen is more like it. Now really, if you don't . . . I have *work* to do."

"So do I," I said, and got up on my feet.

She made a dismissive gesture with the cigarette. And smacked the burning end against her desk lamp and sent another fallout of sparks to the litter of papers strewn over the surface. One of the sparks started to smolder; she didn't notice because she had swiveled her chair around to replace the file folder in the cabinet. This time I didn't bother to smother the sparks. I went away from her instead. There was a thumping sound behind me as I crossed the office, but I did not turn around to see what it was. I didn't want to know.

It takes all kinds, sure. But some kinds are harder to take than others.

EARLY AFTERNOON

I hadn't been to Yuba City in twenty years. As with Vacaville, there was little reason to go there unless you had friends or relatives or business in the area. It is forty miles or so north of Sacramento, across the Feather River from Marysville, and to get to it you take arrow-straight Highway 99 through a dozen miles of rice fields—a crop that isn't usually associated with California agriculture but that grows well in that part of the state—and then either a continuation of 99 or the quicker Highway 70 through Marysville. The countryside around Yuba City nurtures crops of a different kind: peaches, nectarines, apricots, walnuts. Mile after mile of orchards extend away to the south, west, and north.

Yuba City has two other claims to fame. One is provocative: In a couple of quality-of-life polls to determine the most desirable place in California to live, it had come in dead last. The other is notorious: In the early seventies it had been the scene of one of the more shocking massmurder cases—the one in which Juan Corona was convicted of cold-bloodedly slaughtering twenty-five migrant workers after having had homosexual relations with them.

Visually, Marysville is a Cinderella compared to its stepsister across the river. Its downtown is filled with attractive old buildings and it sports a huge shady part with a lake in the middle. Yuba City, on the other hand, has an unaesthetic downtown area sans park and lake, plus a couple of miles of southern California-style shopping centers and fast-food joints. But looks can be deceiving where cities are concerned, too. Marysville also harbors a wellpopulated skid row and has larger crime and substanceabuse problems than its neighbor. Despite Yuba's tarnished image, if you had to live in one town or the other, and you weighed the pros and cons carefully, Yuba City would be the one to pick.

The Toyota's buy-gas light was on when I drove into Marysville a little past noon. I took the bridge across into Yuba City and stopped at an Exxon station off Bridge Street to fill the tank and to look up Elmer Rix and the Catchall Shop in the local directory. No entry for Rix; but the Catchall Shop was listed at 2610 Percy Avenue. According to the kid working the pumps, that address was less than a mile from here, out past the nearby Del Monte packing plant. "You'll find it real easy," he said. And for once, somebody who told me that was right.

The building at 2610 Percy Avenue was big, sprawling, and on the brink of condemnation as a fire hazard. A cyclone-fenced yard to one side was full of things like claw-foot bathtubs, random lengths of pipe, car parts, pottery urns and ceramic garden statues, rusty stoves, a twenty-foot-high carved oak likeness of a snarling grizzly bear. On the warped wood front of the building were several signs, some large and some small, some metal and some wood, all hand-painted by somebody with not much of an artistic eye. THE CATCHALL SHOP, over the double-doored entrance. SECONDHAND ITEMS OF ALL KINDS. BURIED TREASURES. TOOLS OUR SPECIALTY. PAPERBACK BOOKS, 25¢. IF WE DON'T HAVE IT, YOU WON'T FIND IT ANYWHERE ELSE. BROWSERS WELCOME. CASH ACCEPTED FROM ANYONE.

But the most interesting thing about the place, at least externally, was the car parked inside the yard gates—a cream-colored Cadillac Seville, no more than a few years old and probably a 1985 model.

I made a U-turn and parked in front of the building. Walking inside was like entering an incredibly cluttered hermit's cave: gloomy, dank-smelling, jammed to the exposed rafters with shelves and piles and tiers of every imaginable kind of junk. There was nobody moving around in there; but through an open side door I could see someone maneuvering an ancient forklift in the adjacent yard. I could also see what happened to be a dimly lighted office over that way.

There were no aisles as such; I had to blaze a round-about path to the office. Along the way I saw the remains of an ancient buckboard, a beat-up Chinese gong with a faded dragon painted on it, at least a thousand dust-laden and mildewed paperbacks on bowed shelves, a wine cask

that somebody had made into a child's playhouse, bins
overflowing with age-crusted hand tools, a Rube Goldberg
machine with arms and legs and wires and a use I couldn't
even begin to guess at, horse collars and pickle crocks and
rows of cobwebbed mason jars and radios with broken
cases and a Stop sign that had been used for target prac-
tice and a mannikin with a crumbling maroon velvet dress
draped over it. The whole place had the look of a madman's museum filled with exhibits that made no sense and
that had lain unattended and unviewed for decades. There
ought to have been another sign on the front of the building: WE HAVE IT, BUT NOBODY IN HIS RIGHT MIND
WOULD WANT IT.

The office was a wallboard and glass affair, small and as
cluttered as the rest of the place, the glass so fly-specked
and grime-streaked that it was mostly opaque. One of the
jumble of objects inside was a desk; another was a man in
the chair behind it. "Fatter than me and that's *fat,*" Mrs.
Ruiz had said of Frank Tucker's last visitor in Vacaville.
Her description and the Cadillac Seville outside made that
man and this one the same. He must have weighed close
to 350 pounds, and in the weak light from a gooseneck
lamp he looked like nothing so much as a huge toad sitting on a stump. Bald brown head, rutted and warty
brown face, little half-lidded eyes that looked sleepy but
would miss little or nothing of what they surveyed. When
he opened his mouth I would not have been surprised to
see a long, thin tongue flick out and snag one of the flies
that moved sluggishly through the air around him.

The only part of him that moved when I walked in was
his mouth: It curved upward at the corners in a professional smile—a moneylender's smile. He said in a deep,
throaty toad's voice, "Howdy, friend. Thanks for stopping

in. Tell you right off you picked a good day. Bargain specials galore, no reasonable offer refused. What-all you interested in?"

"Elmer Rix, for starters," I said. "Would that be you?"

"Sure would. You got business with me?"

"With someone you know."

"Who would that be?"

"Frank Tucker."

A change came over him, the subtle kind that you might miss unless you were looking for it. Outwardly, nothing at all happened; the smile stayed fixed, the expression otherwise blank and the eyes half-lidded. But beneath the surface he got hard, rock hard: Fat turned to stone so suddenly that he might have gazed upon the face of Medusa. Those amphibian eyes measured me, dissected me with the same emotionless precision a biology teacher uses to dissect a real toad.

He said with false geniality, "Hey, do I look like the missing persons bureau? I sell junk, not information."

"Are you telling me you don't know Frank Tucker?"

He didn't say anything, just looked at me. I looked back, not giving him any more or any less than he was giving me. I had my hand in my jacket pocket, touching the butt of the .22, but it would have been a mistake to put him under the gun. Elmer Rix was no O. Barnwell; intimidation and threats wouldn't work with him. The hardness was strength as well as stubbornness and probable veniality. A tub of guts with guts.

I said, playing it a different way, "Look, I need to talk to Tucker. As soon as possible. He won't mind when he hears what I've got to say."

"What would that be?"

"I've got a job for him."

"That so? What kind of job?"

"Do I need to spell it out?"

"I'm a good listener, friend. Try me."

"Muscle work."

"Bodybuilding, that what you mean?"

"Come on, Rix, let's cut the bullshit, okay? We both know what Tucker hires out to do."

"Man in my business gets to know a lot of things," he said. "Point is, how do *you* know?"

"Somebody I know knows Dino."

"Dino who?"

"Friend of Tucker's," I said, and I didn't have to feign the impatience in my voice. "The word I got was that if I wanted to talk to Tucker, I should come over here and see Elmer Rix at the Catchall Shop. So here I am. Now do you point me to Tucker or do I find somebody else to give my dough to?"

He watched me a while longer before he said, "What kind of job and how much you paying?"

So far, so good. "I own a trucking outfit in Winters. For a while I didn't have much competition; now I got heavy competition and I don't like it. I want the competition to close up shop, go somewheres else. I want Tucker to fix it so that happens."

"Tsk, tsk," Rix said through his smile. "You didn't say how much."

"Top dollar. Plus a bonus if my competition is gone within three months. I'll work out the exact numbers with Tucker."

"Uh-huh. You know my name—what's yours?"

I said, "Canino. Art Canino." And I thought: If he asks for ID, I'll have to put him under the gun after all.

But he didn't ask for ID. He said, still smiling, "Well,

you sure do tell a wild story, Mr. Canino. If I did know somebody named Frank Tucker, and I ain't saying I do, I don't know as I could recommend he take on a job like the one you're offering."

"Suppose we let him decide that."

"Sure. *If* I knew him and how to get hold of him."

Now I saw what he was after. Still a little slow on the uptake; still a little rusty. But the important thing was that it meant I had him hooked.

I asked, "How much do you want?"

"Some of the stuff you see in here, I'm selling it for somebody else. On consignment, like they say. I get ten percent."

"From Tucker? Or from me, extra?"

"From the customer," he said. "Always."

I put up a mild protest to make it look good. "What the hell? That means I got to pay a hundred and ten percent."

"Everything costs these days, Mr. Canino. You want a job done right, you go to the best people. You go to the best people, you pay high prices right down the line."

"Okay, okay. But I'm not putting up any cash until I see Tucker and we settle on a price."

"Hey, nobody's asking you to."

"So where do I find him?"

"Tell you what," Rix said. "You go away someplace, come back here in an hour. No, make that an hour and a half."

"How come so long?"

"I ain't had my lunch yet."

"Listen, this deal is important—"

"So's my lunch," he said, and he was dead serious.

"Will Tucker be here when I come back?"

"Ninety minutes and then you find out, right?"

We traded another long look, him with that amphibian smile pulling up the corners of his fat mouth. Only now it was genuine. Big toad king sitting on the throne in his cave full of decaying junk, holding court and enjoying every minute of it because in this place, this little kingdom, he made the rules and levied high tariffs for the privilege of his favors. I wondered if the local cops knew what kind of business His Bloated Highness was really in. I thought that maybe, when I was done with all this, I would find out.

There was nothing more to say to him, not just now. So I let him win this round of the staring match, nodded once, and left him sitting there looking royally pleased with himself.

It was a quarter of one when I got into the Toyota. I drove downtown, found a Denny's, and picked my way through a taco salad. Not much appetite since I'd come out of the mountains above Deer Run; it would probably be a while before I had one again. But that was all right. I liked the shape I was in now, leaned down and hard-bellied. Once I was home, back into a daily routine, I would have to take steps to ensure that I didn't put weight on again.

When I finished eating I paid the check right away and returned to the car. I had been spending too much time in restaurants lately, drinking too much coffee, brooding too much, and listening to too many trite conversations among strangers. Better to kill the half hour I had left by driving around instead. I took the bridge over to Marysville, toured around there, went up Highway 70 a ways and then turned around and came back. My watch said 2:10 when I recrossed the bridge into Yuba City, and 2:15 when I pulled up in front of the Catchall Shop.

Rix was right where I'd left him—fat toad king on his throne. But there was nobody else in the office, nobody else in the kingdom except for a long-haired kid struggling to load a cast-iron sink onto a dolly: slave or serf, and nobody I was interested in.

"Where's Tucker?"

"Nobody here named Tucker," Rix said through one of his smiles.

"I can see that. What's the idea?"

"Tell you what you might do. You might drive over to Highway 99 and on down there, south, about eight miles. A road'll come up on your left, next to a closed-up fruit stand—Herman's, it's called. Road runs through some orchards toward the river. After a mile or so it hooks to the left, and right there where it hooks you'll see another road, dirt one, that runs straight ahead to the river bank. Plenty of parking space back where the dirt one ends."

"Tucker'll meet me there, is that it?"

The smile, and a delicate shrug to go with it.

I said, "Why not here or at his place?"

"Real private out there by the river. Fishermen and kids and farm workers in the summer, gets pretty crowded. Nobody goes there this time of year."

So Tucker was being cautious. Cautious enough to bring somebody with him as a backup, just in case? Somebody like Lawrence Jacobs? Be just fine if it worked out that way. If it didn't, if he brought somebody else or came alone, that was okay too. I was taking my own company along, my own little backup in case of trouble: the .22 Sentinel.

"All right," I said. "If that's the way it has to be."

The smile, the shrug.

"You'll be hearing from me, Rix."

"Real soon, I hope," he said.
"Yeah," I said. "Real soon."

MIDAFTERNOON

The side road and Herman's Fruit Stand were easy
enough to find. I turned onto the narrow blacktop, past
the boarded-up shanty, and drove in among the orchards
—peach trees on my left, walnut trees on my right, both
kinds just starting to show their spring buds. There had
been plenty of winter rain up here; the ground under the
trees was soggy in places. I passed one group of farm
buildings tucked back among the peach trees, saw no one
there or in the orchards or on the road.

The Toyota's odometer had clicked off nine-tenths of a
mile when the hard left bend appeared ahead, just beyond
where the orchards ended on both sides. The unpaved
track that extended off the paved one was narrow, rutted,
and muddy; it ran in a series of little dips across a brushy
expanse of sand and broken rock and then vanished
among scattered scrub oak. Beyond and through those
trees I had glimpses of the Feather River: brownish spar-
kles where the afternoon sun struck the water.

I eased off onto the track. Its condition wasn't as bad as
it had looked from a distance; I had no problem getting
across the open ground and in among the scrub oak. The
track dipped sharply and at an angle then, into another
cleared area of sand and gravel some ten feet above the
level of the river. You could tell that it was used for a
lover's lane as well as a parking lot; there were used con-
doms and a pair of girl's underpants among the beer cans
and other litter. You could also tell that in the summer,

when the Feather shrank in size, it would be half again as large as it was now. At the moment it was deserted. And I saw no sign of a person or a car anywhere else in the vicinity.

I turned the Toyota around to face the track, braked in the shadow of a scrub oak, and shut off the engine. From this spot you couldn't see either the country road or the orchards. I looked at my watch: five past three. When the hands showed ten past I yielded to impulse and got out of the car; I was edgy and sitting there was causing crimps in my neck and shoulders.

A brisk wind blew here, almost cold and strong enough to make sighing, rattling sounds among the oak branches. Clouds had begun to pile up in the west; some of them moved across the face of the sun, so that the daylight was successively bright and a dull metallic gray. I walked over to where the ground sloped muddily to the water. The river was maybe seventy-five yards wide at this point, a hundred yards wide where it bellied inland farther south. Willows grew down that way, past a fan of driftwood that spread upward against a hump in the bank. Somebody— kids, probably—had fashioned a water swing out of two pieces of rope and a truck tire and hung it from one of the willow branches: swimming hole in the summer. Now the water was heavy with silt, swollen and swift-moving from the winter rains. More driftwood and other flotsam bobbed along on the surface, running down toward where the Feather joined the wider and deeper Sacramento River.

For a time I stood alternately watching the water and the place where the track bled into the parking ground. Stillness, except for the movement of the river and the tree branches. Silence, except for the soughing of the wind. It wasn't long before the cold prodded me away, back to the car—the cold and the mounting tension.

3:20.

Come on, Tucker, I thought.

I got back into the Toyota, sat with my hand kneading the butt of the .22 in my jacket pocket. The track stayed empty, this side of the river stayed deserted. On the other side, half a dozen crows came from somewhere and began wheeling above another walnut orchard over there, creating a shrill racket that penetrated the closed car and scratched at my nerves.

3:25.

3:30.

Maybe he's not coming, I thought—and that was when he finally showed up.

I saw his car before I heard it, because of the wind and the crows. Newish Chrysler, its brown and chrome surfaces dulled by a layering of dirt and mud. The windshield glass was streaked, too, but I could see through well enough to tell that the driver was the only apparent occupant. Somebody hunkered down in back? Not likely. Unless he was the paranoid type, Tucker wouldn't have any cause for that much caution.

He parked twenty yards from the Toyota and a little to one side. But he didn't get out right away: waiting foᵢ me to show myself first. I obliged him, straightening up behind the open door. When he followed suit I stepped around and shut the door and walked toward him, slowly. He edged forward to meet me. There was a kind of ritualism to it all, like a couple of street dogs working each other in an alley.

We stopped with a few feet separating us, about halfway between the two cars. He was four or five inches above six feet and big all over. "Arms like cement blocks," Barnwell had said. Yeah. Popeye forearms, and biceps that bulged and rippled and stretched taut the sleeves of his blue T-shirt. The T-shirt and a pair of Levi's and heavy workman's boots were all he wore: Mr. Macho, Mr. Bad Ass. Maybe so, but his head under its covering of black slicked-back hair was undersized and his eyes, like chips of brown glass, betrayed its relative emptiness. Thinking would never be a hobby with him. Whenever he did have a thought, if he ever had one, it would soon curl up and die a solitary death, like a babe lost in a wasteland.

I said, "Frank Tucker?"

"Yeah. You Canino?"

"That's right."

"I hear you got a job for me."

"Right. An easy one."

"Kind I like best. What you want me to do?"

"Answer a question."

"Huh?"

"Tell me where I can find Lawrence Jacobs."

"Huh?"

I took the .22 out and pointed it at his sternum. "Pal of yours, the one who calls himself Lawrence Jacobs. Where can I find him?"

He stared at the gun for five seconds, not moving. It took him that long to shift gears, to come to terms with the sudden twist in the situation. Then he got mad. His muscles rippled, his hands closed into fists, his eyes got mean and his mouth got ugly, and he said, predictably, "What the fuck's the idea?"

"Lawrence Jacobs. He's the idea."

"You're talkin shit."

"Lawrence Jacobs," I said again. "He lived with you on

K Street in Sacramento last November. Slender, brown
hair, in his thirties. Called himself Lawrence Jacobs."

"Brit? What you want with him?"

Brit. Another name I didn't recognize. "Is that his first
or his last name?"

"Huh?"

"Tell me his full name."

"Blow it out your ass, cowboy."

"Wrong answer. His full name and where I can find
him—those are the right answers."

"Blow it out your ass."

"Tell me what I want to know or I'll put a bullet in
your knee. You've busted some kneecaps in your time,
right? You know how much it hurts."

"You're crazy," he said.

"Sure I am. Now make up your mind. Talk to me or
spend the rest of your life on crutches."

But I wasn't scaring him; he was either too tough or too
much of a Cro-Magnon to be scared. The only emotion in
him was rage. His face was blood-dark and pinched up
with it, the eyes hot and bright. "You ain't gonna shoot
me," he said. "Not with that little popgun."

I thumbed the .22's hammer back. "Try me."

And he did, by God. The stupid son of a bitch said, "I'll
make you eat that fuckin gun," and charged me.

I would have shot him, I had every intention of putting
a bullet in his leg, if not his kneecap, but I made the
mistake of first taking a step backward and to one side to
give myself more room. When I did that my foot slipped
on the loose mix of sand and broken rock; my arm
bumped out to the side and when I yanked it back and
squeezed off at him, the round didn't even come close. I
had no time for a second shot. He was on me by then,

bellowing something, swatting at my right arm, launching a blow with his other fist. That one scraped the side of my head but his other hand hammered into my wrist, broke my grip on the .22 and sent it skittering free. I reeled away from him, still trying to regain my balance. But he was fast on his feet and he caught up with me, swung again and hit me high on the left shoulder when I pulled my head back. The blow knocked me sprawling on hands and knees.

When I came up shaking my head he was right there, trying to stomp me with his goddamn boots. I lunged into him while he had one foot off the ground, staggered him away from me far enough so that I could get back on my feet. Through a haze of sweat I saw him grinning as he came back toward me, not in a rush but in slow gliding movements. He was in no hurry now. This was his kind of fight, this was what he was good at and what he liked to do. "I'm gonna tear your fuckin head off, old man," he said and he meant it. He would kill me if I let him get enough of an advantage.

I took a quick look around for the gun; didn't see it and forgot about it. Tucker was still advancing on me, almost within arm's reach now. I backed off a couple of steps, to gain more room to maneuver, and that made him laugh; he thought I was afraid of him, starting to back down. So I retreated another step and put up a hand, as if to ward him off. He laughed again and then charged me as he had before.

It was just what I wanted him to do. Instead of backing off again I moved in on him, crouching, ducking under the first of his swings, and threw my shoulder into his upper body. Good solid contact, part of it on his chest and part of it on his jawline. He staggered backward four or five steps, to the edge of the sloping river bank. Before he could check his momentum his feet went out from under him and he fell belly-flat, went sliding feet first down the short muddy incline—almost into the river before he could drag himself to a stop.

He came up onto his knees, spitting mud and obscenities. But by then I was on my way to the fan of driftwood along the bank farther down. Tucker scrambled up through the mud, still bellowing; reached firm ground just as my hand closed around a three-foot chunk of tree branch with its bark peeling off. I yanked the wood free of the tangle, came around with it.

Tucker shook himself like a bear, spraying drops of water and flecks of mud, and rushed me again.

I stepped toward him, drawing the branch back over my right shoulder, sliding my hands up on the bottom end like a baseball player choking up on his bat. He thought I was going to swing it like a bat too, and threw his left arm up to protect his head, groping toward me with his right. That opened him up wide from chin to sternum. Instead of swinging the wood I met his charge with a lunge of my own and jabbed the short end hard against his collarbone, felt it glance upward and take him in the throat. I meant the blow to stop him and it did—did some damage to his windpipe and started him gagging—but it didn't hurt him enough to end it. One of his flailing hands clawed at the shoulder of my jacket, found purchase and hung on and swung me around off balance. If he'd let go, momentum would have sent me spinning off my feet, probably caused me to lose the branch when I went down. But he didn't let go. He hauled me in against him, still gagging, trying to hurt me the way I had hurt him. He swiped at my head with his free hand and hit me a solid lick over the left eye,

cut me with a ring he had on one finger. The blow rocked
me backward, but because he still had hold of my coat it
didn't put me down or off stride. And that worked in my
favor: It gave me just enough space and just enough lever-
age to use the branch on him again.

My first jab went in under his breastbone, stiffened him
and knocked out what air he had left in his lungs. The
second jab made him release my coat, staggered him. I got
the club up over my head then and whacked it straight
down the side of his head, almost tearing off an ear, and
hard against the joining of his neck and shoulder. He
grunted like a pig in a wallow. His knees buckled and he
went down on them, hands scrabbling at the air, drool
and blood coming out of one corner of his mouth. I pulled
the wood back and this time I did swing it like a baseball
bat: home run swing, all the power I had left in my arms
and upper body. Too much power: The impact of the
branch with the side of his head created a pulpy cracking
sound and the wood splintered in my hands. Tucker went
over on his back and skidded down the muddy bank again
—headfirst, like an upended tortoise down a greased slide.

When he splashed into the brown water his head and
shoulders went under and stayed there. No way it could
be a ploy to draw me down to him so he could get his
hands on me again; I had hit him too hard for that. I half
slid down to where he lay, took hold of his belt, and
dragged him out before he drowned or the current sucked
him free of the bank and carried him off.

His mouth was open and there was silt-heavy water
inside it, water in his throat that was choking him. I
flipped him over onto his stomach, sank to the mud beside
him, and did some CPR work until the last of the water
dribbled out of his mouth. By then his breath was coming

in a faint rasping gurgle. I put my fingers against the artery in his neck, felt his pulsebeat. Irregular but strong enough. I rolled him onto his side, pried one of his eyelids back. The eye had rolled up in its socket and the white had a glazed cast. Concussion. And maybe I had scrambled what few brain cells he had, too. The side of his head where I'd clouted him was pulpy and bright with blood, most of it from what was left of his ear.

Looking down at the ruin of him, I felt nothing except frustration. He was out and out good; it would be a long while before he was able to talk. If he could talk at all after what I'd done to his windpipe. Would I have felt anything else—remorse, regret—if I'd killed him? Probably not. Funny, but I had gone through the whole fight, start to finish, without fear or anger or emotion of any sort. And so far, none of the usual physical aftereffects of this kind of hand-to-hand combat had set in.

Wetness on my face, dripping down into my left eye: blood from the cut Tucker had opened on my forehead. I wiped it away, got up on my feet and climbed the bank, humped over and using my hands monkey-fashion to maintain my footing. At the top I paused for a few seconds to look around, to listen. Emptiness and silence. The crows were apparently the only ones who had heard the shot and the sounds of the fight, and they were long gone.

It took me the better part of five minutes to locate the .22. When Tucker banged it out of my hand it had skidded over against one of the scrub oaks and was partially hidden by the lower branches. I checked the inside of the barrel, the cylinder, the action; it hadn't been mudblocked or damaged. I started to put it into my jacket pocket, but the jacket was torn and caked with mud. So I took it to the Toyota, set it on the seat inside. Any man

who walks around with a loaded revolver tucked into the
waistband of his pants, the way you see them do it on TV,
is a damned fool.

There was nothing in the Toyota that I could use to tie
Tucker up. The keys were still in the Chrysler's ignition; I
took them out, found one that would open the trunk.
Plenty of stuff in there, most of it tools of the professional
slugger's trade: a couple of lengths of galvanized pipe, an
axe handle, some heavy chain, a coil of strong hemp rope.
I took the rope down to the river's edge, looped it around
Tucker's hands, tied his feet, tied the four appendages together. Then I slithered him up the bank and left him
lying on his belly at the top, making little liquidy purling
sounds in his throat.

Among the other items in the Chrysler's trunk was a
bunch of rags. I used a couple of them to clean mud off
my hands. The hound's-tooth jacket was a ruin; so were
the rest of my new clothes and my new pair of shoes. But
I hadn't thrown away the outfit I'd taken from the Carder
A-frame; it was bundled up in the Toyota's trunk. I got it
out, changed, threw the muddy stuff inside. Then I went
to Tucker again, pried his wallet out of his Levi's. A hundred and nine dollars in cash, a driver's license—that was
all. Nothing to tell me where he was living in this area.
The address on the license was an unfamiliar street in
West Sacramento. Old address, the one he'd had in 1987
when the license was issued.

Back to the Chrysler. The glove compartment was full
of junk; I rummaged around in it until I came up with a
folded piece of pink paper. It was what I was looking for
—a receipt from a Yuba City realty outfit, dated twelve
days ago and made out to Frank M. Tucker for payment
of three months of a one-year lease on property located at

1411 Freestone Street, Yuba City. The total of the payment was $2250. Nice piece of change for somebody in Tucker's line of work, somebody who had been living in a low-income apartment building in Vacaville two weeks ago, to be shelling out in a lump sum. The year's lease was interesting, too, considering Tucker's penchant for moving around from place to place. Mixed up in something with Elmer Rix, I thought—something a lot more lucrative, and a hell of a lot more illegal, than buying and selling junk.

Nothing else in the glove box told me anything. Nor did any of the car's other contents. On the dash was a Genie garage door opener; I looked at it for a couple of seconds and then put it into my pants pocket. In a pouch on the driver's door I found a Yuba City–Marysville street map, put that into my pocket as well.

The trunk yielded one more item I could use—a car blanket, new and from the looks of it, never opened. I brought it over to the Toyota, set it on the roof, opened the rear door, then went and got Tucker. He was too big, too much dead weight to carry; I took a wrestler's grip on him, under the arms from behind his head, and dragged him to the car and muscled him in across the seat. I checked to make sure he was still breathing—he was—and then shook the blanket out and covered him with it.

Reaction was beginning to set in now, though not nearly as much as in the past. A little weakness in my legs, some shortness of breath, sweat running on my face. Or maybe the wetness was more blood; I pawed at it, looked at the fingers. A little of both.

I got in under the wheel. Thought about taking a look at myself in the rear-view mirror and didn't do it. The hell with what I looked like. No, that wasn't smart. What if a cop saw me driving with a bloody face and stopped me to ask questions? I stepped out again, found one of the rags I'd used earlier, took it back into the Toyota and held it against my forehead until the bleeding began to diminish. Then I persuaded myself to look in the mirror. Inch-long gash above the eyebrow, not too deep and not too noticeable as long as I kept blotting it with the rag. Spots of mud here and there that I'd missed, a blob of it matting the beard on my left cheek; I rubbed those away. My eyes . . . I refused to look at my eyes. Instead I took out the area street map and concentrated on locating Freestone Street.

It was in the southern part of town, not all that far from the Catchall Shop. Easy enough to get to from here. I put the map on the seat, leaned up and around and lifted a corner of the blanket for another look at Tucker. Still out, still making those purling sounds in his throat. The whole left side of his face was wet with leaking blood and his torn ear had swelled up to twice its normal size. I said aloud, "I wish you were Brit, tough guy," and let the blanket fall again.

Then I started the engine and went to find out what awaited me at 1411 Freestone Street.

LATE AFTERNOON

It was a brown wood and stucco house in a quiet, older residential neighborhood. Attached garage, wide front porch, budding tulip tree in the front yard and an acacia tree at the rear. Not fancy; substantial, respectable. The kind of place somebody like Tucker would never choose

for himself, but just the sort somebody like Elmer Rix
would choose for him.

I drove by once, slowly, made a U-turn at the corner,
and came back for another look. No car in the driveway
or on the street in front, no sign of activity inside or out.
But that did not necessarily mean the house was unoccu-
pied. Tucker had lived alone in Sacramento except for
Brit's brief stay, and alone in Vacaville, but this place was
a couple of rungs up the ladder from either of those. If he
liked company, and now that he was in the money, he
might have moved a friend or two in with him.

I circled the block. When I came back along Freestone
Street to 1411 I had the .22 on the seat beside me and the
garage door opener in my left hand. Without hesitating,
just like somebody who belonged there, I turned into
1411's drive and pushed the Genie at the same time. The
garage door went up—the interior was empty—and I
pulled inside, braked, hit the Genie again as soon as the
up cycle ended, and was out of the Toyota and leaning
over the hood, the .22 aimed at the inside door to the
house, before the garage door was halfway down.

Nobody appeared at the inner door. The garage door
clicked shut and the Genie switched off; I stood listening
to the tick of the Toyota's engine, the faint fluttery rattle
of a furnace . . . nothing else. But I stayed where I was
for another three minutes, waiting in the thick shadows.
No sounds from the house. Nobody home—maybe.

I moved around the car, went to the inside door,
pushed it open. Empty alcove leading to an empty
kitchen. I eased through the rest of the house, using the
gun as a pointer: living room, dining room, two bedrooms,
one and a half baths, rear porch.

Nobody home.

After I checked the porch I relaxed a little, letting the revolver hang down at my side. All right so far. The place had a vaguely musty odor, an unlived in look, and clutches of old, mismatched, bargain-basement furniture. Furnished house that had sat unrented for a while before Tucker signed his lease; and since he'd taken possession, he hadn't spent much time on the premises. For one thing, there were no dirty dishes anywhere in the kitchen and Tucker was the kind who would always leave dirty dishes lying around. The only room that showed signs of much habitation was the smaller of the bedrooms, and it was a mess of blankets, sheets, and soiled underwear.

It was the other, larger bedroom that I searched first. That one had a desk in it, as well as a TV and VCR combo and an eight-millimeter film projector and portable screen to boot. There wasn't much in the desk, and only one item of any interest: a spiral-bound notebook containing a dozen names and addresses. But it wasn't an address book. In addition to the names, street numbers, and towns —all in this general area—there were dates at the top of each page, along with dollar amounts ranging from $500 to $10,000. And at the bottom of each page were more dates and smaller dollar amounts. You didn't have to be a cryptographer to figure out what all of this meant, or why Tucker had it in this nice respectable house he'd rented.

Tally book for a loan-sharking operation. Not Tucker's; he wasn't bright enough to have set up that kind of business. The toad king's—Elmer Rix's. How right I'd been when I thought of Rix as having a moneylender's smile. Tucker had been brought in to do the collecting, and the enforcing if anybody got behind in his payment.

But loan-sharking wasn't the only scam Rix and Tucker were working. They had at least one other, and it was far nastier than lending money at back-breaking interest rates. When I opened the closet door in there I found a cache of videocassettes, cans of eight-millimeter film, color photographs and color slides—all of it the worst kind of pornography, manufactured by and distributed to degenerates. Kiddie porn. Grown men engaged in atrocities with young children, some no older than two or three, most of them boys. High-priced filth for the exotic-minded voyeur and the discerning pedophile. No wonder there were TV and VCR, movie projector and screen in here. If Tucker didn't watch this sort of garbage for kicks, he damned well used the machines to entertain potential buyers.

Rix and Tucker, entrepreneurs. Rix and Tucker, slimebags.

I slammed the closet door, went out of there with a sour taste in my mouth. Nothing in the other bedroom but Tucker's mess. Nothing in the living room. But in the kitchen, in a drawer under a wall phone, I found a cheap Leatherette address book. Most of the entries were written in pencil in a childish hand. And under the letter B—

> Brit
> 62 Cordilleras
> Elk Grove
> 916–555–4438

I stood looking at the entry for several seconds. Brit, Brit. First name or last? I still had no idea. But one thing I did know now: If the address in this book was current, he wasn't far away. Elk Grove was off Highway 99 south of Sacramento, a town I'd passed on my way to Carmichael from Stockton two days ago. Sixty miles or so from here —not far at all.

There was no need to copy down the address and telephone number; they were burned into my memory. I paged through the rest of the book, but the only names I recognized were Elmer Rix and "Maggie, Sacramento," probably Maggie Barnwell. No entry for a Lawrence Jacobs or any other Jacobs.

I returned the book to the drawer, finished searching the house in case there was anything else for me here. There wasn't. I went back into the garage, opened up the Toyota, and hauled Tucker out from under the blanket and across the garage floor and the kitchen floor to the living room floor, where I deposited him in the middle of an imitation oriental rug. He was still breathing painfully; I wouldn't have cared much if he had stopped breathing altogether. I'd done a good job with the ropes: They were knotted so tightly that I couldn't work them lose with my fingers. In the kitchen I found a butcher knife and used that to cut the ropes off his hands and feet. Then I gathered up the pieces, took them to the Toyota, and pitched them onto the floor in back.

In the kitchen again I lifted the wall phone off its hook, dialed 911 and asked for the police, got through to a sergeant named Eales. "Two things," I said to him. "I'm only going to say them once, so listen carefully. First, an ex-con named Frank Tucker, fourteen-eleven Freestone Street, Yuba City—somebody beat him up and he's in a pretty bad way. You'd better send an ambulance. Second, Tucker and a man named Elmer Rix, R-i-x, owner of the Catchall Shop on Percy Avenue, are involved in at least two illegal activities: loan-sharking and distributing child pornography. Some of the porn is in a back bedroom, in the desk, there's a notebook full of information on the loan-sharking operation. Have you got all that?"

"I've got it. Who is this, please?"

I said, "Fourteen-eleven Freestone Street, Yuba City, don't waste any time," and hung up.

I went out to the car, leaned in for the Genie and pushed its button to raise the garage door, then tossed the thing onto a nearby workbench. Might as well leave the door up, make the cops' job easier when they got here. I had the car started by the time the opener finished its up cycle; I backed out and drove off along the street without seeing anybody except a couple of housewives who weren't paying any attention to me. Drove out of the neighborhood without seeing any police cars. If they used sirens getting to Tucker's house I never heard them. But then, I might not have heard sirens if they had been a block away. I was too intent on my driving, on getting out of Yuba City, on covering the distance between here and Elk Grove.

Here I come, Brit.

Here I come.

NIGHT

Sixty-two Cordilleras Street, Elk Grove.

I had trouble finding it, not because Elk Grove is a big place—it isn't—but because neither of the two Elk Grove Boulevard service stations I stopped at had a local street map and none of the people I talked to knew where the hell Cordilleras Street was. My third stop was a 7-Eleven store; the woman clerk said she *thought* Cordilleras was on the south side, by the cattle auction yard, but she just wasn't sure. She did tell me how to get to that part of town, and once I got there I found somebody—a liquor store clerk—who could pinpoint it for me. It was 7:35, almost two and a half hours after I'd left Tucker's house, when I made the turn onto the street where Brit lived.

It wasn't much of a street. If he was mixed up with Rix and Tucker in their loan-sharking and child-porn scams, or into some other kind of crooked deal, he wasn't making much money out of it. Two blocks long, Cordilleras, dead-ending in a fence beyond which was the cattle auction yard and some kind of rental facility for heavy equipment. Run-down, low-income houses and trailers on both sides, a couple with the rusting corpses of automobiles in their weedy front yards, one with a boxy-looking homemade boat up on davits. Number 62 was a squat wood-shingled cottage with an uneven roof line and the remains of some long dead flowering vine climbing a trellis to one side of the front door. On the other side was a plate glass window, undraped, so I could look into the lighted front room as I drove past. Nobody occupying it just now. But somebody was home: The light and a car obscured in shadow at the rear of a gravel drive made that plain enough.

I went on to the corner, U-turned, came back for another look. Still nobody in the front room. Across the street and a little way down was a vacant lot choked with weeds and high grass and a scattering of refuse; an ancient black oak grew at the near end, its gnarled branches overhanging a cracked sidewalk and root-buckled curb. I made another U-turn at that end of the block, came back and parked under the low-hanging oak branches. It was the best kind of place for a stakeout: dark, protected. And the angle was such that I could still see into most of Number 62's lamp-lit front room.

I shut off the lights and the engine, rolled down my window to let some air into the car. It was warmer here than it had been in Yuba City, the sky clear and bright with stars and a three-quarter moon, but the night breeze was still cool. And I was tired, keyed up, stiff from driving and from the fight with Tucker.

I sat low on the seat, staring across at the cottage. What if he wasn't alone? What if he had a visitor, or he was living with somebody? This thing was between him and me, just the two of us—beginning to end, just the two of us. No way I was going to hurt an innocent bystander. If I did that I would be no better than he was, no better than Tucker and Rix and all the other predators that walk the earth in human skin. Stupid to involve another person anyway—let somebody here get a look at me, maybe identify me to the police later on.

So before I could even think about bracing him over there, I had to make sure he was alone. Another few minutes, another few hours, even another day or two . . . what did it matter? Locating him had been the big job, and now that that was done, he wasn't going to get away.

Five minutes passed. Ten.

And somebody walked into the lighted room—walked in and sat down in a chair and picked up a magazine. A woman. Thin, angular blond wearing a quilted housecoat and of an age that I couldn't determine at this distance.

My hands were damp; I scrubbed them dry on the legs of Tom Carder's Levi's. Relative of Brit's? Girlfriend? Barnwell had claimed the man was a homosexual, but Barnwell was a dimwit and dimwits make lousy witnesses. Was Brit in there with her, in one of the other rooms?

Could be. But it could be, too, that he was out for the evening, or away from Elk Grove altogether, or even in another damn state. If he *was* on some kind of trip I could sit here waiting for days . . .

On impulse I started the engine, swung the car around, drove back to the same liquor store I'd stopped at a while ago to ask directions. There was a phone box out front; I put a quarter in the slot and punched out the number that had been in Tucker's address book.

A woman's low-pitched voice said, "Hello?"

"Is Brit there?"

"No, not right now."

"You expect him back tonight?"

"I guess. He comes and goes."

"What time do you think he'll be home?"

"I don't have any idea."

"Who is this?"

"Midge."

"Midge who?"

". . . Do I know *you?*"

"I'm a friend of Brit's."

"Uh-huh. You want to leave a message?"

"No," I said, "no message."

I cradled the receiver. Midge. Girlfriend, probably. The important thing was that he wasn't out of town or out of state, that he was due back home tonight. But how was I going to get him alone? Lure him out by phone? Foolish move; if I didn't handle it just right it might put him on his guard. Chances were, he hadn't been back to the Deer Run cabin yet. In which case he believed I was still chained up inside, and as long as he believed that he had no reason to be looking over his shoulder, to stay cooped up at home with Midge. Sooner or later he would go out again—sometime tomorrow, probably. Sooner or later there would be a time and a place where he was alone and I could take him the way he'd taken me that long ago night in San Francisco.

I debated finding a room for the night, coming back and staking out the cottage early in the morning. No point in returning to Cordilleras Street now, was there? No . . . except that I wasn't ready yet to close myself up in some box of a motel room, do my waiting in absentia. I ached for a look at him, at his face without the ski mask to hide it. Maybe I could accomplish that much tonight, at least.

Back to Cordilleras, back into the tree shadows next to the vacant lot. The cottage's front window was still undraped, and the blond woman was still sitting there reading her magazine. Brit hadn't come home in the brief interval between my phone call and now: The driveway still had just one car parked on it and the curb in front was deserted.

I waited. I have always hated stakeouts—the monotony, the dribbling passage of time, the tension—and this one was twice as bad as any other in thirty years. I was so tired my eyes ached and watered and I had to keep knuckling them to clear my vision. So wired already that my neck and shoulders felt as though they were being compressed in a vise. Hunger pangs under my breastbone, too . . . I should have bought something to eat at the liquor store. Still not thinking things out as carefully as I used to, still not planning ahead. But Jesus, I was so close to the end of it now, so *close*. It was like an obstruction in my mind that I had to keep squeezing past to get at anything else.

8:30. Headlights behind me, turning into Cordilleras. I eased farther down on the seat, watched the lights approach in the side mirror. But the car went on past Number 62, ahead into the next block, and turned into a driveway midway along.

8:45. The woman, Midge, got up and left the front room. It was ten minutes before she came back, carrying a plate of something and a glass, and sat down again.

8:55. A man came out of a mobile home adjacent to the cottage and directly opposite where I was sitting, took something from his car and then went back inside without looking my way. If he knew I was there he didn't want to know it. That was one good thing about staking out an area like this, as opposed to a middle-class residential district: no neighborhood watch program, no overwrought fear of strangers who might have designs on the family silver, no self-righteous busybodies eager to pick up the phone and call the police at the slightest provocation. People here minded their own business. They had no family silver to protect, shunned the law except in cases of emergency, and avoided hassles whenever they could because their daily lives, scratching out existences on streets like this one, were hassle enough, thank you.

9:20. Another pair of headlights turning in behind me —and another destination on the second block.

9:30. Midge got up and switched on a black and white TV. Sat down again, only to stand a minute later and walk to the window and draw thin patterned drapes: There had probably been some kind of glare from outside that affected her view of the television. I said aloud, "Shit!" Now maybe I wouldn't get a look at Brit tonight after all.

9:50. Cramp in my right leg. I had to go through contortions to pull the leg up, maneuver it past the gearshift and straighten it out across the passenger seat.

10:05. Why didn't he come? Out enjoying himself,

probably; taking in a movie, playing cards, having sex
. . . damn him! Damn his rotten soul to hell!

10:15. God, how I wanted this to be over with. Not just
this waiting tonight—*all* of it. So I could stop hating, so I
could go home, so I could see Kerry. So I could lick my
wounds and start the healing process. So I could begin to
live again.

10:30. Another cramp in my leg. I couldn't keep on
sitting here much longer. . . .

I didn't have to. Two minutes after I massaged the knot
out of my leg, a third set of headlamps appeared behind
me—and this time the car turned into Number 62's driveway.

I sat up, gripping the bottom of the steering wheel with
both hands. The car over there—I couldn't tell the make,
just that it was an older model—went dark and a slender
man shape got out. The dome light was too dim and the
night too dark for me to see him clearly. I watched him
walk through the weedy front yard to the door, let himself
in with a key. There was light inside, and when he stepped
through the open doorway I had a quick glimpse of lank
brown hair, pale face in profile, dark blue Windbreaker.
Then the door closed off the light and he was gone.

Frustration was sharp in me for a few seconds, but then
the edge of it rubbed off against the grindstone of fatigue.
So close to him now, just a hundred yards or so separating
us. And yet there was nothing I could do about it tonight.
Tomorrow, but not tonight. Get out of here, go get some
sleep, I thought, come back in the morning . . . but I
could not seem to make my body respond. I didn't trust
myself to drive yet anyway. My hands twitched when I
took them away from the wheel, as if I had contracted
some sort of neurological disease: too much stress, too

much time cramped up in this small space. I gripped the wheel again, harder this time. Sat like that, waiting until I felt able to handle the car without risk to myself or someone else.

More minutes crawled away—not many, ten at the most. When I let go of the wheel this time my hands were still. I had been taking deep slow breaths; I took several more, ran my tongue over dry lips, tested my reactions by pushing in the clutch, tapping the brake, working the gearshift. Okay now. I reached for the ignition key—

And the cottage's front door opened and he came back out.

I froze with my fingers on the key. In the two or three seconds he was in the light I saw that he had changed clothes, or at least put on a different coat—something heavy and plaid—and some kind of cap on his head. Then he was a shadow shape walking across the yard, opening the car door, ducking inside. The starter ground, a whiny sound in the night's stillness; the headlights came on. He backed the car out of the driveway and turned my way.

I drifted low on the seat, straightened immediately after he rolled past and reached again for the ignition key. He turned left at the corner behind me. I had the engine going by then, and I made a sharp U-turn and hit the headlight switch before I reached the corner. When I completed the turn after him he was only a block and a half away.

Adrenaline had taken away some of the dragging tiredness, made me alert again. I thought: Going after a pack of cigarettes or liquor, maybe. That was fine, as long as he went somewhere that wasn't too crowded. I could wait in his car while he made his purchase; or if he locked it I could hang around in the shadows nearby until he came back.

But he *wasn't* out on a late-night shopping errand. He led me to Elk Grove Boulevard, along it through the middle of town, and out past the chain of shopping centers and service stations and fast-food joints on the western outskirts. I knew by then that his car was an old green Mercury with a piece chipped off one of the taillights: easy enough to keep in sight.

Highway 99 came up ahead. He led me across the overpass, then onto the southbound entrance ramp. He drove in the fast lane; I stayed in the slow lane at a distance of a couple of hundred yards. But wherever he was going, he wasn't in any particular hurry. His speed hovered between sixty and sixty-five.

We traveled down the freeway about ten miles. Then an exit sign loomed ahead—Highway 104, Jackson—and when he put on his directional signal and started off onto the ramp, I realized suddenly where he was going. Knew it in that instant the way you know or intuit certain things, with a sense of utter inevitability. Knew it with a feeling too dark, too full of bitter irony to be elation but close to elation just the same because it was fitting, it was a kind of cosmic justice. I could not have picked a better night to catch up with him or asked for a better place to have it all end.

Highway 104 leads to the central Mother Lode, connecting with Highway 49 just north of Jackson. And there could only be one possible reason for him to drive up to the Sierras alone at this time of night.

He was going to the cabin at Deer Run.

THE LAST DAY

Traffic was sparse on 104—nothing much along most of it except flattish farmland and the Rancho Seco nuclear power plant—so I let the distance between Brit and me widen until the Mercury was out of sight ahead. No percentage in my hanging close to him now; headlights in his rear-view mirror might alert him to the possibility that he was being followed. And I wanted him to get to the cabin well ahead of me, to have time to skulk around outside, let himself in through one of the bedroom windows, find out I had escaped, and think about the implications of that before I walked in on him. Fifteen minutes' head start, at least. That way I would ensure that the last act of our little two-man drama took place inside the cabin.

I drove at a steady fifty, and by the time I covered the twenty-five miles to the Highway 49 junction, he must have picked up ten of those fifteen minutes. Traffic on 49 was just as sparse but I held my speed down along there too. Jackson, Mokelumne Hill, San Andreas—little gold country towns that teemed with tourists in the summer, that were deserted clusters of old wood and brick and false-front buildings at this hour of a March night. No, *morning:* It was twenty past midnight when I made the turn off 49, just outside San Andreas, onto the twisty two-lane county road that climbed to Deer Run.

The sky was clean and moonlit up here, too, the air cold but without the sharp wintry bite of last week. There had not been any snowfall since I'd left; in fact the

weather must have stayed warm and dry. Once I got up
past the snowline, the road was not only clear but in
places the windrows along it had melted completely.
There were dark patches and furrows in the open mead-
ows where the snowpack had thawed and water had begun to run off.

It was fifteen miles to Deer Run this way. In all that
distance I saw no sign of Brit, encountered no other car
traveling in either direction. Here and there I saw lights
from cabins built on ridges or down in hollows or back
among trees, passed through a little cluster of lights that
marked the tiny hamlet of Mountain Ranch; but mostly I
drove through black and moonstruck white, alone in the
night, not thinking much now because there was no
longer any need to think. Transition, that was all this was.
Dead time—the long empty minutes before the condemned man and his executioner come together.

But there was one thing I should have thought about; I
realized that when I reached Deer Run. The place had an
eerie look at this hour of the morning, everything still and
empty. The only lights anywhere were nightlights inside
Mary Alice's general store. The through road and the
ones that branched off it were all clear, shiny in the moonlight like bands of black silk loosely arranged among the
hill folds. As with the terrain below, what had been
mostly unbroken snowfields just last Sunday now showed
ragged black at the edges, as if with some encroaching
fungus, and spotted black in low places that could be
reached by both the wind and the sun.

It was the roads that made me think of the access lane
to the cabin. Last week it had been choked with snow.
What was it like now? And how would Brit travel it—on
foot or in his car?

I made the turn onto Indian Hill Road, braked, cut the headlights but not the engine. If the access road was still packed with snow, and he wanted to go up by car, he would have to stop and put chains on the rear tires; and if he wanted to go up by foot he would have to use snow-shoes. Even if the snowpack had thawed enough so that the road was passable without either chains or snowshoes, traversing it would be slow work. So no matter how he did it, it would take time—probably more time than I had allowed him so far. If I could help it I did not want him to see me coming before he got to the cabin.

I made myself sit there, fidgeting, for ten minutes. I had intended to take a full fifteen but the stress was getting to me again, bunching muscles, putting the twitch back in my hands. Without even making a conscious choice I put the transmission in gear and flicked on the headlights and went on up Indian Hill Road.

Its surface stayed clear and dry all the way up. There was evidence of thaw on the access lanes to other cabins in the area, including the one to the Carder A-frame. All the visible cabins I passed were dark; the only illumination came from the Toyota's headlamps probing the road ahead, the moon glinting off stretches of open snow.

When I climbed to where the tree-clad hillside walled the road on my right I slowed to twenty and rolled my window down for a better look at the snowfield that was opening up on the left. I saw the Mercury as soon as I came around the last bend below the access lane to the Lanier cabin. He had pulled it into the lane by ten feet or so and it sat there dark. If I had seen any sign of him on the road or anywhere else in the vicinity I would have driven on past and out of sight above—just a local resi-dent coming home late—and then waited another few

minutes before doubling back. But there was no sign of
him.

I eased over behind the Mercury, stopped at an angle
that blocked it off from Indian Hill Road. The thaw had
had its effect here, too: Parts of the lane's surface were
visible and the skin of snow on the rest looked to be no
more than eight to twelve inches deep. I could also see
that he'd gone along it on foot, without snowshoes; in the
moonshine his tracks in what was left of the snowpack
were clearly outlined.

I shut off engine and headlamps, got out of the car. The
wind made a thin, preternatural murmur as it blew across
the meadow, but it carried no other sounds with it. I buttoned the bush jacket to my throat, slid my hands into the
pockets and gripped the butt of the .22, and tramped
ahead along the lane.

The footing was slick in places and I had to move at a
retarded pace. But that was all right because he would
have had to do the same thing. Twice on the climb to the
top of the first hill I blundered into pockets of deeper
snow, but I got out of them again without doing any damage to myself. The cold wind slapped at my ears and
cheeks, numbed them a little; but it also braced me, kept
me alert and in control for what lay ahead.

Near the crest I slogged over to one of the spruce trees
and went up the rest of the way in its shadow, to keep
from skylining myself in the moonlight. But I needn't
have bothered. I could see all the way to the cabin from
there and Brit wasn't in sight. His tracks went right up
near it on the left, then vanished among the trees. He
must be inside by now—but the cabin was still dark.
Good. My timing had been just right. He hadn't found

out yet that I was gone. When he did he was certain to put the floor lamp on to investigate.

I moved downslope, hurrying as much as I could. I was halfway up to the cabin on the other side when the light went on; I could see the glow obliquely through the shutters on the front window, more clearly where it spilled out across the snow from the side window. I started to draw the .22, remembered how cold can numb bare fingers in a short space of time, stick the flesh to metal surfaces, and let it stay where it was.

Snow crunched under my boots as I moved up the last stretch of ground to the cabin, but the wind's murmurings were loud enough to cover those sounds. The ground directly in front of the cabin door had been thawed and wind-scoured enough so that I didn't have to walk on snow at all to get to it. I put my left hand on the latch and stood listening: the wind, little unidentifiable noises from inside, the pounding of blood in my ears. The door should be unlocked; I had left it that way and he wouldn't have had any reason to lock it. I took the gun out, drew and held a breath. And opened the door and went on through in a shooter's crouch, both arms out and both hands on the .22.

"Hello, Brit," I said.

He was over near the shelves that contained the remaining few provisions. He whirled, froze with one hand up in an unintentional mockery of a greeting. But I couldn't see him clearly enough yet to identify him. The lamp was in front and to one side of him so that his face was shadowed under the bill of his cap. Shadows crouched everywhere in the room—along the fireplace, in the open doorways, in the corners, among the trappings of what had been my

prison cell. Like phantoms. Like memory ghosts screaming in voices just beyond the range of hearing.

"You!"

"Keep your hands where I can see them. If you move
you're a dead man." The gun was clenched so tight in my
right hand I could feel its surfaces cutting into finger pads
and palm. Just the slightest additional pressure on the
trigger . . .

But he didn't move; he stood rigid, staring at me. "You
can't have got free. Goddamn you, you can't have!"

"But I did."

"How? How?"

"Turn around, lean against the wall with your feet
spread."

He didn't obey. He just kept staring at me out of the
shadows that hid his face.

"Do what I told you. Now."

Another five seconds of frozen defiance—and then the
rigidity left him all at once and he went slack, seemed
almost to shrink an inch or two. In a duller, more con-
trolled voice he said, "I'm not armed."

"Face the wall. Do it!"

He did it. I used my left hand to shut the door, then
went over to him and kicked his legs back and put the
.22's muzzle against the back of his neck. I took my finger
off the trigger entirely while I patted him down one-
handed; I did not trust myself to leave it there.

He hadn't been lying: He was unarmed. I backed off
from him, around on the other side of the cot. "All right,"
I said then. "Come over here and sit down in the light
where I can see you."

He did that, too, without resistance. And for the first
time I stood looking into the face of the enemy.

I knew him, of course, yet it was several seconds before I recognized him. He was thinner than I remembered, his face gaunt, the pale, ascetic features pinched and stamped with changes—ravages, maybe. His eyes were those of a fanatic: wide, shiny, savage with hate.

The look of him was a surprise, but a bigger one was his identity. For more than a week I had been laboring under a complete misapprehension: He had never had anything to do with Jackie Timmons, and his revenge against me had nothing to do with Jackie Timmons either. Our paths had first crossed less than six years ago. I had never once considered him for that reason, and because the circumstances did not seem to warrant such a maniacal vengeance, and because the number thirteen had nothing to do with those circumstances. And yet there had been clues, a string of little clues over the past three days that should have told me the truth.

His name wasn't Brit; he *was* a Brit. That was why his voice had sounded so odd and stilted to me. He had disguised it, Americanized it, to keep me from realizing that he was British.

His name was Neal Vining.

Expatriate son of a London antiquarian book dealer. Twenty-six years old, married to an American woman and working for a San Francisco bookseller named John Rothman when I exposed him as a thief and a near murderer. He had devised an ingenious plan to steal rare books, maps, and etchings from Rothman's shop, after which he'd sold them to unscrupulous collectors; he was intelligent, well educated, amoral, and totally ruthless. When he'd realized that I was onto him he had tried to use his car to run me—and Kerry, who had been with me at the time—off a steep, curving street into Glen Park

Canyon. It had been luck as much as anything else that had kept him from succeeding and almost cost him his own life instead.

But none of that, none of it, warranted or explained what he had done to me here the past three months.

"Recognize me, eh?" he said. He was making no effort now to conceal his accent and it was discernible enough, if blunted somewhat by his years in this country and in prison. "I can see it in your face."

"I recognize you, Vining."

"I thought you would. It's too soon for you to have forgotten who I am."

"I never forget a man who tries to kill me," I said. "When was it you tried the first time? Five years ago?"

"Almost six."

"The judge gave you ten years' hard time. But how many did you serve? Four, five?"

"Four years, ten months, thirteen days."

"You're young—that's not much time behind bars."

"Isn't it?" He shifted slightly on the cot, so that the lamplight struck his eyes; the hate in them burned like foxfire. There was so much hate in this room that it was almost a third entity, a force comprised of pure negative energy. "How did you get free of the leg iron? I still can't believe you managed it."

"Look at me. That ought to give you an idea."

". . . You're thinner. Much thinner."

"Close to forty pounds."

"I don't . . . Christ, you lost enough weight to slip it off?"

"With the help of some soap and Spam grease."

"When? You were still shackled in mid-January. And there's hardly any food left . . ."

"A week ago."

"You stayed here waiting for me to return? No, you couldn't have . . . you got that pistol somewhere . . ."

"Another cabin nearby," I said. "And no, I didn't wait here for you. I tracked you down. Followed you up here tonight from Elk Grove—Sixty-two Cordilleras Street, Elk Grove."

The hate in his eyes seemed to burn hotter for a few seconds. "How did you find out I've been living with Midge?"

"Frank Tucker."

"Oh, of course. I might have known. I don't suppose you shot Tucker, killed him?"

"No. I hurt him some, though."

"Did you? Good! How did you hurt him?"

"I busted his head with a piece of wood."

He smiled; it seemed almost to cheer him. "Will he die?"

"I doubt it."

"Too bad. A slow lingering death—that's what I wish for him."

"I thought the two of you were friends."

"My God—friends!"

"You stayed with him last October, in his apartment in Sacramento."

"Yes, well, I'd just been released from Folsom and I needed a place. I didn't know Midge then."

"What about your wife?"

"My ex-wife," he said bitterly. "She divorced me after I went to prison. My father disowned me at the same time. Not a bloody word from either of them since."

"Why did you stay with Tucker, if you hate him so much?"

Vining smiled again—a dark, unreadable smile this time. "I had my reasons," he said.

"Such as establishing an address so you could rent this cabin."

"That's one."

"Where did you get the money?"

"Oh, I had a bit put away."

From selling the rare books and other items he'd stolen from John Rothman, probably. I remembered that not all of the money he'd received had been recovered. At his trial he'd claimed to have spent it and refused to budge from that story.

I said, "Is that what you've been living on since you got out? Or are you in on Rix's loan-sharking and pornography scams too?"

"I don't know anyone named Rix."

"You gave him as a personal reference to the real estate outfit in Carmichael."

"Did I? Yes, that's right—Tucker's friend. I asked Tucker for the name of someone who would lie for me and he provided this fellow Rix. He also provided the gun I used to abduct you. He was very accommodating, Tucker was."

"Yeah."

"Tell me, is he involved in those scams you mentioned?"

"He was. He won't be much longer. Neither will Rix."

"You've put the police on them?"

"That's right."

The dark smile again. "Quite the detective. Quite the fucking detective."

I didn't say anything.

"But you didn't put the police on *me*," Vining said.

"Instead you followed me up here. I suppose you intend to kill me?"

I still didn't say anything.

"I don't care, you know," he said. "I really don't, not anymore." A thought seemed to occur to him then; he frowned, and the timbre of his voice had changed slightly when he said, "I do care about Midge, though. She had nothing to do with any of this. She knows nothing about it."

"I didn't think she did."

"Not a bloody thing."

Are you worried about her? Of course you are. You're afraid I'll do something to Ms. Wade. His words, on the way up here that first night. The irony was sharp, and yet it gave me no satisfaction, no desire to remind him of it and goad him with it. Maybe because I was so tired and wired, wired and tired, and I just wanted to get this done, the rest of the questions and then the other thing, so I could rest. Or maybe because other of his words that first night had also come back to me: *I could torture you with the idea. Make you think I intend to harm your woman. It's tempting, I'll admit . . . but I don't think I'll do it. No need for it, really. There's such a thing as overkill, after all.*

"I told her nothing about me," he was saying, "not even . . . nothing. She never asked. Knew me only a week when she invited me to move in with her, share expenses—into her house, not her bed. That's the way she is, trusting. Leave her alone, will you? She's been hurt enough in her life."

"I won't go near her."

". . . No, no you won't. I believe you."

"This is just between you and me."

"Yes. Well, then, one other thing before you shoot: Did you suffer? During the time you were chained here?"

"You know I did."

"Tell me how much."

"No, goddamn you."

"Why not? Dying man's last request." Another of those dark, unreadable smiles. "The provisions for thirteen weeks—was that maddening too? Thirteen instead of twelve or sixteen?"

I stared at him. "The number doesn't mean anything. You set that up along with the rest."

"Of course. I knew you'd try to find meaning in it. Such a smart detective. But a good red herring will fool even the best, eh?"

"Why, Vining? Why?"

"Why what?"

"Why did you do it, all of it? Why do you hate me so much?"

"Don't you know? You seem to know everything else."

"No, I don't know. It can't be just because I had a hand in sending you to prison—"

"Had a hand in it? That's a bloody laugh. You were totally responsible. If it hadn't been for you . . ." The words seemed to choke him up; he coughed his throat clear. "You destroyed me, destroyed my *life*!"

"For Christ's sake, you only served five years."

"Five years! You think that's all there is to it? If you only . . . all right, then. I'll tell you. I wasn't going to but I will." His eyes glittered and glistened again. "Eleven days after I was admitted to Folsom, I was gang-raped by four other cons. Have you ever been homosexually assaulted? No, of course you haven't, so you can't even begin to understand what it was like. You have to experience it to know. And that wasn't the only time, no. Some of the cons . . . well, they covet chaps like me. Young, slender, oh yes, we're prime meat. I was raped three more times before one of them, a lovely fellow named Abbot, turned me out. Do you know what punk means in prison slang?"

I knew but I didn't say it.

"A homosexual lover," he said. "Private property, for the exclusive use of one man. I was Abbot's punk for two years, until he was released. Then I became Frank Tucker's punk—I was Tucker's punk until *he* was released last year, six months before I was. Now do you understand why I despise him?"

"Yes," I said.

"Ah, but you still don't understand why I went to him after I got out. Why I would subject myself to more of his abuse. Aren't you wondering that? I could have got the help I needed elsewhere, couldn't I? Isn't that what you're thinking?"

His voice had risen shrilly, almost hysterically. The look in his eyes . . . it was the same kind of look I had seen in mine that day in the Carder A-frame. Only worse, more tormented—the most terrible look I have ever seen in the eyes of another human being. It put a chill on my back, a metallic taste in my mouth.

"Here's something else for you to think about," Vining said, *"I* thought about it, you know. After I brought you up here and chloroformed you the second time and dragged you in here. I thought about raping you as those cons raped me. I wanted to do it, I truly did, but I . . . couldn't. I'm not a faggot, I never participated willingly— I couldn't do that even to you. Besides, there was no way to be sure you'd catch it and I couldn't wait long enough to find out, the doctors said I might have to be hospital-

ized within a few months, I didn't have enough *time* to
make you die that way."

Chills up and down my body now, because now I understood, I knew his motive, I knew what he was going to
say before he spoke the words—

"That's right," he said, "I have AIDS, I'm dying of
AIDS, they gave me AIDS in prison but *you* put me there,
damn you, *you're* the one who destroyed me!"

He came lunging up off the cot, charged me, struck
wildly at my face. But he was no fighter; he hadn't been
able to defend himself in prison against bigger, stronger
men, and he had no chance with me either. I fended him
off with my left arm, hit him under the right eye with the
flattish surface of the .22—not half as hard as I had hit
Frank Tucker with the piece of driftwood—and knocked
him down.

He got up on his knees, holding his head, moaning a
little. There was blood on his lower lip where he'd bitten
through it. "Go ahead," he said, "shoot me, kill me, get it
over with. Do it, you bloody bastard. Do it do it do it!"

But I couldn't.

I could not shoot him.

Something seemed to tear loose inside me. The room
went out of focus for an instant, came back into focus
with a sudden sharp clarity. Ninety days in this place, a
week on the move, all the hate and all the rationalizations
and all the shoring up of my resolve . . . and I couldn't
do it.

He saw that in my face and got off the floor, rushed me
again, screaming, "Kill me, damn you, kill me!" I hit him
another time, nothing else to do, hit him with a little more
force and put him down again and this time he didn't get
up. He groaned, rolled over, lay pulled up into himself

gasping for breath, sobbing. Not a diabolical lunatic, not a mad dog—just a weak and broken man, sick and tormented and dying. Just another victim.

My knees had gone shaky; I made it to the cot, sank down on it, and sat there looking at the floor. The hate was still inside me but it was dying too, now—as if it had burned too hot for too long and consumed itself. Glowing embers that in a short while would become ashes . . . cooling ashes, then dead ashes. Maybe that wouldn't have happened if he had been someone else, if he had had another motive, if he were not dying from the horror of AIDS; maybe then my hate would still be as white-hot as his and I would have been able to go through with it.

And maybe not.

Either way, I would never know for sure.

Sitting there, I became aware of the smell in the room: sour stench of fear, corruption, human misery. And part of it was mine. It came wafting up from the cot, from the canvas that had absorbed it from my body, and it seeped in through my nostrils, seemed to swell my head like a noxious gas. Gagging, I pushed onto my feet and stumbled to the door and pulled it open to let the night in.

But I didn't go out into it yet. I leaned against the jamb, taking in cold clean air until I could breathe normally. The .22 was still in my hand; I shoved it into my jacket pocket. Then I went over to where Vining lay, hunkered down beside him.

He was quiet now; I turned him enough to tell that he had passed out. There was a ring of keys in his pants pocket. I took that to where the leg iron rested at the end of its chain, over near the bathroom. Only four keys on the ring, and the first one I tried opened the padlock. I brought chain and iron and padlock back to where Vining lay, looped the iron around his left calf, adjusted it to a tight fit, locked it in place. Then I straightened and put my back to him and went out of there, away from him, away from my prison for the last time.

I walked along the access lane, not fast and not slow. Walked with the night wrapped around me, the wind cold in my face, the sky immense and lunar-bright and frosted with stars. And I felt . . . free. It was a different feeling from the one last week, after I had squeezed out of the leg iron—as if that sense of freedom had been false, illusory, because it was incomplete. As if for the past seven days I had been dragging around another set of shackles, an invisible set whose binding weight had drawn me down inside myself, made me see things the way you see them through distorted glass, made me believe things the way you believe them in a dream or a delirium.

If I had shot him in there I would never have thrown off those shackles. I would have carried them until the day I died, and they would have grown heavier and more restricting until the burden of lugging them around became unbearable. Vining's revelations and my own internal makeup had weakened the links, and by not killing him, by not being able to kill him, I had burst them. That was what the feeling of something tearing loose inside had been: the last set of shackles coming off, setting me free.

Now it was over, finally over.

Now I could go home.

Epilogue

COMING HOME

I returned to San Francisco at eight P.M. on Thursday, March 10—seventeen hours after I had left the Deer Run cabin for the last time.

Not much happened in those seventeen hours; it was all anti-climax. I had driven to the Calaveras county sheriff's office in San Andreas and told my story to the night deputy in charge, a man named Newell: who I was, what had happened to me, how I had tracked down Neal Vining, and that I had left him chained inside the cabin. The only things I omitted were my original purpose in going after him, and my breaking and entering and thefts from the Carder A-frame. Those were things I would never tell anyone, not even Kerry; they were private crosses for me to bear alone. I had locked the .22 in the trunk of the Toyota, and it would stay there until I could pack it in a box with a couple of hundred dollars in cash and mail it anonymously to Tom and Elsie Carder in Stockton.

Newell sent a couple of deputies up to Deer Run to take Vining into custody. He also notified the sheriff, who came down and listened to me tell my story a second time and then agreed to my request for a twenty-four-hour grace period before any of it was made public, so I could tell Kerry and Eberhardt myself, in person, instead of them hearing it through the media. I repeated the story a third time into the microphone of a tape recorder. After that they gave me a place to sleep, and I was unconscious until midafternoon. When I woke up I shaved off the beard, had something to eat, received permission to leave the area, picked up the Toyota, and spent two and a half hours driving due west to San Francisco.

And now here I was, coming into the city off the Bay Bridge. It was a cold, clear night, the same kind of night my last one here had been. The skyline struck me much the same way it had then: new and clean and bright, real and yet not real, as if it was some kind of elaborate stage set. Not San Francisco, San Francisco Land. But there was a difference in the illusion this time. Ninety-seven days ago, it had had a pleasurable, magical connotation. Tonight it was merely strange, as if I were entering a familiar place that had changed in subtle ways while I had been away. The strangeness was in me, however, in my perceptions; it was I, not the city, that had been altered in subtle ways. Yet even though I understood that, I could not quite make the city come alive for me.

I was home, but I wasn't home. Not yet.

I took 101 south to the Army Street exit, Army to Diamond, then went on up into Diamond Heights. The cityscape, the gaudily lit bridges and the East Bay, had the same odd aspect from this vantage point. There was even a vague peculiarity to Kerry's street and its usual lack of parking spaces.

For ten minutes I hunted for a place to put the Toyota, finally found one downhill two blocks away. Walking up the steep sidewalk to her building, as I had so many times before, I passed the spot where I'd left my car on that last night—and caught myself looking for it among those angled in against the curb. Long gone, of course. Where? What had Kerry done with it? What had she done with my flat? So many questions I had to ask her. So many

questions to ask Eberhardt, too—about the agency, about
his relationship with Bobbie Jean. And so many things I
had to tell both of them.

It had occurred to me on the long drive from San Andreas that Kerry might not be home when I got there. It
was a weekday night, but women sometimes went out on
week nights—to the movies, to visit friends. A single
woman who believed that her boyfriend must be dead
might even have gone out on a date. Or she might still be
working at Bates and Carpenter; she was a workaholic
and she often stayed late at the office. But no sooner than
I'd thought of these possibilities, I rejected them. She
would be home, and she would be alone. I knew that,
intuited it with the same certainty and inevitability that I
had intuited Neal Vining's destination last night.

I smiled when I reached her building, because there was
a light on behind the drawn curtains in her bedroom. I let
myself into the foyer with my key, climbed the stairs, and
went down the hallway to her door. Stood there for a
time, preparing myself. And then rang the bell, rather
than using my key here too, because it would be easier for
her that way.

Footsteps inside. She would look through the peephole;
she always looked through the peephole. I heard her gasp
when she did, even with the thickness of the door between
us. The chain rattled, the lock clicked, the door jerked
open.

And there she was.

At least five pounds thinner, a gauntness to her face, the
skin drawn tight across her cheekbones and pale now,
very pale. Shock in her green eyes, and relief and joy
crowding up close behind it, pushing through.

"Kerry," I said.

And she said, "Oh, thank God!" and came into my arms.

I held her tight, I stroked her hair, I kissed the softness of her neck, and she cried and I cried with her—and nothing was strange anymore, everything was familiar, everything was real. *Now* I was home.

And holding her, crying, I thought: It's going to be all right. It may take some time, I may need some help, but it's going to be all right.

Most days, I'm all right. Close to my old self again.

It has been almost two months since the end of the ordeal at Deer Run. The first few weeks were the hardest. People flocking around wherever I went, asking endless questions—the media, old friends and casual acquaintances, strangers who felt they were entitled to probe into my personal life and private hell by right of public domain. Voyeurs, many of them, and not all well-meaning. I craved human contact, but I did not crave the poking and prodding attention, as if I were some sort of curious specimen on display in a zoo cage. Anonymity was what I needed—that, and Kerry and the comfort and routine of my work.

If it were not for Kerry and Eberhardt, things might have been much worse. They shielded me whenever they could; they gave me stability and normalcy and understanding and love. For the ninety-seven days I was away, chained like an animal to the wall of an isolated mountain cabin, they kept the faith . . . as if those ninety-seven days were nothing more than an extended vacation or business trip. As if they had known all along that I would come home again. My flat and everything in it just as it had always been, waiting. My car put away in storage. My business and personal affairs kept in order. So that when I did come home, it required little surface effort to step back into the mainstream of my life.

The old saw is true: Time heals. It blurs the past, too; today's news becomes tomorrow's recent history and next week's half-forgotten memory. Days go by now without anyone reminding me of the thing I went through. There are the nightmares, of course, but there have always been nightmares and there will always be nightmares. They are part of the job, part of the lives of men like me.

But there are still days when I wake up on edge, with little patterns of dread lurking like goblins in the corners of my mind. Days or parts of days when I can't work, can't concentrate, can't stand to be alone or to be cooped up in an enclosed space even if others are present. Sometimes, on those days, I call Kerry and she comes to be with me, to walk with me on crowded streets or in the park or on Ocean Beach where I can feel the soothing closeness of the Pacific. Other times I want no one to talk to, not even Kerry, so I go alone to walk or sit or just drive. And slowly, gradually, as time wears on, the goblin shapes vanish, and the edginess vanishes, and I am no longer afraid.

Most days, I'm all right. Close to my old self again. Most days.

ONE

When I got home that Friday evening, there were two messages on my answering machine.

The first was from a Hollywood TV producer named Bruce Littlejohn, who had been pestering me off and on for weeks. "Yo, guy, Bruce here. It's heating up, baby, and I mean burn-your-fingers hot. You wouldn't believe who I been talking to. Just one of the biggies on the little screen, that's all, and I do mean a *biggie.* He loved the concept. What I mean, it melted his chocolate bar. No shit, I think we got him in the bag. I'm winging up this aft to see some sugar daddies, talk numbers. How about you and me have breakie tomorrow ayem? Nine-ish, Stanford Court. Think I can get you a consultancy on the flick but we need to rap, get our signals straight. Extra maple syrup on your waffles, you know what I mean? Nine-ish tomorrow, don't forget. Be good until. *Ciao,* kid."

Hollywoodspeak. Mostly as indecipherable to us laymen as a coded CIA message. What it boils down to, I thought, is that they're all as crazy as stoned monkeys down there.

The second message was from Kerry. "Hi, it's me. Five-thirty now and I just tried callling your office but Eb said you'd already left. Can you come over a little early tonight, six-thirty instead of seven? There's somebody I'd like you to talk to—business, not social. Okay? Love you."

Love you too, I thought.

I reset the machine, went into the kitchen and took a

bottle of lite beer out of the refrigerator. One beer a day—that was my limit now. I had lost more than forty pounds in that cabin at Deer Run and I was determined to keep it off. The reason had nothing to do with vanity or even health; losing the weight had allowed me to survive those three hellish months, and my mind had translated the weight loss into something both symbolic and visceral. I *had* to keep the pounds off; the slow mending process, as fragile as it still was, depended on it. So I consumed my one beer a day, I ate sparingly and limited my intake of fats and carbohydrates, and I followed a somewhat less rigorous daily exercise program than the one I had developed in the cabin. And I would keep doing these things as long as I was physically capable of it.

In the bedroom again I put on a clean shirt. Through the window I could see a cold wind swirling leaves and a scrap of paper into the misty overcast sky. Late May in San Francisco and it was already topcoat weather. Tourists come here this time of year with nothing but spring and summer clothing in their suitcases and then register loud complaints, as if they were victims of a conspiracy instead of their own shoddy planning. If San Francisco had weather like L.A., the city would be inundated not only with tourists but with sun-worshiping transplants from east of the Rockies—and then where would natives like me be? The city was changing too rapidly and too negatively as it was. Drugs and drug dealers had the poorer sections in a stranglehold. The politicians had mismanaged all aspects of local government until there was a huge debt that had brought on a cutback in public services. Yuppies and Asians and money-grubbing developers were changing the faces of the old neighborhoods, a few for the better, too many for the worse, and all irreparably. Sometimes I felt I no longer knew the city, that it was no longer mine even though I had lived in it for more than half a century. That it was metamorphosing into an alien entity, and that maybe its new existence would be as vulnerable to destruction as a butterfly's after it emerges from its cocoon. But at least the weather was the same; there was nothing the drug dealers or the pols or the tourists or the developers could do to change that. Fog and chill winds invaded San Francisco from late May until September and always would, and I for one was glad of it.

I finished my beer, got my topcoat, went out and picked up my car and drove to Diamond Heights. When I turned down Kerry's street I felt my hands turn slick around the wheel, the stirrings of apprehension. It was here, on this street, that I had been kidnapped at gunpoint; shoved into the back of a car, handcuffed, chloroformed, and driven away for ninety-seven days. Since I had been back the sweaty apprehension gripped me nearly every time I came here, as if my subconscious harbored fears that it would happen again, or that I might somehow be thrust back in time and forced to relive it. On one of the bad days, I could not come here at all. The one time I had tried it I had had an anxiety attack so severe, it was almost crippling.

My watch said that it was just six-thirty when I let myself into Kerry's building. I thought that if she had company, I had better ring the bell instead of using my key, and I did that when I got up to her apartment. She came and opened the door.

I kissed her. Said against her ear, "Who have you got here?"

"One of the secretaries from the agency." By agency, she meant Bates and Carpenter, the ad firm where she worked as a senior copywriter. "Her name's Allyn Burnett."

"What's her trouble?"

"I'll let her tell you," Kerry said. "I don't know if there's anything you can do for her, but she does have reason for concern. I think so, anyway."

I nodded, and went on into the living room. The woman sitting on the couch near the fireplace looked to be in her mid-twenties. Blond, thin and hipless in a tan wool dress, plain-featured; but for all of her plainness, there was that little-girl quality about her that stirs protective instincts in some men. She wore a solemn expression now, but you sensed that when she smiled, it would be like a light going on to reveal a warm, pleasant room. She would not lack for male attention, I thought.

We exchanged names and small smiles, the way strangers do, and I sat down in one of the chairs opposite. Kerry was a businesswoman and she knew that it was always easier for two people to establish a business relationship one-on-one; she said to me, "I'll get some coffee," and disappeared into the kitchen.

Allyn Burnett cleared her throat. "I read about you in the papers," she said. "About . . . well, you know. And Ms. Wade says you're the best private detective in the city."

"She's biased. And you shouldn't believe everything you read in the papers."

Small, wan smile. There was a little silence; then she said, with emotion thickening her voice, "It's about my brother. David. He . . . a week ago he . . . took his own life. With pills . . . an overdose of pills."

Old story, sad story. "I'm sorry," I said.

"Yes. But it doesn't make any sense, you see. No sense at all."

"What doesn't?"

"That he would commit suicide."

"Well, people on drugs—"

"No, he *wasn't* on drugs."

That was an old, sad story too: the faith and denial of a loved one. "You said he took an overdose of pills . . ."

"Sleeping pills. He never took those things before, never."

"So he bought them with the intention of taking his own life?"

"That's how it seems, yes."

"Do you doubt it?"

"Doubt what?"

"That your brother actually did commit suicide. Do you suspect foul play?"

"No, it isn't that. I can't imagine anyone wanting to harm David. And the police . . . they say it couldn't have been anything but suicide. The circumstances . . ." She shook her head and looked into the cold fireplace.

I said gently, "Then just what is it that's bothering you, Ms. Burnett? Why would you want a detective?"

She sat without answering for a time. It was not really the fireplace she was staring at; it was at something long ago and far away. I waited, listening to Kerry in the kitchen making homey sounds with crockery. Outside the picture window, wisps of fog chased each other across the balcony and the wind rattled glass and made cold purling sounds in the gray dusk.

Allyn said abruptly, as if my questions had just registered, "He had no reason to want to die. No real reason. He was so young, so happy—he had a good job, he and Karen were planning to get married in September . . . it just doesn't make any sense that he would kill himself."

"Did he leave a note?"

"Yes. But all it said was that it was best for everyone if he . . . that Karen and I should forgive him . . ."

Her voice broke on the last few words and I thought she was going to go weepy on me. If she had, I would have sat there like a lump, feeling awkward and helpless; crying women have that effect on me. But she didn't break down. A couple of hiccoughing sobs escaped her and then she caught her breath and leaned forward with her mouth and throat working, as if she were trying to snatch the sobs out of the air and swallow them again. She put one hand up to her face, fingers splayed, and sat there like that: little girl lost.

I wanted to tell her that she was grasping at straws, wasting her time and mine. I wanted to say that in very few cases of suicide was anything sinister or even particularly unusual involved. I wanted to remind her that the suicide rate among young people today was at an all-time high; that kids who seemed to have every reason for living, who seemed carefree and happy on the surface, could in fact be seething bundles of neuroses underneath. Dissatisfaction with their lives, disillusionment with modern society, pressures, fears, private demons—all those and more could and did drive a young person to suicide even more easily than an older person.

But I didn't say any of that. All I said was, "Do you know of anything unusual that happened to him recently? Any trouble he might have gotten himself into?" I have never particularly wanted to be either a father or a father figure, but there are times when my latent paternal instincts get the best of me.

She said, "No trouble, no. But the money . . . it must be the money. Only that doesn't make sense either."

"Money?"

"Two hundred thousand dollars. David won it two weeks before he . . . died."

The amount surprised me. "How did he win that much? One of the lottery games?"

"No. In Reno. He and a friend went up for the weekend and David . . . it was one of those super-jackpots you read about."

"Progressive slot machine?"

"Yes. Something called Megabucks."

"What did he do with the money?"

"Paid some bills. Bought a new car for himself, a Corvette. Bought expensive presents for Karen and me. And then . . . this is the crazy part . . . then he *lost* the rest of it. And more—enough so that he had to sell back the Corvette and return the presents and go around trying to borrow money. I gave him a thousand dollars, all I had in my savings, but it wasn't even close to being enough."

"Lost the money how? Gambling?"

"That's what he said. He bet it on sports events with those places in Reno and Las Vegas . . . what do you call them?"

"Sports books."

"Yes, sports books."

"So he was a heavy gambler?"

"No. No, he wasn't. That's what's so crazy about it. He never gambled much—never. He went to Reno and Lake Tahoe several times a year, but it was mostly to see the shows. He never won or lost more than a hundred dollars on any trip."

"Are you sure of that? Sometimes compulsive gamblers cover up the extent of their losses."

"Then he would've had a lot of debts, wouldn't he? He didn't. Karen or I would have known if he had."

"Well, it could be that the big jackpot changed him— gave him the gambling fever. It wouldn't be the first time a major windfall has done that to somebody."

"That's what everyone says. But David was my brother, I knew him better than anyone. He just wasn't like that."

"Then why would he make large bets on sports events?"

". . . What if he didn't?"

"You mean he might have lost the money some other way?"

"It's possible, isn't it?"

"Anything's possible," I said. "But gambling is the only way I can think of for somebody to lose a large sum of money in a few days." Which wasn't true. There were other ways, illegal and highly unpleasant ways. But I did not want to go into that with her.

"It just doesn't make any sense," she said. "Money never mattered that much to David. What he cared about was sports. And going places, doing things, having fun."

"The more money you have, the more places you can go and the more fun you can have. Theoretically, anyhow."

She shook her head and said, "He wasn't materialistic."

"All right. When did you last see him?"

"Two days before he died."

"How did he seem then?"

"Fine." But then she shook her head again. "No, that's not so. He always put on a happy face, no matter how he was feeling inside. But I could tell when something was bothering him. He was upset about something, I sensed that, but he wasn't depressed. He didn't act like someone thinking about suicide."

She thought she knew him so well. Only he was the type who always put on a happy face to hide his true feelings. And if a person is thinking about suicide, and wants to hide his intention from his loved ones, naturally he'll act as normal as possible. But grieving relatives aren't always capable of sorting out contradictions and looking reasonably at facts. Grief itself is an irrational emotion.

I said, "Was it just that one time he struck you as upset about something? Or did you notice it before then?"

"He was like that a couple of days earlier, too, when he asked me to return the necklace he'd bought and to borrow my savings. That was when he said he'd lost all his jackpot winnings and more with the sports books."

"He told his fiancée the same thing?"

"Yes. She finds it just as hard to believe."

"What about his friend, the one who was in Reno with him? Did you ask him about it?"

"Jerry Polhemus. He and David used to share an apartment, before David moved in with Karen last year. Yes, I asked him. At the funeral. He couldn't tell me anything . . . didn't have much to say at all." She paused, frowning. "It was odd, though, the way Jerry acted that day."

"Odd in what way?"

"He seemed . . . I don't know, angry about something. Almost as if he weren't . . ."

"Weren't what?"

"Weren't sorry David was dead."

"Why wouldn't he be, if they were close friends?"

"I don't know. Maybe I'm wrong. I was so upset that day . . ."

"Had he and your brother had some kind of falling out?"

"Not that I know of."

"You didn't talk to him about it? Then or since?"

"No. I haven't seen him since."

I allowed another little silence to build. She looked so forlorn, sitting there. And I had a soft schedule at present, with more than a little extra time on my hands. And I needed to work as much and as often as possible. . . .

"Well," I said finally, "I suppose I could talk to Jerry Polhemus for you. See what else I can find out."

"Would you?" Relief brightened her voice.

"I'll do what I can. But don't expect too much of me. Detectives aren't miracle workers." Nor clinical psychologists, I thought.

"I know. It's enough to have you try."

It wasn't and we both knew it. Still another little silence descended. Then Kerry came in—she'd been listening in the kitchen, if I knew her—and distributed coffee and gave me an approving glance before she went over to sit beside Allyn.

There was some more talk, not much. I took down Allyn's address and telephone number, the addresses of Jerry Polhemus and Karen Salter, and such other information as I thought I might need. Allyn asked me if I wanted a retainer—they get that word off TV—and I said no, not until I had drawn up a contract for her to sign. She thanked me again, and we shook hands, gravely, and Kerry showed her out while I sat there sipping my luke-warm coffee and wondering why I had never learned how to say no.

When Kerry came back she plunked herself down in my lap and said, "That was nice of you, offering to help Allyn."

"Yeah."

"Well, it was. There really isn't much you can do, is there."

"I doubt it. But I've always been a sucker for stray cats and lost waifs, as if you didn't know. How much does she make at the agency?"

"Three-fifty a week."

"Uh-huh. And the rest of her family's poor as church mice."

"Her mother and father are dead too. All she's got left now is an aunt in Los Altos."

"Christ. I'll be lucky if I make expenses."

Kerry kissed me, ardently. "You're a nice man, you know that?"

"Yeah. And you know where nice guys finish."

"In my bed, if they're lucky."

"I thought we were going out to dinner."

"We are. After dinner you get your nice-guy reward."

"So what are we waiting for? Go get your coat."

She went and got her coat. On the way downstairs I said, "That Hollywood producer called again today."

"What did he have to say this time?"

"Fortunately I wasn't home. He left a message. Things are getting burn-your-fingers hot, he said. He talked to one of the biggies on the little screen, he said, and the concept melted the guy's chocolate bar. Once we get our signals straight, he said, there'll be some extra maple syrup on my waffles."

Kerry shook her head. "They're all crazy down there," she said.

"Yup. He wants me to have breakie with him tomorrow morning."

"Breakfast? Are you going to?"

"Probably not. In the first place, he's a lunatic. And in the second place, I don't want him or anybody else making a movie about what happened last winter."

"Didn't he say it would be your life story?"

"Yeah, sure. But my life story is dull. What happened up at Deer Run isn't dull."

"Well, you'd have the final say about what goes into it, wouldn't you?"

"Supposedly. You think I should see him?"

"Not if you don't want to. I know how you feel about what happened."

No, you don't, babe, I thought. But I smiled at her and said jokingly, because I did not want things to turn serious between us tonight, "The last time I saw Brucie he drank five shots of Wild Turkey for lunch. I wonder what he drinks for breakie."

"Booze is better than cocaine or heroin," she said.

"Marginally. But that's about the only positive thing you can say about him."

"He's produced a couple of movies, hasn't he? He can't be a *complete* idiot."

"His big hit was called *Shoplifter: A Mother's Tragedy.* You think it takes a Rhodes scholar to make a TV movie about shoplifting?"

"I never saw it. Maybe it was good. Who's to say he couldn't make a good, honest movie about *you*?"

"Nobody'd watch it."

"Sure they would. You'd be immortalized on TV."

"Immortalized on TV is a contradiction in terms."

"Says you. Who do you suppose the 'biggie' is?"

"The guy with the melted chocolate bar? No idea. You know how much prime-time TV I watch."

We were outside now, climbing uphill into the teeth of the wind. Halfway to where my car was parked, Kerry said, "I wonder if it's Brian Keith."

"Who?"

"Brian Keith. The 'biggie.' You look a little like him, except that he's fair and you're dark."

"And he's Irish, with a name like Brian Keith, and I'm Italian. How about they get an Italian to impersonate me?"

"Ben Gazzara," she said.

"Dom DeLuise," I said.

She was horrified. "My God, what a thought!"

"It's *all* nonsense, that's the point. Bruce Littlejohn isn't going to get financing to make a TV movie about me, with Brian Keith or Dom DeLuise or Rin Tin Tin or Howdy Doody. Any day now somebody will realize what an airhead he is and put him away for observation."

"Don't bet on it. If they put away all the crazies in Hollywood, there wouldn't be anybody left to make movies."

Now we were at the car. I unlocked the passenger side, went around and got in under the wheel. "I just figured it out," I said.

"Figured what out?"

"Why you want me to see Brucie tomorrow. Why you want him to make a movie about me. You're a closet groupie."

"I'm what!"

"A closet Hollywood groupie. You think Bruce Littlejohn is your ticket to La-La Land and audiences with the stars."

She glared at me. "Drive," she said. "Before you lose your bed privileges, and I don't just mean tonight."

I drove, smiling a little, enjoying myself. This was one of my good days. Even Allyn Burnett's dead brother hadn't changed that.

Robert B. PARKER

"The toughest, funniest, wisest private-eye in the field."*